Feedback

A Novel By
Lisa Montanino

DEDICATION

To John F. Coffey and Patricia Coffey, for changing my life for the better, to never lose faith, and to write. Save me a seat up there. *Requiescat in pace.*

To anyone who has the courage to live by their convictions authentically.

ACKNOWLEDGMENTS

Thanks to my father Robert, for everything. Especially for never judging my 'accidental' desire to live unconventionally.

To Jennie, for all the countless meals, trust, support, and laughs throughout the years.

To Anthony, for the challenge and comedy.

To Frank, Vincent, Michael, and Sherry for putting up with me talking about this project countless times at the dinner table and on the train.

To Judy Turek, for editing this baby.

To Michael Pennachio, for collaborating and bringing my conceptual vision to life.

Feedback (ˈfiːdˌbæk)

n

1. (Electronics)

a. the return of part of the output of an electronic circuit, device, or mechanical system to its input, so modifying its characteristics. In **negative feedback** a rise in output energy reduces the input energy; in **positive feedback** an increase in output energy reinforces the input energy

b. that part of the output signal fed back into the input

2. (Telecommunications) the return of part of the sound output by a loudspeaker to the microphone or pick-up so that a high-pitched whistle is produced

3. (Jazz) the whistling noise so produced

4. (Biology)

a. the effect of the product of a biological pathway on the rate of an earlier step in that pathway

b. the substance or reaction causing such an effect, such as the release of a hormone in a biochemical pathway

5. (Journalism & Publishing) information in response to an inquiry, experiment, etc: *there was little feedback from our questionnaire.*

vb, adv

6. (General Engineering) (*tr*) to return (part of the output of a system) to its input

7. to offer or suggest (information, ideas, etc) in reaction to an inquiry, experiment, etc

"True artistry comes most often, not from the head, but from the heart that has suffered. Enough said."

"Behind a choir singing smile, often lurks the soul of a brooding tortured artist."

– Michael Lutin

CHAPTER 1 / *THE BOMB*

Lobotomy. Also known as prefrontal Leucotomy. Such startling words. I think I need to undergo this psychosurgery. Wait, do they even perform these anymore? Let's see what Wikipedia has to say. "By the late 1970's, the practice of lobotomy generally ceased." That's just great. Now what the hell am I going to do? Hold on, Josef Hassid, the famous Polish composer had one? I did not know that. Why is this red light blinking? Anyway, I need a procedure that can help erase the last eight years of my life so I can move forward as if nothing happened. Maybe a Craniotomy? I need help. A diagnosis by a trained professional is in order, to grant me a similar remedy for my affliction. But can I wait to see one? It's usually a month's wait if not more, to book an appointment with a specialist. Suffer I must, for the time being. *Wounded,* my life's latest album title. If only I could get an interested producer to remix and make sense of this torment. Suffer I must, for the time being. Before I can conciliate my pain by cruising down the road to Wellsville, I must play four hours of groundbreaking music, emulating the renowned radio personality I used to be. My fans rely on me to provide some "Calgon, take me away!" moments; no time for excuses since they have their own issues to deal with. Whether they listen in their cars or commute by train, my New York accent-drenched voice is part of their entertainment, a musical foray they can happily sing along to. Under no circumstance can they know

4

their beloved deejay is on the verge of crumbling while she's currently residing on a lost planet.

Oh shit, the red light is blinking! What the hell am I going to play? I have two minutes and my mind's blank. This happened the other day when I had fifteen seconds of dead air while I was fumbling with deliberation. Fifteen seconds of dead air on radio is like five minutes in light years. I never had a problem like this, choosing my set list before that explosive bomb went off, leaving me emotionally handicapped. Back in the good ole days, I would have tunes readily available in my head to broadcast—gangbusters if you will. Now I'm lucky if I remember to put on deodorant before rushing out of the house. What do I play? One... two... three... breathe and get it together Claire, for fuck's sake! It kills me to use outdated backup discs for times like this, but I have no choice. Three... two... one... on-air button is pressed. It's showtime.

"Good Morning New York, more like good night since it's still pitch black outside on this September morning that has way too much crisp in the air... am I right? Summer isn't even over yet and already autumn is trying to weasel its way in. Don't worry 'bout a thing because you're with me, Claire Convenzionale, and every little thing is gonna be alright. The request lines are now open, so give a call or an email and I'll do my best to play what you want to hear for the next two hundred and forty minutes on 97.2 WLDM. We have a special show for you today... featuring a prize of two tickets with meet and greets for the Foo Fighters concert next Thursday night. I'll be joining the lucky winners as well so if you've been pining for a date with me, this is your chance. Keep in mind, Dave Grohl, my celebrity husband, will be chaperoning so you'll have to be on your best behavior. Stay tuned for the trivia question later on in the next hour... the lucky ninety-seventh caller with the correct answer wins. Now on with the music. See, music is my drug and I'm fiending right now. Without further ado, here's a subtle song by the bad-asses from Hempstead, New York known as Public Enemy, with one of their best, 'Who Stole the Soul?' A loaded question to ponder this fine morning. Now sit back, relax and enjoy the ride."

Mic off. How pathetic was that? I don't know how much longer I can endure this agony. It's getting worse as the days go by, it's supposed to get better, right? I miss him. Maybe I was rash and hasty. Maybe I've made a terrible mistake. Maybe we can get back together and it will all work out. I'm thirty-one years old. I can't be single now. Not in this time of my life when most of my friends are engaged or married. I used to be on the marriage highway with the rest of the cannonballers. I need to get a grip. It's going to be okay. I will meet someone else without the substantial baggage. I know I made the right decision, I think? I just have to get my subconscious to agree with my conscience. How do I do that? Who decided to induct me into the broken hearts club? Why couldn't he and I live the fairytale forever? Dating rules have changed and I don't have time to read the dos and don'ts manual studying this crap, so where does that leave me?

It's hard to believe four months ago, my show ratings were at an all-time high on the third most coveted National Radio Station based in New York. Considering the odds against me, young and female in the man's world of radio personalities, I earned the prestige at age twenty-six, a rare opportunity usually obtained by deejays in their thirties. I had my first intern job at eighteen and the fortune of working with the *crème de la crème* of on-air's most notable legends—my favorite being Scott Muni, aka "The Professor," and "Scotso." In my opinion, he was Yoda of the disc jockey world and I was honored to be his eager Padawan. My relentless passion brought me to this place, absorbing anything pertaining to music down to the erroneous details. Along the way, I won major awards for Best Morning Show, Personality, and Music Supervisor. Now as I'm approaching my eighth year, I'm playing under par facilitating vocational maladies and potential pink slip doom. My ratings are slipping, my mind's congested and I find myself perpetually complaining instead of being grateful for my position. I need to focus now and bring the ratings back up, and um, getting my sanity back would be ideal too. It pains me to acknowledge I have been languidly spiraling into a dark abyss since the bombing. You know the bomb I talk of, right? Understandably you may be thinking of the Military type, but I'm talking about a completely different kind, one that stings your heart crippled. In my case, it entails breaking off an engagement and severing a relationship of ten years that took a nose dive instead of flying the friendly skies. I need to curl up and lick my wounds from the aftermath. If only work could ease up, especially with the new future spin doctors starting tomorrow, and guess who has to be the perfect professor mentoring these wannabes? More like nutty professor in my case, pun intended. I can't deal with this right now. I can't help myself these days, let alone have the strength to mold someone else. Last year was unmanageable with the two spoiled felines my manager cursed me with. I know the station has a limited pick of the litter, but still, it was awful. This year, I was promised hardworking guys only, let's see if management keeps their word.

Well, another mediocre show is done, now onto set list recounts and litanies of station log updates. I hear the door open behind me, who is about to enter my chamber of despair?

"Hey Claire… is this a good time?"

Oh no, it's my Program Director. Am I being fired after the shit show I just aired?

"Hi Lana, sure, just going over recaps. What's shaking?"

"Are you all set for the interns tomorrow? Did you have a chance to go over their background and stats? What do you think? Out of the whole lot, they seemed the brightest with the most radio experience. I handpicked them for you to make up for last year's debacle. Any ideas on what you have planned this year? That one in particular, has an excellent voice."

"I checked out their resumes and videos you sent me. They seem like solid choices… I look forward to working with them. I was about to email you an agenda on some format ideas I have, let me know you what you think."

God bless my years of auto pilot verbal presentation. Now she's looking at me as if I have two heads.

"Great, I will. Can I ask you another question? Where the hell is Claire? Seriously, can you find her and let her know I want my happy talented deejay back. You haven't been yourself for a while and I'm concerned, and please don't feed me your line of impressive bullshit either. I know you all too well and you loathe the training process… so if there's something on your mind, don't be afraid to say it. Had you not reached your breaking point with your last assistants, I wouldn't have known how you felt. I'm here to help you, ensuring you're happy and everything runs smoothly.

"Lana, I am happy and optimistic for the days ahead, especially support from the new assistants. I'll definitely let you know if there's any problem. As long as they're not high maintenance chicks flown in from the West Coast that I have to bottle feed, all will be clutch."

She smirks, buying mostly what I said. "Okay… but how are you doing personally? Are you alright? You're lacking the usual sparkle that seeps through the mic and that's not like you. I'm here, not just as your boss but as your friend. How long has it been now… ten years? So many great memories we've shared. I don't mean to pry, but I just want to say again, how sorry I am hearing about you and Jake …"

Oh no, she brought it up again. Now I'm tuning her out, unable to comprehend what she's saying. Her lips are moving, resonating distorted ramble, like one of those adult characters out of a Charlie Brown special. Help. I need help, please.

"Thanks Lana, I'm okay and really appreciate you checking in on me. You're right... I have been lacking a little bit and I'll turn it around soon enough. It's been busier than usual around here since Barnaby's on medical leave and I've been wearing a producer's hat as well... you know that takes a toll. Look, the personal tragedy I'm experiencing now will work itself out soon, I promise. I won't let you down, have I ever?"

"No you haven't. I'll put Alan on rotation from Steve's show to help you out till Barnaby comes back if you want. I'm glad you're optimistic for the new interns too... but till you have the balls to tell me what's really going on I guess I will let it go. I'm here if and when you need me, so don't hesitate."

"Thanks again. I better wrap up... I'll email that agenda to you, cool?"

Lana straightens one of the hanging pictures on the wall. "Email me when you can, there's no rush. Remember, our meeting starts at 5:00 AM tomorrow... well, you know the drill. Get out of here and enjoy the rest of the day."

I lucked out with having Lana as my boss. From day one, she's always been fair and gone to bat for me, helping me get from being an assistant to where I am today. How can I truly express to her what I really feel which is, Lana, your employee here wants to check herself into cognitive therapy three times a week and swallow supersonic meds because her head isn't right. Oh and the last thing I need now is to deal with testosterone infused boys on my show. I should finish these recaps. On second thought, it's a great task for the new guys to do. Bikram Yoga with my childhood friend awaits. A detoxifying sweat every guilt-ridden-angst-out-of-your-pores session will help numb the pain in my heart. Sandra eyes me through the glass window and comes into the studio.

"Hey Cannoli, you ready to bounce? We can't be late or the instructor won't let us in. How are you doing today... better?"

"Yeah... I know. Better, you ask? Hmm... I'm gonna say no."

"I hope you're prepared for the Nazi instructor... that dude Malcolm, your favorite is on tonight."

"No, not him... he's out of his balls. Can this day get any worse?"

Sandra stands behind me and puts her hands on my shoulders massaging tension out.

"What happened at work? I heard some of your show and thought it was really good."

"Stop lying to me. I thought it was pitiful and then Lana had to remind me that school's in session tomorrow."

"Aww... you're too hard on yourself. This personal hiccup will pass soon. What's it been now, five months? You got me and your family... not to mention new bucks pining after the older hot teacher starting tomorrow."

"What would I do without you, Sandster? You're just... you're just so fucking special."

I snicker as Sandra knows what song I'm referring to as she licks her pinky and rubs her eyebrow, popping up the collar of her shirt.

"And I'm a riddle, radio head. Now let's get the hell out of here."

After ninety minutes of scorching torture, we cooled off over an early dinner with our friend Fez, reminiscing about happier times. I actually felt relief from some of my woes. Maybe it was the *Starmont 2006 Cabernet Sauvignon* induced buzz, mixed with two parts of supportive friends. Whatever it was, it was the first night since the bombing that I enjoyed a full night's sleep.

CHAPTER 2 / *THE INTERNS*

"Good Morning everyone, I am Warren Woods. I'm pleased to welcome this year's interns and what a fine bunch they are. We look forward to our best year yet at 97.2 WLDM New York Hits Radio Station. With the knowledge of our seasoned team, I know our new batch of assistants will surpass our expectations. On that note, I leave you to your mentors, where you will learn all the tricks of this fine trade and be our future voices. Remember, you are in the disc jockeys and producers hands now… what they say goes. Our Program Director, Lana Silson, will introduce you to your managers. Rock on!"

Spoken like a true jackass, station's owner and disgustingly overpaid dimwit, Warren Woods. He doesn't know his so-called musical ass from his elbow—it's this lack thereof that's propelled all under his employ to forever hang him in effigy. He inherited the radio show when his dad Jack, a sagacious and intelligent broadcasting force, died last year. I know that poor man is turning over in his grave, because his only child doesn't even know what a music note is. Utter disgrace since he's not worthy of the empire he owns. I see Lana and two guys walking towards me. Hmm… one is on the cute side with I'd say a 6'1" athletic build, lightly tanned skin, dark hair and green eyes—a winning combination. The other guy is on the too-short-to-ride-this 5'9" ride. He's no more than 5'7" with a paunch frame, pale skin, light brown hair, and also has green eyes. Interesting, we all have green eyes; I wonder what this symbolizes? I believe in signs and metaphysical phenomenon. It makes me think of a funny conversation I had with this dude at Zeitgeist Bar in San Francisco a few years back. I think his name was Mario. He quoted or most likely paraphrased (I'm not really sure since we were both blazed out of our minds on some fine Hash) an old Spanish proverb, *Brown eyes say love me or I'll kill thee. Blue eyes say love me or I'll die.* I agreed with both sentiments yet wondered, what about green eyes? After much thought and giggling fits, we both came to the conclusion that those unfortunate souls were shit out of luck. This explains a lot on my part.

Lana motions for my attention. "Hello Claire, meet your assistants, Jared Parker and Shane Salinger, and yes they have memorized how to pronounce your last name correctly... *con ven see oh nah lay.* Fellas, you lucked out big time working with her; work hard and make us proud."

I thank her as she leaves to go to the next group. "Hello, it's a pleasure to meet you both. I hope you're ready for a unique journey."

They both smile and the short one speaks first.

"Hello, my name is Jared. May I say it's an honor to have the chance to work with one of the best disc jockeys in the nation. I've been a fan of yours since I was a Junior in high school."

Great. Now I feel old, you little bastard. "Thanks, Jared."

The tall one reaches his hand out to shake mine. "Claire... I'm Shane. It's a pleasure to meet you, finally and like Jared mentioned, I'm a huge fan. To have this chance working with you... well, I couldn't be more grateful. In answer to your question, I'm always ready for an adventure.

May I just say, your pictures do you no justice."

"Thank you Shane, that's very nice of you to say. I look forward to a great year ahead for us."

His smile widens and I notice he has subdued freckles on his face. I like freckles. Alright, I will admit, I'm already partial to this kid. He seems cool and has one of the sexiest rasp voices I have ever heard. His audio submissions didn't do him any justice, plus it doesn't hurt that he has the same last name of one of my favorite author's. It's been a while since I've had sincere reverence exuded towards me and it's a mellifluous sound to my ears.

"Alright guys, follow me to the studio. This is the getting to know each other phase so I'll start by telling you a little about myself and what I expect on the work front. I am originally from Reading, Pennsylvania. My family relocated to Garden City, New York when I was seven. In case you couldn't tell by my name, I'm Italian and despite the stereotype we don't all have big hair, wear gaudy jewelry and have goombas for friends. Well, maybe I have a few goomba friends... anyway, how about you Jared, where are you from?"

"Roslyn, New York."

We may have a spoiled brat on our hands. "And you, Shane?"

"I'm from Shoreham, New York."

Not as bratty. I reread their resumes. "Jared, I see you went to university here at Hofstra... good school and you interned at Walk 97.5. Shane, you attended George Washington University... great school as well. Impressed to see you helped out at BIG 100.3 in DC. I knew Paul over there, cool cat. Considering you never left Long Island, Jared, you don't have the typical accent that trickles through with some words like me or Shane."

He looks up as he clears his throat. "It's weird… sometimes I think I sound Midwestern. I lost remnants of it by my third year studying communications."

Shane chimes in, telling us about his background of being part Italian, English, and Irish. Jared mentioned he's half Scottish and Lithuanian. Coincidentally, they each had two siblings and like me, they were the youngest of the brood. See in my opinion, a dynamic team needs to have commonalities. Lana lost the big game last year pairing me up with two rich girls that drove a poor man's Mercedes. I recall one was a product from Daddy's second flavor of the month. The other one had a silver spoon shoved so far up her ass, she didn't want to file any of the play list logs, which just so happens to be the number two job description for an intern at WLDM. They both couldn't catch onto the lingo, radio terminology, a key element in being a successful broadcaster. It was torture dealing with their cattiness, let alone their obscenely bleached-blonde hair. The guys are in front of me looking curious. This is my chance to set the tone.

"So let's get down to business… what I expect from you while assisting me.

Number One: Work hard. Get all of your work done and then you can have fun, pretty much carte blanche.

Number Two: Research. Feed your knowledge with music… all aspects from who wrote what, when, and why. Delve into the full spectrum from who produced it to how the band sounds live. Use all the perks this job gives you, which is free shows, events, and resources up the yin yang.

Number Three: Challenge me by putting my knowledge to the test. In fact, if you can enlighten me on something I don't already know about this business… not only will you impress me but I'll be your biggest fan.

Number Four: Know and speak radio terminology. For example, I expect you to know what the terms: gain... liners... drops... front-sell... and hit the post means. Also, familiarize yourselves with the FCC website, which will become your best friend and worst enemy.

Number Five: Leave your attitudes outside our studio door. This is my Buddhist sanctuary that we share for four plus hours... then another three in my office to go over song lists and other tasks that come along with the unpleasant portion of this job.

Number Six: We must do our best to never, under any circumstance let interference, static, miscues, and feedback happen on our show. I will test you randomly so please study the assistant manual.

I want greatness, determination, alacrity, positivity, humor, no whining or arrogance, and lastly... respect for one another. Let's treat each other with kindness by keeping our contained atmosphere light since the on-air tends to get heavy at times, if you catch my drift. I have more on the list but that will be addressed as we get rolling along in the coming days. Do you guys have any questions?"

Shane grins confidently raising his hand as Jared looks a whiter shade of pale.

"Is there any type of reward for us being the best damn interns you'll ever have?"

"Your confidence is bigger than Texas dude, and I like the enthusiasm but do realize you're dealing with a pragmatist to the third degree. You need to understand this will be a grueling gig, and you have to be okay with that. As for a reward sure... you're looking at it. Working and learning from me. And trust me, I can be very generous. We have ratings to bring up, as much as it pains me to admit they've slipped. I need to put this show on another level and I'm counting on both of you to help me. You dig?"

"Totally. I understand everything you said and you'll have no problem with me, I'm there two hundred percent."

"Thanks, Shane. And can we include you, Mr. Silent?"

Jared clears his throat. "What if we don't meet all your expectations?"

Shane interjects. "Why are you having doubts, Debbie Downer? We're a team, we need to be optimistic."

"Hold up, let me address Jared's concerns... he's asking a good question. Well it's simple, if you don't make the grade in here then you'll be dismissed as an intern with no shining referrals. The station has strict guidelines we all must adhere to. I can say if you listen and learn from me, you will not have an issue and most likely have a lot of fun in the process. My track record is pretty good as far as job placements go. Does that answer your question?"

He sinks back into his chair as if a load of tension just flew off his shoulders. "It does... thanks. I don't mean to be a drag but I... I guess it's just overwhelming, surreal for me to be here. I don't want to let you down."

Okay, I now see Jared in a new flattering light. "I give you credit for admitting that since the usual work robots are programmed to exude positivity at all costs. I too have insecurities and I think it's integral for success... to be realistic."

Shane sighs. "Am I the only one, who doesn't have doubt or insecurity?"

As the three of us look at each other, our unspoken words feed him his answer.

"Also, is cursing allowed?"

"Yes, as long as it is not directed at each other in a negative connotation. You can say whatever you fucking like... off-air of course."

We chuckle as Shane grabs my mic shaped award to speak into. "This is going to be a hell of a ride and I'm lovin' it already."

I notice it's 5:45 AM. "Okay fellas, let's get started. I need your help with the voice tracks we'll be using during the show due to start in fifteen minutes, so let's giddy up."

"Aye aye, Captain, whatever you need."

Aye aye Captain? Is he a *Dead Poets Society* fan? Interesting, considering Shane must have been five when it came out. I had never been called that before but I like it, so it can stick; his audacious manner is encouraging. I whisked them both through a crash course of dos and don'ts as they watched, writing down notes as the show went off without a hitch. For the first time I could see light at the end of my dark tunnel, snapping me out of this funk, considering I didn't think of the bomb once that day. Another peaceful night's sleep. Nothing like the power of distractions.

Day two for the interns and already I won the bet, compliments of their tardiness. It never fails as I too arrived late on my second day. The unforgiving rooster shift—it's a tortuous adjustment. It takes a good month before your body becomes accustomed to it. As soon as I played the first song, Peter Gabriel's "Big Time," Shane dashes into the studio in a fevered panic. His face and shirt are sweat stained as he gasps for air.

"I'm so sorry Claire, I missed my train by a minute and

had to get the next one... it won't happen again."

Jared rushes in with the same excuse before I could answer Shane.

"It's okay for today fellas. Proceeding forward, please make sure to be here on time, unless you have a good reason. The main part of this job entails the show's prep fifteen minutes before we go live."

I knew they understood as they both answer yes in an obedient tone.

"Go get yourselves some breakfast if you haven't already; you're going to need the energy... we've got a big day ahead of us."

Shane insists on staying with me, to help man the control board as Jared volunteered to pick up our breakfast order.

"Do you see the playlist so far? I need to add flavor to it for the next segment, one hour of free-form music. Do you have any suggestions?"

"Do I? How do you feel about a little hip hop mixed with some classic rock here and there?"

"I'm listening. What exactly do you have in mind?"

He pauses to answer as he queues up the first set of songs we're about to play. "How about Fabolous's 'Young'n,' segueing into Rolling Stones 'You Can't Always Get What You Want' for starters?"

I liked it but changed the song to "Under My Thumb" since it was what I was feeling from the Stones instead. We made sure all of the rap songs Shane suggested were edited versions, we had to manually tweak two of them, another task I trained them on the mixing board. We played tunes I hadn't spun in a dog's age, bringing a fresh sound to the show. The bomb only crept into my noggin for a brief moment when Jared suggested songs from Pearl Jam and Bruce Springsteen. It seems Shane loves hip hop and rock and roll. Jared on the other hand, has an eclectic palate from classical to world music, very similar to mine leaning heavily towards alternative rock. I am finally warming up to Jared. I don't want him to irk me, but he does with his skittish lack of confidence that I need to help him build. And build it, I must.

CHAPTER 3 / *THE LONELY HEARTS CLUB BAND WITH SPECIAL GUEST: GREEN GOD*

The first few weeks manning the ship with my two latest prodigies flew by as we acclimated to each other's work styles, smoothing out the usual kinks while building a synchronal dynamic. Day by day, the formality evaporated as we talked more on a social level. If it's one thing I have in common with these two, it's the gift of gab. Seriously, we may be the three most communicable souls on the planet because there is never dead air around us. The guys were grateful that I am cool with them talking freely, without any female sensitivity screen. I've always been fond of hearing guys uncensored banter—not only is it entertaining, it's a sure shot way of learning what really goes on in their minds. During one of our rap sessions, Shane inanely revealed he's an avid pothead. So avid in fact, he smokes every few hours or as he put it, *enough to kill a horse.* Jared and I were taken aback since he doesn't look or seem like the typical red-eyed lifer.

"How about you Claire, do you indulge?"

"I do every so often, especially when I need to chill out. I used to enjoy it regularly during my college days. What about you, Jared?"

His pallor blushes. "Yes, usually on the weekends with my friends but not on a daily basis."

21

Shane has his heads down looking at the control board with a frowned expression, as if he's the odd man out.

"If it upsets you, I won't smoke on my breaks while we work."

"Get the hell out... you've been working all this time stoned? Honestly? I can't believe you function that efficiently. I'm jealous and ambivalent as long as it doesn't impede on your job performance. Let's keep it on the down low here since the bosses don't need ammunition on you."

"Will do... and yeah I know, it's sick, right? I've kind of been blessed and cursed at the same time. Thanks for being cool with it... you're the best boss ever."

Okay, so the borderline wanton attention turns me on, despite the subtle tones of kiss-ass. Who wouldn't get off on it?

"You're the god playa... I don't know if I should bow or salute you. Jared, we have a green god in our midst."

Jared claps and whistles. "Shane, do you have a girlfriend?"

Before Shane answers, he hands me a note that reads: If you ever need greener pastures, just say the word. Good to know and one could interpret that as a double entendre. I give him thumbs up.

"Yes J bone. A dime of a girl, going a year and a half... how about you?"

I like how Shane already had a nickname for Jared. I'm a sucker for hypocorisms, they're tokens of endearment.

"I had one for a few years... she broke up with me three months ago, ruined my life, and I've been miserable since."

I am dreading them turning the klieg light on me regarding this subject. I was finally feeling relief by distracting myself and I didn't want to fall back into dangerous minefield territory.

"Claire, who's the lucky man?" Shane asks.

"Well... I... I broke up with my fiancé roughly five months ago, so... "

Both their mouths dropped. Why did I answer that question honestly?

"I'm sorry to hear that, are you okay?" Shane asks in a soft consoling voice.

Great, how do I answer this one? Should I divulge I'm a goddamned wreck? Jared puts the caller line onto voicemail and asks me what happened.

"Forgive me guys, but I'm not in the mood to talk about it right now. It's still sensitive... I need some time."

They both gave me a free pass on the interrogation and Shane's calm façade turns red with heavy eyes.

"I just got my heart ripped out by the love of my life."

Jared looks as confused as I am. "Wait a minute, didn't you just say you had a dime of a... "

"I lied... sorry... I didn't want to bring it up, since it happened a few nights ago and there's no chance of reconciliation. But when I heard the both of you say it, I figured I should come clean."

"We understand, Shane. I know it's not easy... I'm

glad you told us. Well, add another one to the... we can relate to each other list. Which gives me an idea, in honor of our unfortunate circumstances, we're going to express our grief... feelings through the show. Yes, we'll use the show as our outlet for all the lonely heart dwellers out there like us. Of course it doesn't have to be all sad pathetic sap tunes... nuh uh. We can each have two songs on the show conveying how we feel. It'll be therapeutic and off-air we can have a so-called therapy session where we're free to vent, saying whatever will make us feel better. Channeling our peaceful states before our bombs hit us. What do you guys think?"

Jared gets up stretching his arms. "Brilliant idea Claire... I could really use someone to listen to me."

"Oh Jesus Jared, if you could be any more of a sensitive sap. I..."

"Hold up Shane, now wait just a minute. From this moment on, we're the same unit. The three amigos fighting the good fight of self-preservation and I won't stand for comments about whose sappy and yada yada... screw that. You need to get over yourself and show your fellow El Guapo there, the much needed support and 'plethora of presents' he deserves. What say ye?"

Shane stands up putting his hand to his head in a saluting position. "Aye aye, Captain."

"I didn't hear you. What say ye?"

Jared stands next to him as they scream. "Aye aye, Captain!"

If someone had been watching us at that moment, and didn't notice the milestone we just reached in our short time together, they would have been blind. Heartbreak will do that to you. It guarantees a compassionate bond with others who can empathize. Now we had to decide what songs to play for our recovery sessions. By their fervid smiles and extra bounces in their steps, I know they're having as much fun as I am, choosing which ones to feature. Shane is feeling hip hop by picking Usher's "You Don't Have to Call." Bastard took one of my picks. Jared's on the gooier side with Sinead O'Connor's "Nothing Compares to You." So what am I feeling today? Should I choose a song that evokes the whole aforementioned situation and expose myself? Come to think of it, there isn't a song for my misery. I'm in a throwback mood and figure you can't go wrong with a classic. I went with one of my favorites by the late great Lou Rawls, "You'll Never Find Another Love Like Mine." They both give me thumbs up approval. For our second choice, Shane chose Aerosmith's "What it Takes." Another solid choice. Jared chooses wisely with Radiohead's "Fake Plastic Trees." I ended off with two because I couldn't decide between them: Bon Iver's "Skinny Love" and Beck's "Guess I'm Doing Fine." As we were about to finish our day's work, I reflected on how I was feeling. Zealously inspired would summarize it best. It felt comforting working with these two, discovering their significant potential, making the days fun again, after such a long scourged winter.

Out of nowhere, a female caller requests a song that Jared relays to me, as soon as I hear the three word title, my heart stopped for a few seconds. I knew this day would come. Jake's song, the one he used to sing to me.

"When can we play it? Maybe we can make it the last song? Or should we wait till tomorrow?"

Uh-oh. How do I blow this one off? I have no plans to play or listen to that song ever again.

"Probably not Jared, we're about to wrap up so… don't worry about it."

I could feel the intensity of Jared's doubtful eyes stare at me. His fear prevailed in lieu of the consequence he would sustain if he pressed me at that given moment. Shane, in his normal charismatic fashion, asked us offbeat sometimes hysterical questions piquing his curiosity.

"Question of the day… what's the significance to your parent's picking your first name?"

"I was named after my grandfather who was the best man ever."

"Perfectly played, Jared. I was named after my favorite Uncle, who died way too young. How about you, Miss Claire?"

"Well, story has it… upon my mom's superstitious mind… she named me after her favorite craving during her pregnancy. Éclair pastries." They both chuckle.

"Yeah… ha-ha anyway… she had never liked them, until she was pregnant with me, so she took that as a sign when she had me and switched the first letter e and put it at the end. It's really fitting since I have such a sweet tooth."

Shane looks at me with furrowed brow. "I'm glad she did that; imagine if your name was Éclair? I bet you love them, right?"

"Actually I can't stomach them. I'm more of a not-fully-cooked-chocolate-chip-out-the oven-chick as opposed to your froufrou pastry type. Oh before I forget… my parents will be stopping by later this week, so please be on your best behavior and save your appetites."

Shane throws the stations logo foam football to me. "Look forward to meeting them. By the way, would you say you're close with your siblings?"

"Yes, with my sister, Bianca. There's room for improvement with my brother since there's times we want to ring each other's necks. What about you?"

"I'm really close to mine… parents too."

Jared looks up and catches the football I threw to him. "I'm close with my brother but the rest of us have friction; I wish we could get along better."

Before I can respond encouragingly, my cell phone rings. When I see the name on the display, I shake in a panic. I contemplate if I should answer it or hope they leave a voice mail. Voice mail it is and Jared asks who I'm avoiding.

"It was my ex's sister… I don't feel like dealing with any ripple effects right now."

I notice Jared's judgmental eyes look at me with acumen as he threw the football at me. Before he has a chance to say anything, Shane beats him to the punch with another question.

"Who is the current number one on your celebrity fuck list?"

This is the first time he brought up sex. This should be good.

Shane points the microphone in my direction. "Ladies first, Ms. Convenzionale."

"Well it changes sporadically, but currently I'd have to say Yoda. Yeah… I've always had a thing for that little green god." Between our laughs, Shane throws the football to me again.

"Okay, now for real. Which guy and no Jedi Masters please."

"Why are you player hating on Jedi Master Yoda? I wasn't kidding, he's on my list… but to honor your said Jedi-less stipulation, it's a tie between Ryan Reynolds and Ewan

McGregor."

"Ewan McGregor, really? I'm impressed with Mr. Reynolds since he's overtly hot and funny but…"

"We need to set up rules on your forum of questions… no peanut gallery bullshit allowed. Ewan is a fine specimen… plenty of appeal and he's one of the best actors of his generation. Two words: *Trainspotting*."

"Actually that's one word, Captain."

"Yes, I know Jasta… you need to acquaint yourself with sarcasm."

Jared throws the football at me. I need to calm down these days; I've been overly snappy and I shouldn't expose the sexual deprivation I am currently experiencing. Presently, my libido resembles a shaken bottle of champagne that's about to have its cork explode hitting the ceiling, squirting its liquids everywhere.

"I think they're good, tall choices."

I felt bad for Jared and his sensitivity about his height.

"Yes, they sure are but don't forget Yoda; he's the shit." He smiles and winks.

Shane stands up and motions to Jared. "You get a ten for your enthusiasm, C note. J Bone, what say ye?"

"Does the person have to be living?"

"Only you would ask that. Yes… they have to be living since there's a slim possibility of actually dancing with them intimately."

I am in the mood to have fun with this. "Wait. If

that's the case, then I need to trade in Ryan Reynolds for John F. Kennedy, Jr. My God, he was the hottest man ever. He'll always have a special place in my… hmm… dreams."

Shane walks over to the mini fridge and hands me an ice pack from the freezer to "cool off."

Jared clears his throat. "Alright, I guess I'd say Jennifer Connelly… but the fuller version, not skinny Jennifer. Oh yeah… "

"Impressive choice. If I was gay, I'd do her."

Jared cracks up. "That's awesome, Captain."

Shane has a big smile on his face. "Now that's hot. Okay my turn. The lucky lady to get Shane lovin' at this point is the sweet beautiful Beyoncé."

"Another solid choice… very nice fellas and yet again, if I was gay… I'd also do her."

Jared chuckles. "You don't have to be gay, Claire."

Shane covers his mouth to prevent spitting out his coffee as I grab the microphone without turning it on.

"Ladies and gentlemen… I'm proud to announce we have just established the proper and dignified, Jared Parker, does in fact… have a libido. Praise, Jesus!"

Jared stands up and takes a bow while Shane hands him an ice pack. We decided to take a break together, walking to the kitchen to get drinks. When we got back to the studio, the overall tone had become surprisingly heavier.

Jared seems uneasy, slightly twitching. "By the way, there is no way in hell you could ever tap that famous ass."

Shane snaps back. "I so have a chance with her.

Obviously, not while she's with the Hov... but if she should ever leave that Rappa Don, I totally have that. Just put her in front of me."

The kid was right. He was smoother than a sheet of ice; he carried himself with a dauntless aplomb like no other Casanova I had ever seen. Jake at his age was charmingly confident, but far more reserved outside the bedroom, his depths only showed through intimacy. Shane is an alpha male that has a lascivious intoxication perspiring out of his pores. He eschews debauchery in his look let alone his voice. The fact that he loves women more than anything else doesn't hurt—it's his Wonka's Golden Ticket. I wouldn't be surprise to read about him and Beyoncé down the road in People Magazine. It seems Jared wasn't sold since they were still discussing it. Why is he starting in? I needed to change the subject, extinguish the situation.

"Hey fellas, I need some PSA's set up for tomorrow. Oh and don't forget we have a meeting with Lana as well after the show's done. Why don't I play something we can sing along to and... "

The guys ignore me and Jared is relentless. "Dude, I don't care how many babes you've bagged, you aren't snagging her. Even the best of them can't always get what they want."

I could see smoke coming out of Shane's nose, just like Ferdinand the Bull, about to charge Bugs Bunny.

"Jared, you're out of your balls thinking I never have a chance with her. In fact, that's your biggest problem... you're always, *no I can't* instead of yes I can, you pessimistic shithead!"

This has to stop. They've been berating each other for the past ten minutes and I am officially pissed.

"Fellas, I will repeat this for the last time, can we please get back to work and end this ridiculous slur-fest now.

Remember rule number five? Leave your attitudes at the door. There's no verbal mudslinging at each other. This studio's my Buddhist sanctuary. Please let's be respectful of each other. Shane, are you packin' some bowls? Why don't you take a break and go blaze for me. We'll all walk to the train together after we wrap up... pretty please?"

Jared sets up two songs while Shane downs a water bottle and I hope for the best.

"Oh that's right Shane, you're the *I can get anything I want* asshole. Correction, delusional asshole."

That's it. I've had it. They're not going to listen to me, so what to do? I remember a code red situation similar to this a few years back where the banter had roared to a screeching crescendo within seconds. What's up their asses? We were having such a good time till their conflicting egos came into our studio. Damn Jared and his annoying Jekyll and Hyde bullshit. Desperate times call for desperate measures. I think the super soaker water gun will do the trick. Now, if I can just remember where I put the damn thing. As I feverishly look for my hydro lightsaber, they're still at it, bickering like an old married couple. Ha! I found it. Fully loaded and ready for action. I turn my back on them so they can't see what I'm armed with. I get into position and focus on Jared's face to mark my shot. In one swift finger motion, water streamed out quick and hard right onto his forehead. He never saw it coming till the first loud splash, he yells "Ouch. What the hell?"

Shane notices I'm the sharpshooter and cackles. Jared grabs paper towels to wipe his face. I turn around and walk back to my chair. Before I sit, I quickly swivel around and shoot Shane square in the neck, I laugh at my shitty aim and his expression went from lively to bothered within a millisecond.

"Ay Mami. So not cool, he's the one that started in...

why am I being doused?"

I sit down as he dries himself off. "I don't care who started it, I don't like being heard on deaf ear. I asked nicely twice, and both times went ignored. Now that's not cool. I was desperate, so addenda to rule number six, listen when I speak and adhere to rule number seven, don't fucking fight. Can I get an amen?"

"Yes." Muffled under their disgruntled breaths. I made the final announcement as they set up the last batch of songs to play. While we tried deciding on what the last song should be, the overall air was strained, their moods could be cut with a knife; I needed to abate the situation. I notice Shane staring out the door's window that looks out into the hall.

"Who is that fine looking petite blonde with the big brown eyes, talking with Kurt?"

"That would be my best friend, Sandra. Paws off dog... she's too old for you."

"Excuse me, Miss Morally Rigid... I have no limits in regards to age. What words would you say best describe her?"

"I'd say gullible and caring. So let me get this straight, you're not an ageist? I could set you up with my Grandmother's friend, Jocelyn? She's recently widowed and could use a thorough cobweb cleaning."

Shane spits out his drink as Jared and I giggle at my inappropriateness. He clears his throat through coughs, struggling to speak.

"You're a bad... bad ol' putty tat."

"You said it, man."

Sandra whisks in, greeting me with her usual sugar laden

salutation "Cannoli." The boys look at each other confusingly.

"Hey Sandra, meet my charismatic interns, Shane and Jared."

"Pleasure to meet you both... I've heard good things. It's nice to see Claire finally got a pair of decent assistants this time. Make sure to annoy her as much as you can."

Jared offers his seat to her. Shane predictably begins the verbal query.

"Thank you... the pleasure is ours. So you grew up with Claire? Tell us, how did she get that name you just called her?"

Before Sandra could answer I intervened. "That would be my mom's favorite pastry which means it's only used by family so it's off limits here."

He rubs his eyebrows as if he has a tension headache. "I thought we were family, Captain." We smile at each other and I wink.

"Sandster, we have to boogie out of here. We'll chat another time with the guy's."

Sandra eats tortilla chips out of the bag we had left opened on the control board unmotivated by my impatience.

"Okay, I am ready to rock and roll."

I scurry grabbing my stuff. "We have to jet off to a class. Please finalize for tomorrow's program, and free reign on what the last song should be."

Shane looks Sandra up and down with his hand stroking his chin as if he's undressing her.

"In lieu of today's events, how about ending on a kind note, say The Beatles 'Here Comes the Sun'?"

Sandra jumps. "Ooh that's a good one, I say go with it."

I'm not convinced. "Great... one vote from Sandra Dee what about you, J Dizzle?"

Jared nods yes. "It's alright but on second thought, it's way overplayed. How about 'Happiness is a Warm Gun' instead... more fitting I think."

"Better choice... touché. Let it roll, provided it's satisfactory with your counterpart."

Shane answers in a strained voice. "Aye aye."

On our ride to yoga, Sandra expressed the noticeable change in me since she saw me last. She emphasized how the glow in my face was coming back and I didn't appear as sullen and frail since the explosion.

"Seriously C, you seem like you're bouncing back... I'm happy because I won't lie... we were all scared about your wellbeing for a while. First time in all the years we've known each other, I've never seen you so dispirited. Now we just need to feed you some fat burgers and you'll be back in shape in no time. By the way, phenomenal job yesterday, the show was on fire. I like those guys... they seem to be contributing to your upswing."

I agreed, thanking her. The days have been improving, especially on the work front. Later that night while straightening up my apartment I couldn't help thinking, what the hell happened to me? How did I become so morose, lacerated with doubts and abandonment? I know I'm not out of the woods yet, and there's a chance I may never be out of them completely. I just want the strength to make peace with Jake and most importantly, myself. Sandra was right about Jared and Shane; they are calming forces, pulling this fallen soldier out of the smoking debris. Now I need to plan for my parent's visit in a couple of days. My parents tried visiting me last month but I couldn't face them at the time. I was in no shape to mask my alarming pain, not even for them. They would have been highly concerned since my weight dropped and the sight was sickly. I had to literally fake every phone conversation since the breakup, assuring them I was fine. I would be damned to have them affected by my misfortune. Bianca is in agreement with me, that when it comes to my parents, the school of "Ignorance is bliss" is the ticket. Every parent obviously wants their kids to be happy at all times, no matter what. Of course when the times get rough for their children, parents have to be there for better or worse. When it comes to Italian ones, they take that obligation to another emotionally draining deep-end-of-the-sedimentary level. I was already drowning and didn't need to drag them into the ocean with me. God forbid they knew their *bambina* has a psychiatrist appointment on the calendar. Talk about being scared and doubtful, that there is a remedy for what seems like a lost cause condition. As sad as it ended, there were amazing times as well prior to doomsday, hence why I have no choice but to shrink the conflicting battle my mind won't stop fighting. I put my headphones on listening to my cyber competitor Pandora, which is currently playing Duncan Sheik's Radio Station. First song is Coldplay's "Life in Technicolor" then Duncan's "Barely Breathing." They roll out another Coldplay tune with "Lost." What a fitting trio—theme songs of my life at the moment. Note to Pandora: you may want to skip playing the same artists two to five times after ten minutes or so on one station. Just a thought, since it's annoyingly irritating, considering the myriad of song options available. It makes me physically ill, knowing with the onslaught of *Jack* and *Brad* and whatever else blow-me prerecorded FM's out there, will inescapably send pink slips to disc jockeys across the nation with their automated bullshit someday.

CHAPTER 4 / *THE INFAMOUS RUBDOWN*

My anticipated spa day with Sandra was finally here. We were overdue for a spoiled session of soothing indulgence. I scheduled a Facial and Deep Tissue Massage for my sore congested body in hopes that all the tension will be released in about ninety minutes. I must admit, when I saw my massage therapist at first, I doubted she could work out one kink. Standing at 4'8" and weighing a whopping eighty pounds, lilliputian Asian woman walks in eschewing a friendly hello, instructing me to lie face down. I noticed through the side of my eye, her upper diaphragm area stood level with the table. I usually have Charlie, whose hands are spun from gold—he was out ill and replaced with a quarter his size. Well never judge a book by its cover because this little krill was a rock star in the kneading of the dough.

"Claire, how great were those facials? Now we're getting massaged in the same room with a view of Central Park and how delicious is that wine? Now I know what J Lo feels like."

"More like hey ho… ba dump bump."

After a few minutes, I see Sandra has nodded off. I too relax into Never Neverland, feeling looser compliments of my ambidextrous foo fighter working out all the knots. All of a sudden, I feel a warm slimy pressure on the upper part of my right butt cheek. Why? Isn't she supposed to be focusing on my hamstrings? The towel covering my ass unexpectedly lifts and the midget starts aggressively rubbing it. Why is she ruining my moment of Zen? By the time I reach my hand for the towel to cover my backside, the molesting squid prevents me from grabbing it and places my hand back down on the table.

"Thanks, but no thanks. Please don't massage me there. Please… for the love of God!"

Sandra wakes up mumbling "What's going on over there?"

"Help… please help."

When I look over at her, she sees what's happening to me and falls into a cackling fit.

The violating shrimp shouts with an accent *"You no like? It work out hip thigh… hip thigh veyee tight… veyee tight!"*

Upon hearing her speak with lack of pronunciation, I join in on Sandra's giggling frenzy, gasping for air. This did not go over well with the petite piranha. She finishes abruptly having an assistant lead me and Sandra to the showers. I wash the jasmine and sea kelp oil residue off my skin. My joints felt tight and again, I am need of another massage. The deranged dwarf was right about my *hip thigh… veyee tight.* Of course they are and why shouldn't they be? I haven't had an internal rub down in what feels like forever, and the last thing I needed now was that sea urchin to advertise it. It's not like I can't get laid, it's not that at all. Presently, I have five turbo fueled gents ready to launch me at any time. They're just waiting for me to clear them for takeoff. The thing is I have no desire to be ignited by any of them. Isn't that a bitch. I want Jake. I want his hands. I want his lips. I want his mouth. I want his arms.

I want his body. I want him. Maybe because he's all I know? He is a disease I yearn to be infected by indefinitely. Why? I need help. I need sex. I need sex with a guy I have smoldering heat with. It has been way too long. It has been over six months too long. Is that desire so much to ask for? I didn't know the definition of intimacy before I met him. And now a moment of interlude as I tearfully recall a significant time in my life eight years ago...

Many moons ago at a university far far away in New York City, there were two biology lab partners who found themselves at the end of their school semester. As they were walking away from what would be their last class together, naïve girl (that'd be me) said "I'm going to miss this class and you as a lab partner. I hate to admit it... I'll even miss that bitch, Veronica. Then the courageous boy (whom I'll refer to as Mr. Unconditional) said fast and nervously "So... I think you need to go out with me and I think this is the weekend... yes, there's a party my friend's having... so how about I pick you up beforehand and we'll grab some sick sushi on Bleecker. It's a great place, you'll love it. No reason we should start missing each other." I remember vividly being in shock because A. He was charmingly handsome, tall and a hell of a good guy. He had the most gorgeous gazing pair of cornflower blue eyes I've ever seen. His thick dark brown hair complemented his golden peach skin tone that he thanked his "Black Irish liquor mixed with French vanilla ice cream descent" for. And B. I couldn't believe a guy like him actually liked me like that. Blame it on my inane insecurity and lack of dating experience since I didn't have a boyfriend in high school. But there I was, in disbelief that he was interested in a pale preppy doe-like me, and all I could muster up was "You like me, really?" He smiled, nodded no and said "Yes." Then he hugged me. Like it was yesterday, I can recall the feeling of being comfortable and safe enveloped against his broad chest, arms wrapped firmly around me. How his warm hands would defrost my iced ones within seconds. Before he let me go he said with his chin over my head "Since the first day of class, you beautiful naïve girl." From that moment on, the word safe had a new definition for me when I was with him, no one could harm me in his presence. The way he touched me with his eyes let alone his hands and body, smothering me with affection, fun, adventure, and companionship. It was the only time in my years breathing I experienced being loved unconditionally, relationship-wise and did I mention he was my first, sexually speaking? You know that has a little something to do with it, right? We were living proof that biorhythms exist; it's in the pheromones and ours were one hundred percent in synch. There are certain people in your presence that will make you go obsessively crazy at the mere subconscious scent of them, leaving you scorched hotter than Georgia asphalt. Jake had that effect on me. He loved sex, which in turn made me love it. I know for certain his addictive personality helped him in that regard. That same trait also aided in our break-up along with personal evolutions and my failure to love him unconditionally. There were substantial reasons why I lost the courage, succumbing to defeat. We embraced our flaws and accentuated our strengths, till the inevitable implosion that night and all was lost.

I need an internal rubdown with a guy I'm lusting over. I know I've crushed Jake horribly and he still hasn't forgiven me. I don't blame him. We made a promise to be with each other forever and I couldn't keep that promise. My inadequacy will haunt me for the rest of my life. Until I receive help. Therapy is scheduled but it's not soon enough. I want to call him and make him understand my side of the story. I don't know if I will ever have the chance to set things straight with him. I hope he's alright. I don't want him to hate me. I want to kiss him. I want to touch every cell of his body. I want to taste him. He had such a delicious taste. He is tragic for me, yet I still burn for him. I am willing to admit one of my greatest fears is never having unconditional love again. Great loves come along yes, but most likely containing contingency clauses with exhibits attached to them deeming it anything but unconditional. What about passion? One could only hope that their new found love is rated above a ten on the passion meter. Considering how significant unconditional love is, I'm grateful to have had it at least once, intimately. Proceeding onward I will keep striving to get back to where I once belonged and maybe, just maybe, gain faith falling in love again. I am channeling with tenacious effort for inner peace and courage to accept the prognosis of no antidote available to remedy my confounded condition. I want to be content with my decision, acceding it was the right choice and quench this uncontrollable fire inside that used to have Jake as a resident. I need a new occupant, a new flame to project my fever on and dwell over. The only other guy I can think of is an old friend of mine, Ethan Kilgore.

Before I salivate over him, I recall my last trial and tribulation a couple of months ago in the pathetic dating scene since the bombing. I have been out a couple of times and people, I can assure you, it is slim pickings out there. Case in point, this guy that hit on me at Trader Joe's in San Francisco, two years ago when I was out there for a work convention. This cute man standing behind me on the checkout line, whom I will refer to as shithead, chatted me up. As I was ready to leave, he had asked for my phone number and to take me out that weekend. I told him I was happily spoken for and only visiting for a few days from New York. He was disappointed but asked to keep in touch by friending me on facebook. I thought it was a weird request since we didn't know each other but abided him with a limited profile view. A few months ago he moved to New York and saw my literal broken-heart picture status of no longer engaged. Which by the way facebook, do you know what that does to a potentially suicidal person? Take that atrocity of an option out now, it's not amusing, it's just plain cruel. Anyway, shithead sent me an email shortly thereafter asking me out. I had reservations understandably with why was he still single after all this time? Was he stalking me for the past two years, wishing for my relationship demise so he could hook up with a famous deejay? I had no ambition of responding to him till Bianca and Sandra insisted I *give him a chance*. I emailed him a week later and we wound up meeting at a hotel bar, where we enjoyed a couple of drinks and surprisingly, had great chemistry. I lied saying I had a thing to go to after our date, he walked me to my car and we had a sizzling make-out session. I could've kicked myself because I wanted to rip his clothes off right then and there and would have, had I not told him about fictitious plans. I looked on the bright side that the wait would make our hookup even hotter. It also gave me the chance to snoop by finding information about him on Google. I figured he would pass inspection as long as he wasn't a rapist or a murderer and didn't have any STD's. My desperate need to finally have fun with no strings attached, after months of a dry spell, and a pressing need to be naughty clouded my typical prerequisite list to date a guy. By the time our second date rolled around (he rescheduled two times), he was drugged out of his mind on Percocet's for a *sporting injury* and opted to drink like a fish at dinner. Before the plates were taken away, he passed out face down on his rigatoni alla vodka. I was mortified. The owner came out and helped wake him up as I watched everyone around me pointing and whispering at my fallen dud of a date. After he regained consciousness, I helped clean his face as he apologized, insisting *the booze and meds were a bad mix.* You think? Astute prognosis, shithead. I kept saying to myself, why couldn't he have sucked it up for one night and take a goddamn Aleve? A kink in the arm could have easily done wonders on Naproxen Sodium. I looked hot that night, dammit. I justified his mishap to myself while we walked out of the restaurant by forgiving his passing out episode as long as he made it up to me in bed. Instead, he quickly pecked my lips and whisked off grabbing a cab home to sleep on a Saturday night at 9:30 PM. I was dumbfounded because this guy obviously liked me, and kept telling me so even during his narcoleptic break. What the fuck? Or in my case, lack thereof. Maybe he had another booty call lined up and didn't want to cancel out on a sure thing since he couldn't bank on me this early in the game? Little did he know. He called me fifteen minutes later while I was driving and too disgusted to answer, I let it roll to voicemail. Instead of calling it an early night, I stopped by Bianca's party with her married friends. My brother-in-law, Mark greeted me at the door with left-handed optimism: *Why in God's name, are you here alone right now, looking as*

41

hot as you do?

I was flattered, yet I wanted to throw darts at him as I responded: *That's the question I've been trying to answer for the last hour, Mark. Now give me an unforgiving drink or joint, before I drown myself in your pool.*

Later on in a drunken daze, I told the whole party about how my date went and they were all unanimous with Mark's sentiments: *he's either gay or the biggest idiot on two feet and totally gay.* Bianca asked: *What did the shithead's message say? Put your phone on speaker and play it.* I raised the volume on my speaker phone and played it for everyone to hear.

Hey Claire... I am so sorry about bouncing after such an embarrassing episode... I hope you don't hold it against me. I'm so groggy and need to sleep it off. I'll be better next time we go out. How does next weekend look for you? Give me a call during the week. Miss your gorgeous face already.

All the guests laughed and yelled loud boos. Bianca clanked her glass with a spoon: *Listen up everyone. I vote Claire kicks this flakey shit-head to the curb... he doesn't deserve another chance. Who's with me?* Everyone raised their hands, including me. Later on, in the wee hours, the party narrowed down to a couple of Mark's friends from college, who added wood to the fire pit in the backyard. Someone was clever enough to bring marshmallows and roasting sticks. It wound up being a glorious night after all; the sky was lit up by the full moon and flickering amber flames. After we downed two bags of roasted sugar puffs, we all fell asleep outside on lounge couches and hammocks. The one time I decided to have sex without a relationship, it bit me in the ass and unfortunately, not in the fun literal sense. As for shithead, I made the partygoers proud and kicked him to the proverbial sidewalk, expressing how disappointing his abrupt exit on our second date was. Naturally, he didn't like hearing my directness—well too bad, you drugged out moron. This would be my life from now on, dealing with consistent ridiculousness of so-called pursuers. I was convinced Jake had put a curse on me. If he couldn't end up with me, then no other guy would. Does his curse entail me never getting my groove on again? I should just bite the bullet and go to church, light a candle praying for this abominable hex to be lifted. I should also pray to make love again with a lothario I am pining to go down on. Which brings me back to the reference I made earlier; the only guy at the moment, I would love to get to know in the biblical sense.

Ethan is hot. Ethan is extremely smart. Ethan is in a famous band. Ethan knew me before his notoriety. Ethan is one of the coolest guys on earth. Ethan is a classically-trained musician and consummate guitar player. I want Ethan to play me like his beloved guitar. Ethan has amazing hands. Ethan knows how to use his hands. I know Ethan would be a rock star in bed; I just know it. Ethan can command naughty boy band ass. Ethan is not the typical boy band slut; he's selective and loyal. Ethan thinks I'm stunning. Ethan is no longer involved with his girlfriend, I hope. Ethan has sort of expressed how he feels for me in subtle flirty ways. Ethan is a good man. Ethan is hyper intelligent and yes, I know I alluded to this before. Ethan is one of my oldest friends—will this ruin our friendship? I'm willing to take that chance. Ethan needs to contact me soon, vibrator city till then. I know I need help and promise to get it, but I need to be touched all over first. Internal rubdown must happen, soon. Lord, hear my prayer and please grant my request in this horrible time of suffering. Why did that oriental octopus have to touch my ass?

CHAPTER 5 / *INCONTRARE I GENITORI (MEET THE PARENTS)*

Claudio Convenzionale
Height: 5'7"
Weight: 170 lbs.
Hair Color: Gray/Brown
Eye Color: Emerald Green

Fiorenza Convenzionale
Height: 5'1"
Weight: 135 lbs.
Hair Color: Dark Brown
Eye Color: Gray

So how can I best describe my parents? Well they're just adorable really and I mean that in every sense of the word. When anyone crosses paths with them, the typical reaction is *they're so adorable.* I think it's because they are petite and have the sweetest cherubic faces, epitomizing dark-haired angels. Considering me, my sister Bianca, and brother Dante are between the 5'9" and 6'5" range compared to my compact-size parents, it's hard not to wonder where the hell we Neanderthals came from? Was there a hot Herculean milkman prowling in the discrete picture? Did our dad have clandestine affairs with Amazonian women and now leads a double life? No one really knows for sure, but since the lot of us look like both our parents, we're going on the theory that Mom was on supersonic prenatal vitamins resulting in gargantuan offspring.

Their slight Italian accents aide in the adorableness as well. Even though I'm immune to hearing it, the rest of the population has a field day listening to them. Although it pains me to be submerged in any type of stereotypical cesspool, there is one that I will gladly submit to bending over with, and that's the food. Italians = food. Food is omnipresent. I repeat, food is omnipresent. Food, upon food, upon food, and upon more food. I'm not just talking your basic three square meals here or some shoddy leftovers. I'm talking about skilled prepared perfection at your beck and call twenty-four seven, featuring the richest most opulent feasts. Most of the ingredients like fruits and vegetables are handpicked from their homegrown garden, to make pies, cakes, cookies, pastas, and breads. Another great example of the food phenomena was the last time I met my dad for a bike ride. He just so happened to have a giant jar of kalamata olives with him that his *paisano* Giuseppe randomly gave him when he saw him biking by his house. I don't know what was crazier—my dad having the jar of olives in the first place or him successfully biking while holding it? I wish I could make this stuff up. It's unbelievable to the layman's eye, but anyone of Italian or European descent knows this to be comically true.

Since as far back as I can remember, all of the family holiday gatherings which guaranteed a six-course meal were held at my parent's house; this still holds true. One of my fondest memories as a kid was sitting at the dinner table in awe of the picturesque food display, aka glorified food porn. The kaleidoscope of colors and entrancing aromas that permeated into my pores seeping and swirling into every cell. Then the inexplicable taste, oh that taste that would send me into a feeding frenzy. And the portions were big. So big, you would expand a bunch of inches after consumption. When I was growing up, I was, how shall we say? On the fuller side? Pillsbury-dough like? The best description would be, I was a fat ass kid—a spade's a spade, remember that. It makes sense as I recall my younger years and the exorbitant amounts of food I ate. My childhood would be best described as swimming in a pool of ostentatious edible delights. When I met Jake and saw the nutritional light with the amount of nakedness our relationship required, it helped me dwindle down from five portions of pasta to hardly one. It kills my mom (let alone me) whenever I follow her back to the pot, scooping out three quarters of what she just put on my dish. I had no choice at the time since I used to gain weight if I didn't eat like a bird and run like a racehorse. Now, I have issues trying to gain weight since Jake and I crashed; the irony I tell you. Of course in my parent's eyes, I'm now too thin. They prefer me with more meat on my bones which means anytime they visit, they bring trays of meals in high hopes of me indulging every morsel. Utter failure on my part and I admit it happily since my stomach has shrunk and I can't consume half of what I used to. It's fine by me, I love my body now and I'll be damned to ever be a pork chop again, strip of bacon is where it's at. The only exception I wouldn't fathom blowing a fire extinguisher on is my birthday cake. My annual tradition of unadulterated dessert sin and trust me, I go at it like a pro. In fact when I broke off my engagement to Jake, he asked for the recipe because and I quote "I will eventually get over you, but I cannot live the rest of my dying days without ever having your birthday cake again. You owe this to me." Since I was in a guilt-ridden state, I had no choice but to fiercely persuade my mom to give him the handwritten gem. Keep in mind I don't even have it; she has all her recipes in her Last Will and Testament. She made a promise to her family that as long as she is breathing, she will cook. That is why everyone who celebrates with me knows their piece of cake is on the small side. It's my only time to enjoy mounds of sweet significance for a couple of days after, worth any potential weight gain. An obscene concoction of all my favorite sweets compiled into a gorgeously crafted work of edible art. Allow me to elaborate.

Claire's Birthday Cake

First layer – Mom's gooey chocolate chip cookies
Second layer – Mom's spicy devil's food chipotle fudge cake.
Third layer – pumpkin pie with roasted marshmallows and graham cracker
crust (you read that right)

Toppings
Hot Fudge, Almond Butter, lemon Curd, nuts, and whipped Cream
(scoop of peanut butter ice cream optional)

Well there you have it, my annual treat of tooth cavity explosion. On that note, they will be here soon. I hope my parents like the guys. They are expected at noon which means they will arrive at 11:40 AM because Mom will be early for her own funeral, God love her.

"So fellas, my parents will be here in a half hour... do me a favor... no cursing, okay."

Shane shoots a piercing look at me with an, *are you kidding me right now... how could you have ever doubted us you crazy bitch?* look.

"Claire, you're stressing for no reason and I'm highly insulted you would think we wouldn't be on our best behavior. I pride myself on good standings with all the 'rents I've met. Trust me... there isn't a mama out there that doesn't love this face."

I am a crazy bitch. "It's not you I'm worried about... haha... just playin' J Dog."

Jared smiles and gives me the middle finger.

"They'll be bringing lunch and you can take home

leftovers... if you can do me another favor. Please tell them when they ask, and they will ask both of you, if I've been eating substantial lunches and doing well here. Please give me a stellar report card; it's important to me and I'll explain their concern another time."

Shane gives me two thumbs up and Jared responds "What's in it for us? I mean... I don't like lying to anybody's parents. Besides you don't eat enough and don't get me started on those puke green whatever liquid crap drinks you down, yuck!"

"First up Jasta, you wouldn't be lying... it's just your definition of a substantial lunch includes twenty piece hot wings with bacon dripped suicide sauce, fries and beer. You know I'm a healthier nut than you, so our views are different and those super green smoothies I get are delicious, by the way. Secondly, did I not say you will be given a bunch of food to bring home?"

Jared looks unimpressed. "Food is overrated."

Shane scratches his head in disbelief. "Dude, speak for yourself. Do you realize these people about to stop by are off the boat Italians? Do you have a clue to the significance of that? I'm in Captain. I'll lie, cheat, beg, steal, and whatever else you may need... I'm your go-to guy. Maybe we should give J Dog the rest of the day off so I can bask in more food glory."

"Hmm... good point Shane. Thank you from the bottom of my lyrical heart. I knew I could count on you. So what will it be, Jared... yes or no?"

Jared knows he's lost this battle. "Aye aye, Captain."

You've got to love men and the simplicity of their requirements to a happy life. I remember what an old family friend, Ginger Cofflin, had said when she was asked at her dinner gathering, what the secret to her successful marriage of twenty-five years was. She answered candidly, *Fuck them and feed them.* The guests couldn't contain themselves with hysterics, especially Jake, who spit out his bite of beef bourguignon from laughing. She was a fun omniscient firecracker and her advice figuratively speaking, is pure gold for the ladies. In regards to my work comrades, the former was completely ruled out, so the latter it was. As I relayed her words of wisdom, the guys agreed along with Jared's two cents.

"Also, good conversation and kindness, too."

"I'm impressed Jaster, usually that's a prerequisite for women."

"And your point being, Claire?" Shane quips.

I receive an IM saying they have arrived. Italian inquisition starts now. The door opens shortly thereafter.

"Hey Mom and Dad... how are you? We were just wrapping up, how was your drive in?"

I hug them both as my Dad answers. "We're doing good, there's was no traffic... smooth sailing. How are you, *bellezza?*"

"Doing real good, thanks. Mom, gorgeous hair as usual."

She touches the back of her hair. "Thanks lovey. I swear CC... you look like you lost more weight from the last time I saw you. Have you been eating well?"

And there it is, like clockwork. I see Shane smile and wink at me as he intervenes.

"Claire orders the best lunches for us. I think we're shaping up with all the running around we do here. Hello Mr.

49

and Mrs. Convenzionale, it's a pleasure to finally meet you both.   On behalf of me and my counterpart Jared, it is an honor to work with your lovely daughter."

Laying it on thick Shane, I love it.   "These are my extraordinary interns, Shane and Jared."

My parents beam as they shake the guy's hands and get acquainted, especially my mother who's enjoying the infectious charms of Shane.

"CC… guess what I just picked from the garden."

"Peaches?"

"Nope."

I'm at a loss. "Plums?"

He smiles. "You're getting warmer."

"Oh wait, it can't be. No… it's too soon. Pluots?"

"Bingo! They're delicious, not bad for my first crop. Probably the best investment out of California in a while, thanks to you stumbling upon them. I just ordered a few more trees from that grower we found online. They're washed, try it."

He throws me one and it's stunning. The texture is smooth and its color is vibrant with rich blush and cabernet tones. The smell is sweet with essence of honeysuckle. I bite into it and immediately teleport back to California, the first time I tried one of these heavenly hybrids.

"It's perfect, Dad. You've outdone yourself on this one."

Dad looks over at Mom. "*Fiore dare le borse calde e fredde termico del cibo e abbiamo fatto si prega di, Claire. Facciamo colazione.*"

Translation: it's lunch time.

"Okay kids, what are we feeling today?"

The guys look at me like deers caught in headlights.

"Well fellas, Mama asked you a question."

Shane looks at Jared. "Whatever you would like to have for lunch. We have no preference, we eat anything."

Mom grabs Dad's shoulder. "I love it, Claudio... the boys are shy. Okay, I'll make it easy for you and let you know the choices. We have chicken cutlet parmigiana, lasagna, penne ala vodka with bacon and shallots, puttanesca, broccoli rabe in garlic olive oil and lemon. We also have baked rabbit with assorted sweet and purple potatoes and marinated string beans."

I couldn't help snicker to myself at the guys expressions. They both had the look of having the most incredible high—their eyes had that notorious glaze over them and I knew they refrained from smoking out of respect.

"In this bag... are poached red snapper with sun dried tomatoes, field greens and dill lemon olive oil dressing. Escarole and beans, braciole, insalata, mashed red potatoes, and pork chops with spicy apple ginger chutney. We also have assorted antipasti and olive bread I made this morning. Would you like anything specific or a taste of everything?"

Now at this point, the guy's mouths are open. They have beads of sweat on their faces, looking as if they are extremely turned on in a state of carnal bliss. Shane notably looks like he just received the best head of his life—first time he's ever been speechless. They both didn't say anything which is a typical reaction for newbies hearing my mom's daily lunch menu for the first time. Mom looks at me with an impatient smirk and I answer for them.

"We'll try a little of everything... thanks."

Little did they know, they were in for another climax with the upcoming dessert choices. We ate lunch in the communal canteen while the guys became acquainted with my parents.

"Oh my God... this food is amazing. I can't believe how good everything tastes. My compliments to you, Mrs. Convenzionale."

"Thanks Jared, but I can't take all the credit, my darling *sposo* helps me in the kitchen."

Shane took second portions of everything and didn't say a word until he finished eating.

"Well Mrs. C., you have ruined me. I thought my mom was a good cook but after this, there's no comparison. Please don't tell her I told you that. Now, I'll be on the hunt for a wife that can wreck a kitchen half as good."

After exchanging some stories, we finished lunch and the boys volunteered to clean up so I could catch up with my parents. Dad puts his arm around my shoulder while we walk down the hall.

"They're nice guys, Claire. You were right. They seem smart and determined which is good. You all have a good camaraderie."

I lead them through the hall into my office. "Thanks Dad, we really do... a welcoming relief from the fiasco last year."

Mom raises her eyebrows. "I remember that... oh I didn't like those snotty girls. They weren't raised right. Remember the stories Claire would tell us, Claudio?"

He pulls chairs out for both of us. "Yes... they

weren't very kind... nothing but *porca putanas!*" I love when Dad says that, his tone with such vigor.

My mom motions for my attention. "So now that we can talk, tell us, how are you doing? Have you heard from Jake? Is he still recuperating? Please don't get upset and take this the wrong way, but you are painfully thin. Baby, you need to put weight on, we're worried seeing you like this."

"I'm not upset Mom and you're right. I have lost some weight and it wasn't intentional... it's just stress took a toll on me. Honestly, I'm feeling better these days, especially this past month. In regards to Jake, I don't know. He made it perfectly clear he doesn't want me to reach out. It was hard at first to accept since we left some things unfinished... I had no choice but to adhere to his wishes. I got a phone call from his sister Greer; she left a message and I haven't even listened to it yet. The last time I spoke with him, his heart condition was improving and he had said the doctor's anticipated a decent recovery despite the irreversible damage. I will call her back and let you know what she says. I want to thank you both for being there for me. I know I wasn't myself during that time and you stood by me with no questions asked, as always—my security blankets. You never put unneeded pressure on me throughout the whole ordeal or bashed Jake when things fell apart between us. You could have understandably, but you supported my decisions instead and I'll never forget that."

Dad put his arm around me. "*Bellissima,* as long as you're happy, then we're happy. We've always said that from day one for all you kids. Whatever you decide we're here for you. We're proud at how far you've come. Don't worry as you deal with the aftermath, because this downturn will pass. You need anything, just let us know. Do you remember what I've always said about life?"

"Life's a rollercoaster ride. Lots of ups and downs, fun, turns, adventure, and challenges. No matter what's behind the turn, always have faith on your journey and enjoy the ride as best you can."

"That's right, CC. Just know things will fall into place as they are meant to. You'll be back to your old self in no time. Promise us you'll reach out if you need anything... no matter what."

"Yes." My eyes were swollen with gratitude as I hugged them. My dad's words were reminiscent to the lyrics of the song Jake used to sing to me. This is a promise I intend to keep.

CHAPTER 6 / *THE NOOSE*

(Heard over the loudspeaker in Pennsylvania Station)

All aboard Track 21. Babylon Train making stops at Woodside, Forest Hills, Kew Gardens, Jamaica, Saint Albans, Valley Stream, Lynbrook, Rockville Centre, Baldwin, Freeport, Merrick, Bellmore, Wantagh, Seaford, Massapequa, Massapequa Park, Amityville, Copiague, Lindenhurst, and Babylon. Change at Jamaica for connections to Oyster Bay and Ronkonkoma.

I can recite this announcement in my sleep. I've heard it since I first went to Penn Station as a kid. I usually follow along with the announcer out loud as I'm walking through the corridor that leads to the Seventh Avenue exit. I had thought for a long time that this was prerecorded in the early 1980's, till I figured out subtle differences from the unenthused announcer each day. For example, how one or two words are occasionally dropped or the vocal rhythmic flow differentiates at times. I swear it's the same old dude with his flat monotone voice. I need to meet and give this guy friendly pointers on how to improve his speaking skills, since I will be commuting for the rest of my dying days—I'm way too spoiled to live in a Manhattan box. I like that a forty-five minute train ride grants me five times more living space for my buck conveniently located next to the beach. Luckily, I was able to keep the spacious condo Jake and I purchased together four years ago. It was his decision for me to wind up with it since he felt horrible for what he put me through. During our happier times, we decided to keep the lease on the first apartment we shared as a couple, a cozy one bedroom in Gramercy that resembled the one in the movie *Barefoot in the Park*. We wound up subletting it when Jake's job moved us to a swankier one in the West Village. After he switched jobs, we moved back and utilized the Gramercy spot for when Jake worked late and didn't want to commute to the beach. The last I heard, Jake was in the process of finding another place without our memories. In the whole time we spent in that city apartment, I never slept peacefully. Maybe it was the street noise or the hustle and bustle. Looking back, I think it was a sign. On my way to work, I notice an old friend from college coming out of Andrew's Coffee Shop. It has to be at least two years if not more since I have seen her. I knew Rosalind from Columbia, I had met her in a Philosophy class our sophomore year. We kept up our friendship for the rest of our college days, gaining a lot of mutual friends. Interestingly, we never quite had the solid connection to sustain keeping in touch exclusively after we graduated.

"Hey Rosalind, is that you?"

"Wow, Claire… how are you? It's so good to see you after all this time… you look great."

"Thanks… you do too. It's so nice to see you. What are you doing up at this hour?"

"I couldn't sleep so I figured I'd go for a jog and get some coffee. Are you on your way to the station?"

"Yes, which way are you headed? We can catch up walking together."

"That'd be great, I'm going uptown."

We walk up Seventh Avenue. "How long has it been, Roz… two years or so? You look amazing by the way. I'm digging the short hair on you; it's a nice change."

"Thanks Claire. Yeah, I finally had the nerve to cut

off the long mess... and gosh, I think it's been three years since we've seen each other. Wasn't it at Iris's going away? Even though we don't see each other as often as we should... I feel connected to you through your show. I religiously listen in... I love it. I always knew back at college you would be one of the greats."

"Aww Roz, thank you. That means so much. Did you ever wind up getting that residency at Lenox Hill?"

"Yes, and I wish someone would've talked me out of becoming a doctor."

Roz's eyes look heavy suddenly as her voice becomes low with a somber tone.

"Claire, I just want to say it was so sad to hear from Jake's sister about you two and what happened. Then, sadly with his shocking suicide attempt a couple of weeks back, well you still must be devastated. Oh my God Claire, are you okay? You're flushed... you poor thing, here I got you... sit down on the bench."

Suicide attempt, what? It can't be. I feel like I'm hyperventilating. This can't be true. I need to speak with him.

"Roz, what do you mean suicide attempt? I didn't... I don't... know what are you talking about? What happened? Where did you hear this?"

"I'm so sorry... I didn't realize you didn't know. I ran into Greer at Whole Foods last week, she was so distraught... hysterical about it. She had said Jake was recuperating in the hospital after downing a bottle of painkillers. She told me about what happened between you two and his stay at St. Vincent's six months ago after you guys broke up. Greer said she had called you about it... I presumed you knew. I am so sorry you had to find out like this. Claire, from what we've heard, please know everyone's on your side. We all would have done the same thing. It's hell dealing with someone who has a drug problem. You know I love Jake... all of us do, but he always had that crutch unfortunately. You were great influence for him... we all thought he had kicked his habit for good when you guys became official but..."

I am at a loss for words, like someone has sewed my lips shut.

"Claire, please let me help you... I'll grab us breakfast and you'll feel better."

"Roz, thank you but I have to get to work so let's meet up another time. I'm okay... I just... I just need to get to work."

Roz holds me commiseratively while hailing a cab that drove us to the station. She escorts me inside and goes next door to the deli to get me something to eat. I didn't want anything, all I wanted is to hear Jake's voice. She comes into the studio and forces me to have a piece of a croissant egg sandwich. I felt like I was going to vomit after a few bites and sips of coffee. Shane and Jared showed up and I told them I wasn't feeling well and needed to lie down for a bit in the lounge. They assured me they would cover the show using the prerecorded disc we have on file. I had to talk to Greer. I never listened to her voicemail when she had called that time. Why didn't I listen to it? I love his sister; I should've listened and called her back. My hand won't stop shaking as I struggle to call her. Roz does the honors for me. My stomach feels like another bomb went off. Please pick up Greer. Please pick up.

"Claire, did you ever get my message?"

"I never listened to it and I'm so sorry... it had nothing to do with you. I was just trying to heal up and wasn't ready to talk to you. I regret not listening to your message... I just found out from Roz who's here with me now. Greer, what happened? Please tell me he didn't do it… I'm so torn up."

"It's true… such a nightmare for all of us. Jake is finally seeing a psychiatrist due to our insistence… we've been supporting him through this. I know this has been horrible for you since that night and his stay in the hospital the first time. Please don't blame yourself."

"Thanks for saying that, Greer. It helps shed some layers of guilt I have on me. How are your parents? I feel so bad for them."

"I know… they're holding up with antidepressants. They figured you didn't know because you would have called."

"They're right… please apologize for me. Is it possible for you to meet up today? It would help me to see you."

"Yes, of course… I can swing it. I miss you, Claire. I'm just so sad he had to cause all of this. I love my brother but…"

"I know all too well. He'll work this out… he's owes it to all of you."

"And you too. I can stop by for a little now… oh but you're working, right?"

"My interns are covering for me, come by whenever you can."

"Okay, I'm actually close by… I'll be there soon."

I felt relieved, yet I still couldn't fathom Jake committing suicide. What happened to the man I was engaged to? He was a stranger to me now because no way would the guy I knew, ever attempt something like this. I felt split in half—remorseful and atavistic rage. I want to push him against the wall and scream at his selfish propensity. That familiar feeling of frustration over his callousness has seeped in all over again. Shortly thereafter, Rosalind left and Greer showed up, continuing our conversation from where we left off.

"Why did he do this? It doesn't sound like him... I just can't believe it."

She nods as she dries her eyes with tissue. "I know Claire, I'm still in shock. He finally opened up about it last week to me. He said he just didn't want to go on anymore and he was embarrassed by the devastation he caused all of us. The good news is he's progressing forward with his therapy treatment, slowly getting back to his old self."

"I'm glad to hear that, I just can't get over the fact he got to that point. I don't mean to put you in an awkward situation but do you know if... if he hates me?"

"He doesn't hate you, Claire. He hates himself for driving you away... that's why he doesn't want to see you. I have begged him many times to talk with you for closure, but he says it's too painful right now and he only blames himself."

The pangs in my gut weren't beating as hard. Hearing Greer relay his message sufficed since I couldn't hear it from him and she's always been honest with me.

"Greer, I want you to know this hasn't been easy for me either. I am also going to therapy, my first appointment's next week. I wish this would've never happened... his relapse and our breakup but I had no other choice. You realize that, right? You know I love your family like my own and it hurts me that I can't see you and sustain the great relationship we once had because of this mess."

Greer looks down at the floor with her hand on my

back. "I feel the same way… we all have nothing but love for you. We know it's his fault. As much as it pains us to have to point a finger, it is what it is. We only hope that you two can make peace with what happened eventually. I feel he will get there, talking with you someday… only he knows when. It's sad to hear you have gotten to the point where you need to see a therapist also. If he falls into the bell jar one more time, I'll be seeing one with you. I just want you both well."

I escorted Greer out and we promised to keep tabs on each other. She will keep me in the loop on Jake's progress. I felt heavyhearted hugging her goodbye. Severing close ties with loved ones against your own will, leaving them behind with the wind to your back as you bravely march forward, is no task for the weary. I head back to the studio, to help close out the show. I am in desperate need of a mood changer. Outside the door, I overhear them arguing over the errors Jared has made.

"Hey guys I'm back. Thanks for covering. How did everything go?"

Shane is fidgeting with nervous energy. "Not bad till Jared screwed up the prerecorded show we taped yesterday. It appears we've lost everything and have to start from scratch now."

"Not necessarily… let me see what magic I can work, so no worries. This antiquated piece of crap machine always acts up, I heard we're getting a new one by January. How you doing… Jared?"

"Not bad, but I'm sick of hearing shit from him anytime things don't go perfectly his way. My forte is manning the control board."

"Fair enough and agreed. Shane, please do me a favor and try to have more patience when things don't go as planned, okay?"

"Aye aye, Captain... sorry J Bone, I don't mean to lose it. By the way, did you know we have a noose hanging high above us... right above your seat?"

They finally noticed and it only took them six weeks. The noose was a souvenir from the late great Eli "Wolfman" Peterson, a charismatic long bearded deejay, reminiscent of the late Wolfman Jack. He used the noose as a gag for his daredevil guests that frequented his show. The adrenaline freaks would hysterically hang from it for amusement; it was painful to watch—precisely the reaction they were looking for. Our whole crew decided to keep it up as a symbol of his celebrity after he died in a snowboarding accident. I miss you, Wolfman, you bought the farm way too young.

Jared raises his hand. "The late great Wolfman? Who is he... how did he die?"

I had no time to get into it, as we were about to start from the commercial break.

"Jared, when in doubt, Google it. Okay fella's, where we at?"

Shane IM's me: Looks like I'm not the only one who has no patience for his clueless ass lol.

I type back: True, but I can get away with it. How much time do we have before we go live?

Shane says "Thirty-five seconds and counting."

I advise Shane he would complete the on-air show portion and he couldn't have been happier. I felt it wouldn't have the right flow if I came aboard with less than two hours left. I join Jared in manning the audio consoles and production board. I tell him he is about to learn the art of crossfade and his face lights up. I am also in the mood for a little old school cue burn and broke out my reliable record, David Bowie's *The Rise and Fall of Ziggy Stardust and the Spiders from Mars*. I alert Shane to follow my lead by watching my hand signals for his cue to announce. Jared puts the caller line to voice mail as we're about to have some fun. Being a producer is a rewarding job and I was relishing the rare opportunity of doing it full time. I set up a slew of killer songs that would make Jake proud. Some notables included Soundgarden's "Fell On Black Days," U2's "Tripped Through Your Wires," Depeche Mode's "Flies On The Windscreen," Weezer's "The Good Life," Bryan Adams "It Cuts Like a Knife," Live's Unplugged version of Vic Chestnutt's "Supernatural." Along with The Pretender's "Talk Of The Town," The Black Crowes "Remedy," and The Police's "I Can't Stand Losing You." I also set up a half hour flow of two plays with the same song title from two different bands such as The Bogman and Bad Motorcycle Club songs "Suddenly." I also included two versions of Huddie Ledbetter's "Where Did You Sleep Last Night" using the original and Nirvana's gut wrenching cover version.

Jared looks at me. "Kick-ass choices, Captain."

Shane messages me with IM's: **I don't know what you're smoking, but this music set is off the charts, you're on fire!**

I hand Shane an edited copy of his close-out script to look over and relay on-air.

"This next set goes out to all the suffering souls that are in strong need of being remedied. Whether you're nursing a health ailment, lack of funds, fear of being shot by madmen on the loose, or whatever woes it may be. How many of us can relate? I know it helps me, having empathetic company in my current hardship… I hope it does for you too. We're all trying to get by as best we can, but let's not forget to look out for one another out there. We're in this together. I want to thank you for listening to me, Shane Salinger, on 97.2 WLDM. I can safely say, things can and will get better. On that note, enjoy this one from Howard Jones."

I pressed play in synch with Shane's last sound and it went off without a hitch, his delivery was flawless. I knew Jake listened to the show sometimes post breakup; Greer had mentioned it to me. I am hopeful he tuned in today, because behind Shane's voice, he would know the message was mine. For this segment, we three amigos had never worked better together. It was a welcome relief having a break from my talking head performance; time behind the scenes is what the show needed. Shane is a natural. Anytime I speak on-air my stomach clenches up a bit from nervousness, a trait I've never been able to shake. Not for him, you can hear his excitement as soon as his first word rolls out. Jared is his polar opposite, preferring back office production mechanics. Though his researching could use improvement, his technical capacity is unmatched. He is a consummate engineer who excels under pressure, having the patience of a saint, which Shane and I lack. I have allowed him to soar in production but in order to be an unmatched producer, he needs to master all aspects of this job. It is time to throw him into the announcer's pool without a life preserver. Shane IM's asking for the last song. I already had it set and write back: "**Chloe Dancer / Crown of Thorns.**" **If you don't know who the band is, I pity you.** He looks up at me smiling with his thumbs up while he enchants his audience crediting, Mother Love Bone's finest. After the show wrapped, Jared's enthusiasm is in overdrive.

"Is it just me or was that show fanfuckingtastic! Claire, I can't believe you did that spontaneously and bravo Shane... you nailed it."

Shane walks over to Jared, grabs his arm leading towards me and gives us both a big bear hug—embracing us in his clenches. He expresses his gratitude for being able to air the whole show. I pat them both on the back, feeling like a proud

Mom.

"Claire, what inspired that phenomenal set?"

"Tragedy." Shane gulps as Jared puts his hand on my shoulder consolingly.

Shane clears his throat. "Well I reckon there was a little positive inspiration mixed in too... superb job."

We gather our belongings to leave and I stare at the noose, unable to look away. I wondered what it would feel like around my neck. I don't know what provoked me to step up on my desk underneath the hanging contraption, but here I am with my head through the opening. It feels uncomfortably scratchy. Shane calls out with his back towards me.

"Clairista, are you ready to bounce?"

Jared turns around, looks me up and down with his eyebrows raised to the ceiling in disbelief. "Um... Claire what are you doing? Please come down from there."

I am frozen, unable to feel anything, not even the rope anymore. I try to speak but nothing comes out as I stare at the door. I hear the guys mumble in a serious tone but I can't articulate their words coherently. They are clever enough to know I am in legitimate trauma. I finally feel something, warm tears stream out of my eyes. My arms are heavy, preventing me to wipe my face. Seems the shell-shock of Jake's demise has hit me again, despite the reprieve of that commemorative song set. The guys are standing below my hip.

Shane softly whispers "Alright sweetie, everything will be fine... I'm going to help bring you down from there. Please don't move. What happened today? Can you speak? Does it have something to do with those girls that were here earlier? We'll take care of you. Don't be afraid... I'm just taking this thing off your neck so I can carry you down. I won't let you fall."

I don't know what has come over me. Slowly, I feel blood pumping in my veins, as if I was thawing from being cryogenically stored in a pose. I feel Shane's warm fingertips touch my neck as he takes the noose off. Jared stands below with his arms out as a point guard to be our net in case we topple over. Shane wraps his arm around my waist and takes his other arm around the back of my knees and lifts me. He steps down on the chair Jared placed in front of the desk.

"Jake tried to kill himself. I'm sorry I... "

"I had a feeling it had something to do with him. He really messed you up, didn't he? Sorry to hear... it's terrible. We'll make sure you get home safe... J Bone, when we reach the Island, we'll share a cab to our houses from Claire's, is that cool?"

"Absolutely. Captain, whatever you need, just say it."

I had no choice but to take them up on their offer as they whisked me in a taxi to Penn Station, we then boarded the train together. For the first time in my life I didn't want to be alone—I felt debilitated. The guys dropped me off at Sandra's instead; she lived close by and was readily available. I didn't want to stay at my sister's because my niece and nephew wouldn't have recognized their aunt in my present state. I'm glad I have the weekend to veg out and regain the surge of positive energy I had before hearing the lamentable news. I kept thinking back to the guys on our train ride home and how they effortlessly made me laugh. They didn't mention my mishap once, kept our train talk light, reiterating their fondness over our touching show and Shane's friend's Hamptons Beach party tomorrow night. He boasted how lucky he is to have a rich friend who throws sick parties and how much fun it will be, insisting Jared and I had to go. I always made a concerted effort not to fraternize with the interns, for fear of creating awkwardness in regards to getting the job done. After my freeze frame moment earlier, I knew they were different and had nothing to worry about. Besides, Sandra and I were in dire need of a mind-blowing party to go to.

CHAPTER 7 / *GLAZED DONUTS AND A BOTTLE OF ANYTHING TO GO!*

Oh... oh... oh... ahh... oh... (beep beep beep beep) Damn you alarm clock! Wow, I can't remember the last time I had a sex dream so vivid. Word to the wise, Billy Joel; sometimes a fantasy isn't all you need. I'm still on the fence about attending Shane's party tonight. I don't know if it's a good idea for me to expose another side of myself in front of the guys. Then on the other hand, it would be sweet to inhale some la-la and Lord knows at that party, they'll be rivers full. How long has it been since I've climbed the green mountain—a year? No, it was longer, almost two years ago at Greer's Birthday Bash. Man was I out of my skin that night, I was so lit. I remember being so aroused I couldn't keep my hands off Jake, he had to pull over on the shoulder of Hutchinson State Parkway to avoid having an accident. We wound up getting it on in the back of our Range Rover. Even though we were roughly a half hour away from the city, I couldn't wait. Naturally, I am uninhibited behind closed doors, but I become an exemplified wilder version when I'm baked on weed. That in of itself is a strong argument on why I shouldn't attend the bash, yet I keep convincing myself I'm due for a far-out unadulterated time. That's it, my mind is made up. Sandra will chaperone me, making sure I am taken home before I howl at the moon.

(Phone rings) "Hello, you have reached the autumn of my discontent."

I hear Sandra breathing. "Claire, is that you?"

We have been friends since we're four and she knows my voice. Her iPhone clearly states my name when she rings me, actually it reads Cannoli bitch. Why does she ask me this every time I answer her call?

"Sandster, this is Claire... who else would it be? Why do you always ask?"

"Well, you never know these days. Maybe that crazy dude from *A Clockwork Orange*, has ganked your phone... so I want to make sure I'm speaking to the right person. Anyway, what time shall I pick you up and where exactly is this place? I think you mentioned East Hampton, right?"

"Great, now I have the willies thinking about Malcolm McDowell from that movie wearing a bowler hat. Hold on... let me check Shane's e-mail. Yes, it's East Hampton, right by Georgica Pond. My, that's a snazzy spot. You sure you're down to drive?"

"Yeah... no problem, I'll stay awake and get us home. We can't rely on you, since you'll be passed out by midnight."

"Yes, damn occupational hazard. Cool Sands... and do me another favor... make sure I don't do anything stupid. Please. Even if we wind up too blitzed to drive home and have to crash in the bedroom Shane's reserved for us... please make sure I don't let the inner slut out."

"Okay, but can I let mine out? I could use a man in a big way. There will be guys our age there, right? Can you skip the *Cosa Nostra* brunch tomorrow morning? It would be cool if we could just crash there and sleep in."

She had a good point but I had dodged my family too many times since the breakup and Bianca threatened me with my head on the line.

"I wish I could Sands, but I have to be there. I appreciate you sucking up the night call. Oh and yes... Shane said his friend's older brother has a bunch of friends going so no danger of being a MILF. Just ignore Shane if he puts the moves on you."

"No prob, he's not my type and I hate your family right now. What are you planning to wear?"

"Don't know yet... maybe my pair of Diesel's and that frilly crocheted peasant top I have. What are you thinking?"

"Something comfortable yet border line slutty... you know, my usual."

"Listen Sandster, just have fun tonight. If anyone needs a good time it's you and I'm running right behind... in fact, we may have a photo finish. But please promise me, you'll lock me in the car by myself if my fangs should show... before you potentially get your freak on. I don't want to do anything stupid in front of my work buddies."

"I promise. Now, let me know when you want me to bring you home to get ready. You do realize you crashed at my place."

"Oh right... yes, I figured you were out but now I see you're downstairs and the jokes on me. Let's blow this pop stand and go get brunch at Allegria, my treat."

After we ate and walked the boardwalk, Sandra dropped me home to shower and get ready. I noticed I had a whole bunch of voice messages on my phone. Half were from my family, mostly from Bianca reminding me to be at the family get together tomorrow and wondering if I still exist anymore. I couldn't make out who or what was being said on the next message, delete. Another message from the pharmacy with an automated reminder to renew my birth control prescription. The last one is from Shane checking in with a warning: *I am not accepting any bullshit excuses*. I texted him back saying we would be there soon. I finish putting on makeup when I hear Sandra let herself in with the key I gave her. She gallops up the stairs looking gorgeously hot to boot. What a difference a blowout and some face art makes. I add another layer of shadow to my eyes and compliment her for the inspiration.

"I brought a case of Mike's Light Hard Lemonade and an overnight change as a contingency plan. What about you? Do you need to stop at the store for bevs?"

"No Sandster, I'm good. Mike's Light, eh... my condolences. I on the other hand have a bottle... make that two bottles of anything and a box of glazed donuts to go... I'm talking about a Yankee Rose."

"I love that song, I'll blast it in the car."

"That's my girl. No offense to Hagar, but Van Halen died for me when Diamond Dave left. You know that, right?"

She smirks while she picks lint off my blouse. "All too well my friend... oh my God, You really do have bottles of *Anything* wine and glazed donuts. Actually, that wine is really good. Screw Mike's, I'm picking up two more of those."

We gather our stuff, pack the car and head out. The drive out there is one for the memory books. Cruising tunes, picturesque scenery and the weather was unbelievably warm for November. Seems Shane had the god Zephyrus in his favor this fine night. We took our time driving and stopped at one of those old farm stands where we ate savory corn on the cob and sweet caramel apples. I got four texts from Shane reading: Are you here yet? Jared arrived and texted same along with: Man there's a lot of people here... where can I find you? I'm by the pinball machine. I didn't respond since we were close by and figured I'd surprise them with our arrival. As we look for a place to park, I couldn't help admire the sunset ocean view; it ran chills down my spine. Sandra suggests we leave our overnight bags in the car, to ensure her promise to me. The game plan is to drive home by 2:00 AM, giving me five solid hours of sleep before breaking bread. I see Shane helping one of his friend's carrying a keg out of the car parked a few spaces away from us.

"Well Ms. Convenzionale, it's about time you graced us with your elegant presence. How are you? May I say you both look extra gorgeous tonight."

Sandra blushes as my ego inflates. "Thanks Shane, you're not looking bad yourself and hmm… is that *Curve* I smell?"

Shane has that infamous look on his face that guys get when they are given a compliment from a captivating girl they admire. I can't peg the adjective to describe it, but it's a fetching visage to marvel at. Like he's a teenager all over again at the high school dance and the girl of his dreams says yes and waltzes away with him. After we hug each other, he leads us up the long driveway without saying a word—unusually reserved. Sandra and I gush like fifteen-year-olds when we step into the grandiose mansion fit for Gatsby. Shane puts the keg down.

"Alright ladies, let me give you a tour. To the right, we have the wine bar and to the left, beer and booze. Everywhere, specifically in the corners… there's enough weed to kill Jeffrey Lebowski. Get out! You brought glazed donuts from my favorite bakery and two bottles of *Anything* wine. Well, its official… do you want to get married? I'll do whatever you want for the rest of my life."

We smile at each other. "Shane, if you can hook up a date with me and the Jolly Green Giant… that would make me oh so happy."

"You shall wait no longer."

He reaches into his pocket and pulls out a chocolate bar with a ribbon on it and hands it to me. All I could think was, where's my joint?

"Real funny Shaneous... where's the bowl, spliff or the fun-loving blunt?"

He puts his arm around my neck and talks softly. "This is so much sweeter... it's an edible." He sees we're perplexed.

"A little piece of this baby will have you high all night and possibly tomorrow too. I had my friend from Big Sur ship them to me, a small token of my appreciation for being the best boss ever. There's two more bars waiting for you upstairs... Merry Christmas."

I express gratitude while he guides us through the palatial digs to an ocean view bedroom to put our purses down. I see two more ribbon wrapped *Blaze... Get the elevation!* bars.

"Ladies... this room is yours. No one will bother you, so enjoy yourselves and stay the night... leave after breakfast cooked by *moi.*"

Sandra looks over asking me with her eyes to take his offer.

"Thanks for the option... we'll see where the night takes us."

Shane suggests we go downstairs to the main floor.

Sandra pats my back. "Alright, let's have a piece of that puppy and start feeling all Kanye and shit by touching the sky... high."

"Shane, where's Jared? He should join us."

Shane looks around and says he'll find him. Sandra already had a hot guy that resembled a young Harrison Ford talking to her. Hip hop is blasting with Biggie's "Party and Bullshit" as I stand in the middle of the floor, gazing at all the vignettes around me. If I had a movie camera, I could shoot scenes that would make an avant-garde fanatic drool. The convivial energy around me is contagious. Each of the small groups clustered throughout the room have different expressions of arousal on their faces. The couple to the right of me, are looking into each other's eyes so intensely, I reckon they'll be sprawled out on something horizontal in about five minutes. The trio off in the far left corner had little pink pills in their hands. You could hear their giggles over the music as they egg each other on to swallow the illusive candy circles to funland. Finally, the stout curly-raven-haired chick took one for the team and the rest soon followed. I'll check back with them in about ten minutes to see how far they go. The group behind me are discussing quantum physics, impressive but out of place in this festive forum. I didn't feel strange waiting alone. On the contrary, I felt highly entertained. This crowd doesn't realize I'm waiting for my own ribald experience to kick in; which doesn't include sucking someone's face off or downing E. Nuh-uh, just a psychotropic Purple Haze hit that can give the ecstasy freaks a run for their money. I see Jared in the distance skipping towards me along with the others close behind him.

"Claire, there you are, you ready to fly? You look beautiful by the way." Jared, at his sweetest, hugs and kisses me on the cheek.

I give our group pieces of the candy bar. We migrate to a plush couch outside while Shane acts as bard, entertaining us with a story about these two girls he knew back in college, both are expected to show up soon. He used to be intimate with one of them, who's now dating his hockey friend and the other is interested in hooking up with him. Seems the girl he used to have sex with had bragged to all her friends that Shane is the *ultimate fuck fix*. Upon hearing this, we can't contain our hysterics. Houston: We are officially lit. Shane didn't know what was funnier—the wicked title he was christened with or the fact that his buddy has no clue that Shane fucked her senseless before and during her relationship with his former teammate. Shane describes his friend (who also remains nameless) as a fiery type A sort, who wouldn't be pleased to learn of his girlfriend's hardcore porn days, especially with one of his friends. Shane could take him if it came down to blows, but he figured what the dude didn't know couldn't hurt him. Jared asks Shane if the term creator was great in bed, Shane shakes his head with a piercing no. We asked what constituted his harsh response and he rationalizes to our group.

"She wasn't enthusiastic enough considering how easy she is… and she lacked depth. I know for a fact I made her, excuse my inappropriateness, gush every time and it didn't matter. She's a cold lover who never gave encouragement. I was young then and didn't know any better than to put up with her bitchiness. A guy needs assurance when he's getting a girl off, and any dude that says differently is kidding themselves. Also, I had to guide her through all the steps of a proper blowjob. Considering her vast experience, it kind of sucked the fun out it… pun intended."

The four of us fall into cackling fits. At this point, I can't feel my feet, as if I'm suspended on a cloud. So far, this is the most brilliant high I have ever had. My compliments to the designated deejay at the moment for playing Lupe Fiasco's "Paris, Tokyo." 4/4 tempo time resonates throughout the mansion. The visuals of luminous candles are flickering, projecting shadows of people dancing on the monumental walls. Their sinewy images flowing rhythmically with the music on such a sensuous night.

CHAPTER 8 / *WHO BE? WHAT E? WOODY?*

"Claire... Claire... Claire! Wake up, your phone's ringing."

My head feels like a frozen cantaloupe being picked at with a fork. "Who in God's name is calling me? Where's my phone?"

I get out of bed and fall down. Where are my legs? My legs are wobbly. I crawl on the floor scrounging around for my bag. I can't feel my arms either. Now what's happened to me?

Sandra groggily replies "Well it doesn't matter now... ringing's stopped so go back to bed."

"Good idea... Jesus, I'm spent."

I climb up onto the bed and lay down closing my eyes. A surge of warmth coats my back. Did Sandra want to spoon? It's not like her and besides she's not this hairy. If memory serves correct, she is unable to have morning wood as well.

"Um whoa... um Sandster... Sandster."

"What?"

"Who in God's name is in our bed... and where the

hell are we?"

Sandra jumps up looking at me then looking down at the sleeping prince. Her face turns beet red as she rolls her eyes back to me.

"Wait a minute... Sands, what time is it?

Claire Convenzionale
You are cordially invited to attend Family Brunch
Sunday, November 16th at 10:00 am at
Adelina's
159 Greenpoint Avenue
Brooklyn, NY 11222

"Oh my God... I have a brunch to go to... help me! Why is this dude naked? Wow, he's a fine looking specimen... oh no my phone's ringing again. It's probably my mother... oh my God, what should I tell her? Sandra, answer the phone please."

Sandra looks at me as if I'm deranged. "Are you fucking crazy? Your mother will ban me from the house if she knows I'm involved with your absence from the mob brunch... hellz to the no."

Press green button and turn on auto pilot: "Hey Mama... I was just going to call... how are you?"

"Are you on your way? We're all here waiting for you and they won't seat us till the whole party is here so... why didn't you answer your phone before? I called three times."

"Mom, I'm so sorry... there's a very good reason why I'm unfortunately held up, so please let the hostess know that I'm unable to make it, and have her seat you all. I promise to be at your house after you finish and see everyone. I should be home within two hours."

I could hear by my mom's breathing, she is perturbed.

"Two hours… why are you not coming? What happened? Where are you?"

If only I knew friends, if only I knew. Enter another moment of interlude:

If I tell her the truth she'll be horribly pissed and question my drug and alcohol use. If I lie, she may catch on to me since I'm such drivel under pressure. Either way I'm screwed so why not just be respectful to her and go with it. I'm thirty-one years old. I'm not a child anymore. I'm prepared to suffer the consequence since presently I can't feel anything. In fact with the exception of my head, I feel groovy and what's this wrapper, Medicinal Edible? I'm flying, that explains a lot, but why can't I remember anything? Alright, enough lollygagging and be done with the execution.

"Mom… I went to one of my intern's parties last night and I had to nurse poor Sandra. She wasn't feeling well from drinking and eating an edible. The poor thing slept till now and I'm about to drive us back home. I'm so sorry for missing brunch, it wasn't my intention."

There, that's my story and I'm sticking to it.

"Oh Claire, is she okay and why did she drink so much? Are you okay? You didn't drink, right?

"No Mom… you know I hardly drink, I'm fine so no worries. Let me help her get ready and we'll be on our way."

"Okay baby, just be careful driving home and *che se deci…* edible?"

Oh shit. "I'll explain later… give my best to everyone and let them know I'll see them this afternoon. *Ciao*, love you."

Okay, that wasn't as bad as I was expecting, she must be softening up in her years. Anyway let me get back to the situation at hand and oh shit, Sandra is charging towards me.

"You're an asshole, you know that."

"Yes, I know but I had no choice… you know she would have sent a search party out on my dazed and confused head if I said it was the both of us, so please don't be angry."

"Why did you have to mention the edible?"

"I know, right? I don't know why I stupidly said it. There's no problem because she'll forget and if she doesn't… I'll just tell her it's some fancy schmancy hors d'oeuvres. Trust me, she won't care and I really appreciate you taking one for the team."

"Fuck you, Claire."

"Yes… I thoroughly deserve that, but I have one question. Why am I in my panties and bra? Why's he naked? And why on earth are you topless?"

She puts her hand up and shrugs me off unconvinced.

"That was three questions and oh my God, I'm topless! Jesus, why can't I feel or remember anything?"

"My sentiments exactly, my friend… I think it's because we're still lit from whatever was in that wrapper. May I just say, that is one of the finest looking asses I have ever seen in my life. I don't know who sleeping beauty is… but damn he's smokin'."

"Agreed… can you help me find my bra."

"Of course, right. Let's start motoring Sister

Christian... not."

I laugh as Sandra turns a brighter shade of red.

"Fuck you, Claire."

"Maybe you did."

I hold my stomach from giggling as Sandra trips over a shoe, falling to her knees and onto her side cracking up. At this point, sleeping beauty wakes up and proceeds to tell us we shared another Blaze Bar and did shots of Patrón. He continues, telling us his name is Tomasz, and his accent stems from Poland. I estimate he's about 6'1" and can make a girl salivate just looking at him. It seems we wound up chilling in the hot tub after drinking and splitting an E pill three ways— so wrong. The night went on with the three of us making out with each other in our imbibed states. He said the highlight was Sandra kissing me at one point—oh Jesus. I guess that would explain this nasty-massive-purple-red hickey on my neck, but they didn't fess up. Sandra asks him if we had a threesome and he said it was close but no cigar. He elaborates that they were about to get down, till she passed out cold and he prides himself on being a gentleman. I asked what I was doing at that point and he said after we fooled around, I went off with Jared and some of Shane's friends to sing karaoke in our underwear—so, so wrong. I am curious as to what I had sung, he recalls hearing "That's Entertainment" by The Jam. Of all the songs to sing, why and how did I choose that one? He said it didn't end there. Supposedly I segued into Gypsy Kings *"Bem, Bem, María."* I don't know one word of Spanish, really? His story revealed further details of Shane being the mix master on the souped-up computer stereo while I sang in front of everyone dancing. After Tomasz tucked Sandra into bed, he joined me to dance for a while and then we migrated to the downstairs kitchen and made pancakes. We were interrupted by Shane who needed help with a "situation" in the living room. Apparently two freaks from LA were coked out of their minds and got steamy in front of the peanut gallery. The fornicating couple is supposedly famous B actors, but only a few bystanders recognized them. Tomasz changes the subject suggesting we take it from where we left off by having morning sex. I politely excuse myself to shower as Sandra is about to get lucky; she deserves this attention.

After I dry my hair, I put my ear to the door to hear if the coast was clear to enter. Silence = green light. I give a courtesy knock and she answers "Come on in." I peek out slowly to see her by herself, looks like cowboy stud just left on his horse to ride the happy trails. I am curious to know how the sire preformed but didn't know if this was the opportune time to ask.

Sandra is graciously forthcoming with "Wow, I mean wow."

On our drive back she keeps mentioning the sick chemistry she noticed between Shane and I, convinced he likes me and I agree with her. Honestly, if things were different and we were closer in age I could see that happening, but at this point in my life, it's not an option. I keep cheering her on with how happy I am about her and the cowboy and she thanks me for not joining in. Even if I wasn't selective, group sex is not how she or I rolls. Besides, if I did swing that way, I wouldn't have the heart to intrude on her moment. I could tell by the way she looked at Tomasz, she was jonesing for him. She wonders why I didn't hook up with anyone. I am a free agent now and should be engaging in carnal fun, but for some strange reason, a gnawing angel on my right shoulder throws a gavel at the one on the left whenever temptation blinks its tawdry red lights.

We arrive at my parent's house and Sandra puts the car in park. "Thanks again for the invite and a mind boggling fantastic time."

I hug her tight. "You are so welcome, my dear. My only regret is not remembering most of it. Note to self, do not eat an edible till the end of the party. Any chance you will be seeing Cowboy Tom anytime soon?"

"Yes… he invited me out next weekend so we'll see. Ooh, Claire… ouch, you better cover that thing up, it's growing by the minute. Here… use my scarf."

I turn the rearview mirror. "Let me see… for Christ's sakes. Thanks to your new boyfriend."

She helps position the scarf. "He's not guilty… he said we definitely weren't responsible… we were trying to figure out who branded you. Say hi to *la famiglia*."

I wave bye as she reverses out of the driveway. Alright, time to put on a brave face and make sure the scarf doesn't move an inch. I see Bianca through the window motioning me to come in. It's showtime. Seriously though, who the fuck sucked my neck off?

CHAPTER 9 / *RUH-ROH*

I will be late for work today, still feeling baked remnants from the other night, not even the Epsom salts bath and celery juice detox has made a dent. I need to call in and have them cover for me.

"Hey Jared, you just got in right? Cool... I'm running a little behind so set on auto pilot or have Shane run the show. What? He's not in yet? Did he call or email you saying why? That's not like him... maybe his train's stuck in the tunnel. Well no problem, just cover. I'll be in about an hour or so, thanks."

Where is Shane? I text him on the train and get no reply. For some strange reason, Penn Station is swarming with people today like the President's in town or something. I bustle through the crowd and feel a vibration from my blackberry, maybe it's Shane. Whoa, it's Ethan Kilgore. Creative visualization is no joke. I haven't talked to him in well over a year; I wonder why he's reaching out now. It can be one of three scenarios:

- His band's touring locally and he wants to hang out while he's in town.
- He heard about my demise and is reaching out.
- He's engaged and wants me to go to his wedding.

Please don't let it be C. A little part of me is reluctant to read his message. I'll be crushed if it winds up being about his pending nuptials. I muster up courage on the escalator to read it.

CC—

It's been a while, how are you? I just passed this coffee shop in DC and it had a framed picture of the Cupping Room, what are the odds of that? Remember when you introduced the gang to that sweet SoHo spot years ago? I thought of you and had to reach out. We just added an AD show at The Beacon. I have passes for you and Kurt, so no excuses. How about a midnight diner run or whatever you're feeling afterwards to catch up? You have my digits so call or write me soon. I miss you.

—EK

His thoughtful email has already made my day, partly because he didn't mention an engagement and he misses me. How do I respond without sounding like a drooling idiot? I'll figure it out when I get to work. I dash down the hallway and see Lana outside of our studio. Hopefully she's not in a bad mood or my tardiness doesn't put her in one. I think I can slip in without her noticing as she's distracted by the repairman in the hall. Don't make a sound as you squeeze behind her, open the door and in, *voila*. I'm impressed to hear Jared announcing, with only two botches, he's definitely improving. It's still nails on a chalkboard hearing him mess up Beck's song title, saying "E=MC in the next hour." Instead of "E-pro." Can you not read? He needs to correct that as soon as the commercial is done.

"Good Morning, Captain."

"Howdy… I appreciate you covering for me. Do me a favor, after the commercial break, please make a correction to Beck's 'E-Pro' you said E=MC."

He puts his hand over his mouth. "Will do, I apologize."

I think I was fair since the old me would've ranted over one of my biggest pet peeves, making him crawl into a self-deprecating hole. I couldn't do that now, not after all we've been through already.

"Have you heard from Shane yet?"

"Yes, he called in from home just before you came in. He's lost his cell phone, that's why he wasn't able to contact us sooner. He's on the train now and should be in within a half hour. I can't wait to hear how the rest of his weekend went... awesome party right? My only qualm is we didn't get to hang more after eating the fun stuff."

I could feel heat surge on my face, embarrassed over the fact these guy's most likely saw me in my underwear. Maybe Jared was too blitzed to recall.

"I know, right? Sadly, I can't remember anything either. Thanks to that Blaze Bar's intensity. Do you remember seeing me afterwards?"

Please say no, pretty please. "Oh yes Miss Claire, I remember we were all in our underwear dancing and singing at one point. You sang amazingly by the way, great rendition of Britney Spears 'Radar.' Then I left to go make-out with Paige and we wound up doing it in my car. That, I fondly remember."

Alright, don't let him notice you're a little mortified right now. "Look at you player... hooked up in the car, you classy boy... nice. I really sang that song? I don't know any words to a Spears tune."

"You did that night. It was awesome."

"Really? Oh boy."

Well, at least I wasn't donning racy underpinnings that night, smart enough to wear hot pink La Perla resembling a bikini bathing suit. I wish I remembered seeing the guys in their skivvies.

"Jared, do we have any almond butter left? Is there another one on the shelf behind you?"

He looks around. "Eureka... do you want a spoon or crackers to accompany, Mr. Butta?"

"Ooh, just a spoon. I have a pear to pair it with... ba dump bump."

As soon as I took the first bite, Shane runs in breathless and sweat ridden.

"Nice of you to join us comrade. Remind me next time to oversleep with a bombshell and avoid coming to work on time."

Nicely put by Jared who hands him the list of PSA's. Shane replies by giving him the finger and sits down. He isn't his usual self, seems uneasy as if he's on trial for murder. He won't look or even gesture at me. What gives? For the next half hour, he studiously works ensuring all the details are covered for the show with no words spoken.

Jared IM's me: What is wrong with him? The only time he'll ever be silent is at his funeral and even then, he'll most likely talk."

I respond agreeing with Jared; I didn't have a clue to what could be wrong. I send Shane an IM and ask him if he's okay.

He responds: Yes, thanks for asking, just a little frazzled with the aftermath of the party and all. Sorry I was late I'll make it up tomorrow. You and Jasta can come in late and I'll cover.

I was about to type back when Jared left to use the restroom, a perfect opportunity to talk instead.

"Don't worry about coming in late… I did as well if it makes you feel better. For the little I can remember, I had a great time at your shindig. Sorry I bolted without saying good-bye. We had to hightail it out of there since I was way late for my family's gathering. How did the rest of the weekend go for you? Seems you and Jasta got lucky." He stares off at the recording machine behind at me as if I should know what his eyes are saying and I'm at a loss.

"Lucky? Oh you mean that slut Paige and Jasta? Yeah they got it on in his car of all places. I… I hooked up with an old college dime I hadn't seen in a while. Claire, do you remember hanging out by the pool?"

I wish I did, I couldn't recollect my own name let alone any other details from that night. He stares again with a blank face and it's making me paranoid.

"So what happened? I know we were all in our underwear, Jared informed me. What craziness happened after the situation?"

He puts his head down and I can feel the tension.

"Not much… there was a lot of drinking and sucking face, that's all. It's cool."

"I have doubt in your shaken response. Let me set you at ease; tell me what happened and I promise it will be okay. I won't say anything to anybody and besides, it can't be that bad so just spill it. You slept with Paige also? I know I sang at the top of my lungs making a complete jackass out of myself… so, what's the dish?"

"There won't be any repercussions if I tell you what happened after the situation? You promise you won't freak

87

out?"

Oh no, I'm freaking out with his questions. "Okay, but it depends on what exactly happened."

He sighs and looks at the control board. "Well, I needed help breaking up the toxic couple from LA... the dude was convulsing from all the E he ingested and we had to call for an ambulance. You stayed with me and waited till they showed up. I got us a blanket to share since you were cold and we were both in our underwear. Claire... are you there?"

"Yes. I'm listening."

"So as I was saying, you were consoling me while I freaked out... I'm indebted to you for that because I thought I was getting arrested, no joke. The EMT guy took care of that reject and said he would turn a blind eye to the booze and drugs that were around the party. You were making me laugh... helping me calm down from stressing out."

Okay, so far not so bad though it seems he's alluding to something else. I know I didn't sleep with him because Tomasz assured me of the events that night. But then again, how would he know for sure? What could it be? I motion for him to continue.

"So after the EMT's left with the couple, you and I... we went to go swim in the heated pool next door to the party. Unexpectedly... for some strange reason... we..."

Oh no, please don't say what I think you're going to say.

"... we started making out while we were in the pool. Please don't freak out, Claire. Oh no, you're turning violet, just like that girl in *Willy Wonka*. Please don't be upset with me... it just happened and I don't know how... I'm sorry."

We were practically swimming naked and I don't

remember a stitch of it. I need to hide my uncomfortable reaction since he looks another level of worried.

"Shane, we didn't... um... you know. It didn't go further, right?"

"No... no we didn't."

There is a God. "So how did we leave off? Was anybody else there?"

He looks down at his keyboard. "Well... when we were swimming, we started talking about our exes and how it's hard to find quality in the dating world and we started... "

"Stop hesitating. Started what?"

His shoulders tense up and his eyebrows widen. "You really don't remember? Okay, okay... don't look at me like that, I don't mean to piss you off. We just started kissing... and it was mutual, I swear. You believe me, right? Claire? Please don't be upset. We were close to having sex but one of my friends with his girl jumped in and talked with us. I kind of got my bearings back and carried you out of there. You fell asleep in my arms... so I put you down in your bedroom and closed the door. That was it. I told Sandra to keep an eye on you. I was hot and bothered, so I sucked down a red bull with vodka and went to town on my college friend. Please don't hold this against me since I love this job and working with you. I don't want this to jeopardize anything. Understandably, this is awkward for us but we can get past it. Look, it's obvious I adore you so... I'm okay and respect the fact if it isn't mutual."

I made out with this fine young creation and I don't remember a sliver of it? I don't know if I'm more pissed with having no recollection or out of everyone at the party, I wound up making out with my subordinate.

"That was very brave, Shane. I appreciate you being

honest with me. I can't remember unfortunately, so why don't we forget it ever happened. All is fine, no awkwardness necessary, okay?"

He finally looks me in the eye. "Okay... but I remember and wish it was that easy to forget. You're a big deal Claire, much bigger than you realize. Can you not see me shaking from the overwhelming hold you have over me?"

Oh no. What do I do? This kid is eight years younger than me and I'm his boss for the next nine months. I don't want to crush him with rejection. This is why you cannot fraternize with your co-workers, the exact situation I had hoped to never deal with.

"I apologize… I didn't mean to leave an inappropriate impression on you. I messed up, letting my hair down, partying irresponsibly. I know in time, we'll right this wrong."

That's the thing… I don't think it's wrong. Why, because you're my boss?"

"Yes and the fact I'm way older than you. Look, I'm still knee deep in the whole debacle of my break-up and you're still recovering from yours so it's understandable that we're both extremely vulnerable. Trust me, this is not a rejection, it's just a situation that sucks and it will bear more crosses if we were to ever think about foolishly proceeding. We obviously have an attraction towards each other and it's normal since we share space for most of the day. My first priority here is the job and providing a productive work environment, without personal entanglements. Let's be cool, okay? I wish I did remember some part of it though."

Why did I just say that? That's opened Pandora's Box even more, giving him a glimmer of hope. Yet, I can't help wonder how his kiss was. What the hell is wrong with me and my perverted mind? Why has my lonely frustration clouded my judgment? Stop being curious and take a Valium, Mrs. Robinson. I can tell by the way he's gripping his baseball that he's disappointed.

"Okay Claire, it will be fine. I just have to say you're an amazing kisser. There, I said it. I won't mention it again."

That was sweet of him to say. I wish I could be as foolish as he is right now. Such an audacious talent to have— I'm envious of him. He doesn't have to be a conscionable role model like I do. If I could throw everything to chance without any consequence I would, but I can't, no matter how loud my yearnings cry within me.

"Thank you, Shane. I appreciate you being a gentleman... a fine one at that. Alright, go eat something, I got it covered here." He nods yes but works instead. I need to make him laugh and alleviate the tension in the air.

"Hey buddy, I have a question for you. Is this your wonderful work of art?"

I slowly take off the scarf off and he squints to see the love bite that's taking up half my neck. His eyes widen.

"Am I allowed to recollect our forgotten night? That be me... guilty as charged. What the hell did I do to your neck? You would think I had fangs and shit. Wow, I'm so sorry and I don't mean to laugh but..."

We giggle, already making progress on the road to less awkward-ville. We hear Jared outside talking with one of the afternoon interns and we pinky swear to keep our poolside romp between the two of us. We didn't want to deal with the potential overreaction from Jared. He bustles through the door with pieces of what looks like ice cream cake.

"Sorry I took a while... they're having a party for Kurt's birthday. He asked for you, Claire... saying *where the hell*

91

is conventional? You should pop your head in. I bought back pieces for you two."

"Mighty kind of you... it's never too early for ice cream cake. Yeah I haven't seen Kurt in a while. I used to hang out with his crew a lot more back in the day, when we frequented three to five shows a week. See what you boys have to look forward to... slowing down as soon as the big three-o hits. I better go visit him... I'll be back in before the next set starts."

I eat the cake as I walk down to Kurt's office and in the distance, I see him jumping up and down.

"Convenzionale... or should I say stranger. Why don't you give me love anymore, women. I need a hug... there we go, I feel better already. So what's shakin'?"

"Doing well old friend and you know you'll always have my admiration. The past few months have been a whirlwind, things have finally simmered down."

"I know... I just like to make you feel guilty. Oh, did you hear that Acoustic Division just added a surprise show at the Beacon in a few... we have to go, no excuses.

"Coincidentally, I just heard from Mr. Kilgore this morning via email, I'm definitely down, it'll be a blast."

"There's no chance of reconciling with Jake, right? You should go out with Ethan. In fact I'm begging you to go out with him... he's perfect for you."

"Definitely not getting back together... no. You really think Ethan and I should date? Interesting... he is a rock star you know. Do I really want to succumb to the whole boy band girlfriend cliché? Besides, isn't Ethan still with Inez? Just out of curiosity, how long have you thought this?"

He cuts another piece of cake and talks muffled through bites. "Correction Clarabelle, he *was* joined at the hip. Oh that's right, you weren't around when he was here last. We hung out and he told me they fell apart right before your split. Fortuitous coincidence, no?"

"Really? No I haven't spoken to him in a while. So now you're branching out into new age matchmaking, hah? Bravo maestro."

"Huh, huh, huh. Alright, maybe I put my big opinionated nose in many corners but listen up, because this is very important. In regards to you and Ethan, it's now safe to admit, I have always seen you guys together. Anytime the two of you hold a conversation, well there seems to be an unspoken admiration emitting from you both. I witnessed many times how he's looked at you while he was with Inez—why do you think she was always a bitch towards you? She couldn't have been more jealous. I know she approached him about you on a few occasions, and even though there wasn't anything physical, he was guilty of emotionally cheating on her. In my book, that unspoken love... thoughts kept contained is a far worse crime than the deed itself. Mind my candidness, but I think you would be a scorching couple, so think about it. Yes, he is a rock star but he's a genuinely grounded dude who you have mega history with... knowing him before the hoopla. I love you like a sister, so please don't take offense when I say you splitting up with Jake was the best thing you ever did. Claire, you were way too good for him. He was mad cool, no doubt, but you were too good-hearted for his type."

Kurt has a charismatic gift when he talks, especially to you. I am an eager, curious listener anytime he speaks. Yes, he is chock-full of candor and meddles a little too often but his heart is gold and that's what redeems him and his opinionated mind. He's right about that unspoken attraction. Not being able to express it physically is a staple ingredient for a quintessential love song recipe that becomes tragic if never expressed. Kurt isn't the first person to tell me Jake wasn't good enough for me, as rough as it hearing his name slurred, there is some truth to it. I have a strong feeling Kurt won't be the last to say it either. Ethan is unattached—my heart is fluttering with elation. I can't let anyone know till Ethan confirms what Kurt said is true.

"I could never hate you Kurtis, come on. We started out in boot camp here… earning our stripes together so you have carte blanche talking to me. I didn't know Ethan was unattached. Did he ask you to put the feelers out?"

"No, he has enough guts to do his own lobbying. This is me… acting as a catalyst for you two, begging you to have courage to throw it out there to him, because I know it would go in your favor. If you don't have feelings for him, please don't tell him what I told you."

"That's mighty kind of you and of course I won't say anything. For now, we'll see what happens… anything's possible. Anyway… how's Mandy doing? You guys finally decide on a wedding venue?"

"She's doing well and wants to have a get together soon… you'll definitely see her at E's show. We're between two places, The Pierre and The Waldorf."

"Fine haughty choices sire… give my best to her and yes, let's get something on the calendar soon. I gotta race back and close out the show. Happiest of birthdays… Kurt Cobain."

He grabs my arm. "Don't run off without giving me another hug… and there we go. Ooh C note… what happened to your neck? Jesus, it looks like a leper gnawed at you… what the fuck?"

I am going kick the shit out of Shane. "That's exactly

94

what happened to me Kurt Vonnegut... can you believe it? A vampire out of nowhere mauled the shit out of me the other night."

He snarls. "Ha-ha you're friggin' hilarious... you smart-ass-leper-loving-ho!"

"You know it, Kurt Russell."

I run away with my middle finger up as he blows a kiss at me. This Halloween prop needs to be healed before I meet up with Ethan or anyone else I potentially want to share sheets with; repulsion is not an effective aphrodisiac. What are the odds of finally having the right time to potentially snag Ethan? Time was never on our side. I had met him a few months before Jake and at the time, I found him attractive but was crushing on a dude named Lance. Ethan attended Columbia for a year before he transferred to Georgetown; I got to know him through my roommate's brother, Hillel. We didn't share classes but we would run into each other at mutual friends parties and immediately got along. We had similar taste in everything, from books to furniture style. I remember he was dating this Spanish exchange student who sounded exactly like Penelope Cruz—he has a penchant for fiery Latin types. As the years went by, we kept in touch as his band soared and frequented my radio show. I didn't think of Ethan romantically till Jake and I had our first downfall of many. It's crazy how you can know someone for ten years without a hot flash ever. Then all of sudden you find yourself pining for them, feeling as if you are flying towards the sun, sizzling just thinking about being in their presence. I approach the studio and see Lana, who looks agitated with pursed lips.

"Claire... do you allow them to mess around playing with the noose while the show's running?"

"I'm sorry Lana... I don't understand, what's going on? We sing along to a song here and there and maybe bounce around but no there's no noose playing and…"

"Well, while you were out, I passed by and noticed them doing just that."

"I would like to hear what the guys have to say about this? Can you fill us in on what happened while I went to wish Kurt a happy birthday."

Shane looks at Lana as Jared bravely takes the floor.

"I apologize to you both on behalf of Shane and myself. We didn't mean to behave unprofessionally, we were just goofing around and it inadvertently went too far. We won't put our heads in the noose again… we were just paying respects to the Wolfman."

"Okay Jared, let me intervene here. Lana, I apologize on behalf of the guys, please know I do not condone (bullshit) this and no, it's not normal practice when we work. We take full responsibility and I'll make sure this never happens again."

"I appreciate that. I will let this one offense slide, Jared and Shane, as both of your reviews have been exceptional. Please understand my concerns… frolicking around the noose is a liability we can't afford. Claire, I'll talk with you later. I have a meeting to get to, so let me run. See you all at the holiday party." The three of us nod bye to her, I gave her a wink assuring her tough ass performance was not taken personally.

"Okay… it's just us now. Tell me what really happened when I left."

Shane got his tongue back from the cat who stole it.

"Honestly, we were just fucking around; you asked us to play a three play from Stone Temple Pilots… when 'Trippin' on a Hole in a Paper Heart' was on, I may have lost control. Kind of like when we all bopped around to Phoenix's '1901.' I didn't realize she was passing by and saw me through the window. Can we cover that by the way? It would be nice to have some privacy."

"Okay guys… yes we get stupid dancing sometimes and that's fine, but why the noose?"

Jared walks next to Shane. "Yeah Shane, why? I said it was the both of us but it was just you, I think that's what set her off."

Shane looks down picking lint off his jeans. "I don't know, I guess I had a moment of crazy dealing with some bad news earlier… let's just let it go. And Jasta, please don't ask me what the bad news is."

Uh-oh. That was obviously intended for me. Time will heal our accidental mishap. I just know it. It has to.

CHAPTER 10 / *ONE MAY* (OR MAY NOT) *FLY OVER THE CUCKOO'S NEST*

The moment I have been waiting for has finally arrived—psychotherapy. And yet, I want to hightail it back to the elevator; I'm already panic-stricken, requiring a shot of something to relax me. I stand in front of what appears to be a whimsical door which has two Etch A Sketches adhered vertically and out of state magnets sprinkled about. I clear the canvas with the smiley face and write HELP on one, ME on the other. Whoever innovative mind designed this entrance gets my seal of approval. The door abruptly opens and a man, who I could only presume is a patient, just went out through the in door. He holds it open for me as if he knows I'm planning to escape. I walk in and see a young woman wearing yellow scrubs, looking in my direction.

"Hello, do you have an appointment today?"

"Hi, yes for 3:00 PM. My name is Claire... thanks."

"Oh yes, Ms. Convenzionale, please fill out the forms and answer honestly to the best of your knowledge. You can have a seat in the waiting room. Dr. Groundz will be ready for you shortly."

"Miss... I actually went over these very questions with

the medical representative, when I scheduled the appointment. Do I still need to fill these out?"

"Yes you do, I apologize for the inconvenience. We need to have a hard copy signed by you for our medical file here. Thanks for your understanding."

I hate filling out medical forms, especially ones with ridiculous questions that nine times out of ten I have to answer no to. Are you taking drugs? Are you suicidal? Do you have a drinking problem? When I relayed my answers to the guy on the phone, I expressed doubt if I was applicable to see a psychiatrist. He assured me that everyone is, it's just some people are stronger than others—we'll see. I wish I had a Xanax to take the edge off, convincing myself this will be positive. Within a few minutes the nurse calls out my name and escorts me into a comfortable room reminiscent of the Library Bar at the Hudson Hotel. Not nearly as big but similar vibe with books, couches and those cool cow photos by Jean-Baptiste Mondino. On the bright side, at least I have a hip atmosphere to pour my crazy out in.

Nurse Gladys offers me water. "Please make yourself comfortable. The Dr. will be in shortly."

I remember being asked if I preferred to see a female or male doctor. I was apathetic so the representative referred me based on geography. Close proximity = Dr. Groundz. I did research on him, he seems legit—renowned therapist background and published author focusing on Cognitive Therapy with seven years in practice. Impressive five-star ratings and over a hundred positive reviews on the web, I am convinced. I notice a framed picture of him, his wife, and son. He's good looking, reminiscent of a brown-eyed David Duchovny, and doesn't seem as old as I imagined. I hope he doesn't come in with a white coat and that mirror thing on his head, I forget what they're called. There's a knock at the door. And again, it's showtime.

"Come in. Hello, you must be Dr. Groundz. It's very nice to meet you, I'm Claire."

He shakes my hand while clutching a folder of papers under his other arm. "It's very nice to meet the extraordinary voice of WLDM. I'm a huge fan... please have a seat."

He's a fan? Now this is awkward. "Thank you, Doctor. I can't believe you're an avid listener on my show... kind of strange as I'm here for therapy and all."

"I've been listening for years and it's not strange at all. I care for one of my favorite hockey players from the Rangers and a handful of famous actors as well. I myself have seen a therapist which benefited me. I pride myself on providing a comfortable atmosphere with the utmost privacy for your sessions. I hope that lessens any awkwardness."

It didn't actually but I couldn't bring myself to tell him that. It's just weird for a fan to see the private side of me. I already feel violated.

"I appreciate that... we'll see how things go."

He looks at my chart and recites all the numbers I checked off and he's complementary, acknowledging I have more resolve dealing with my problems than his usual patients.

"So Claire, what would you like to gain from our sessions? I ask because it's important to address a patient's concerns and needs. I'm here to work with you on that. While we're in session, feel free to say anything you want as there is no judgment or bias here." I breathed a sigh of relief after he said that. Just to know someone could listen to my problems without me worrying about their reaction felt comforting.

"Well, I had a life changing experience about seven months ago. I terminated my engagement of two years stemming from a relationship of eight years. It's left me

100

bruised and anxiety ridden. I lost weight from stress… constantly reminded by loved ones on how malnourished I look. My sleeping patterns are messed up as well. I want to be healthy again and have the scar its left on me removed. Can you work a miracle, Doc?"

He nods while he finishes writing. "Miracles? Probably not. But I can help you alleviate all the symptoms you mentioned, to find resolution and get you back on a stable healthy track. As for the scar… well, there really is no removal of it I'm afraid. A healing or suppression absolutely, but scars are embedded deep. We can analyze how the scar got there and help you heal from the pain of it."

"I also have guilt problems. I would like to even that energy out or get rid of it completely. And I would like to find unconditional love again."

This poor guy doesn't know what he's in for.

"I like your growing list and of course I can help. Guilt is a prime emotion… challenging but feasible to balance it out. As for the rest, I have a good feeling once we tackle the primary sources of discord, everything else will follow a more positive suit. Before we get into what happened with your relationship, let's go over some things that can make these sessions more effective. First, please call me John… Doctor or Dr. Groundz is formal and I want to set a relaxed pace for you to say what's on your mind."

He reads my chart again. "Chest pains, anxiety, exorbitant amounts of stress and tension, depressed, and fatigued. Okay, we have some work to do."

"Yes we do."

"Let's start with how your life was before your relationship… any upbringing or parent issues? Good childhood and school experience? The reason I ask is so I can build a foundation… layers if you will, bringing you to today."

The thought of my birthday cake pops in my mind when he mentioned layers. When I tell him about it, his bright eyes widened in disbelief which is understandable because it's pretty ridiculous. I summarize my Italian upbringing as nurturing and safe with mostly pros, a few cons such as the excessive restrictions on my social life, leaving it mildly unbearable at times. I address relationship patterns with my parents and siblings truthfully. He listens and writes down in his notebook attentively while I record a compilation tape of my life thus far.

"So John, what do you think?"

He pours us a glass of water. "Good question. From what you just told me, it seems there is a distance between you and your brother Dante, whereas you're closer to Bianca. You seem to have a close healthy relationship with your mom and dad, which is helpful for patients in general. Was the apparent dissention with your brother always prevalent? Or was there a time you had a closer relationship with him?"

"Sadly no, I never had a close relationship with him. Since I was a kid it seemed we just didn't synch… a shame really. I think our mentalities are too far spanned in order to mesh. It was frustrating when I was younger but as I got older, I made peace with it and keep things light when I see him. Even though he goes out of his way to push my buttons in some ludicrous way… I turn on autopilot ignoring him. There's never been a deeper level of conversation other than the weather or general stuff. It's dysfunctional, yes, but it works for me. Go ahead and tell me how wrong I am to act superficially with him."

"I wish I could… from what you've described it sounds like there's jealousy and/or animosity that he's harboring, his actions and treatment towards you prove so. I am an advocate of strengthening a troubled relationship but in your particular case, you are better to be laissez-faire. In regards to relationships, it's a two-way street. They don't work unless both parties cooperate. Having a peaceful existence as opposed to a destructive one is always the right decision no matter how shallow it may seem. You stated you were concerned about being unconventional... overall I don't think you're as atypical as you think. You may perceive yourself to be since your lifestyle is different than your siblings, but they are older so that's par for the course. You said you're drawn to the road less traveled, maybe out of curiosity or it's just how you're wound. Instead of seeing it non-traditional or 'I have a problem,' try to embrace your philosophy instead. Do you agree?"

"Yes. You've made strong points, especially with my crutch of harsh criticism. You're definitely onto something... I'll try working on that. I think breaking up with Jake left me feeling more isolated than before we were together... not being part of a unit."

"We're going to look into all facets and sources that have hindered you and deduce what caused your failed relationship. Sometimes our greatest stress comes from places we don't think of as culprits, yet they turn out to be contributing factors of our weakened condition."

"So... are you saying my strained relationship with my brother has contributed to my doomed relationship?"

"Considering you haven't told me what happened between you and your ex-fiancé, I wouldn't be able to give a clear distinction of exact causes just yet. What I am suggesting is your anxiety symptoms may not be the sole result of your breakup with Jake. Other secondary factors are very likely to exacerbate your stressful condition."

"I'm impressed with your analysis so far and it's only

the first session."

He turns slightly red with a faint smile. "Thanks Claire. Sometimes the first session can be the most painstaking; I like to gather as much of a foundation to make the upcoming appointments more cohesive. Anytime I have therapy, my stomach clenches up right before the session starts... but as soon as I start talking with my patient, the comfort level balances out and I feel better. I am happy to hear you're having a similar experience."

"You just explained word for word how I feel when I'm about to speak on-air. The butterflies swirl in my gut every time before I flick the switch. After the first sentence rolls out, I'm stabilized and complacent."

John's eyebrows arch in disbelief. "I would have never gathered that, your presentation is flawless every time. I remember one of your shows, where you were having technical problems a couple of years ago. I think the station had a tower down from a storm that night and distortion... white noise was an issue. The deejay before your show, um... what's his name?"

"Stephen."

"Yes, that's it... he screwed up a few times towards the end of his show and you could hear his nervousness throughout. Not you though, you just rolled with it in a comedic way and it went off without a hitch, especially when that bout of feedback wouldn't stop screeching. Remember?"

I nod yes, entranced by his detailed recollection of my show.

"It wouldn't stop and you were trying to mimic it... singing along, going with the flow of an inconveniencing circumstance instead of buckling under pressure. I listened with my ex-wife at the time... we were highly entertained. It's in my top five list of your best shows."

Apparently, he didn't hear my fifteen seconds of dead air a few months ago.

"Wow, I'm floored. So you were serious when you said you were a fan, hah?"

His smirk turns into a smile. "Good one, Claire."

I always use humor mixed with self-deprecation when I receive a compliment. I know why I do that and a reiteration from my newfound shrink isn't necessary.

"Thank you, John. It's always flattering to hear someone express fondness for my offspring. Tell me, what drew you to it? Considering, it's on at the crack of dawn."

"My ex-brother-in-law, he's a huge Gypsy Kings fan and noticed WLDM played them… your show in particular and he became an enthusiast. After he raved about you, I listened in and was hooked."

"Who are your favorite groups? I'll be sure to play the shit out of them."

We snicker and I notice how the sun shining through the curtain opening illuminates his amber eyes.

"I like mostly everything you play, but I especially like Tom Petty, The Clash, Garbage, A Perfect Circle, and that group Gomez… how much fun are they?"

"Loads… great bunch of guys. They were on last year for an interview when they played Roseland."

He looks at his watch. "We have another few minutes left… if there's anything you want to address? Kyle, the medical assistant you talked with over the phone, advised you were undecided if you wanted to make this a recurring appointment. I hope you will return next week."

"I'll definitely be back. I wanted to gauge if this could work and after talking with you, I feel comfortable continuing."

"I'm glad to hear that. Maybe we can tap into your job a little and any pressures it entails. Earlier you referred to your job as your offspring. Care to elaborate?"

"Well it is really. When I started my own program... my life changed. The hours, the nurturing, constantly making sure everything's running smoothly. The hours especially were a killer at first... I lost about a year's worth of sleep when I started that gig. Like an infant, the show had to grow... constantly be tended to. I could only imagine that it's similar to having a kid. You always hear parents professing how having a child changes their lives, for most people, it's their greatest accomplishment. I can relate to that in regards to my job. It kicks my ass every day, but I love the hell out of it."

He nods yes. "You basically summed it up. How is your relationship with your co-workers? Good? Bad?"

What are the odds of him judging me making out with my infantile co-worker and not recollecting a second of it? I'm wagering ten to one.

"It's good, especially with my interns. In fact, they've become a sort of salvation for me. It's the only time I don't think about my inner turmoil. They're good guys and funny... I admire them. I would have never thought they could help me heal but they have and I'm grateful. It's not unhealthy to feel that way or rely on them as I do, right?"

"Not at all... seems the dynamic naturally took its course. It's not like you asked for their help or there's any inappropriateness. Next week, I want to explore why you doubt yourself with instances you reveal. We'll work on that underlying insecure association. Try to encourage your feelings instead of questioning them and we'll see if that helps you. Till then, anything that can happily distract you from your unfortunate life event... revel in it."

I wonder what his thoughts are on recreational drugs and prevalent inappropriateness with my subordinates.

"Thanks again, Doctor, I mean John. You've given me hope."

"You're welcome and I look forward to resuming next week. Claire, what do you think of Arctic Monkeys?"

"They're pretty solid and they're from England... those bastards know music."

"I know, right? Can I add them to my list?"

I nod yes waving goodbye as I close the door. There are four people ahead of me to pay their co-payments. Is it just me or was there a hint of flirtation there? Where does this come from? That unexplainable vibe, that suddenly draws you in. It doesn't help when I'm fed attention, especially in the state I'm in. Just my luck to find a great therapist and we're kind of attracted to each other at our first meeting. Why couldn't I be attracted to him on the fourth or fifth meeting, when I'm almost done with this chore of self-evaluation? From my quasi-stalking assessment, he is approximately six years older than me. I'm not being presumptuous by thinking this therapy will be done within six visits, right? I'm free to date who I want and if something doesn't happen with Ethan, I would totally date John. Like me, he seems to be a play it safe type. Only I would suffer Freudian transference after the first treatment, how cliché is that? What the hell is wrong with me and my perpetual libidinous thoughts? Now I'm hooking up with John in my depraved mind. I think I should scratch therapy and check into a sexual addiction rehabilitation center for an extended stay. Or maybe find a new therapist. And here he comes, walking towards me, looking so good and tall in his jeans, taupe-colored sweater and black button-down shirt.

"Claire, if you need to leave, we can mail you an invoice... I apologize for the line."

See how he's already singled me out. Granted, the people before me are either under eighteen or over sixty years of age, but still.

"No apologies necessary, I appreciate that. I'll head out since I have to meet my friend for soccer."

He leans in. Please don't lean in John, pretty please.

"You play soccer, so do I... what position do you... oh, what's this on your neck? I have a good dermatologist to recommend if you need one."

I'm mortified the scarf moved, revealing the evidence again. I'm at a loss for words as I shrug, giving a *no need to worry* look as I walked out backwards. I hate you, Shane. Only a fucking amateur would leave a watermark!

CHAPTER 11 / *NUMBER 3 WITH A BULLET*

I feel good at the moment, especially physically. I've been sleeping regularly, the dark circles have evaporated and I'm a few pounds fuller. Things overall have improved since attending therapy. Work is doing well and me and the guys are getting along commendably. We have been focusing on fine-tuning the show the past couple of weeks; it's slowly climbing back up the ratings ladder. Luckily the awkwardness of Shane's and my momentary lapse of reason are behind us. I had a discussion with the guys last week about being solo and how certain types must have someone attached to their hip 24/7. The guys agreed that we didn't fall into that criterion, which Shane comically branded *The J-LO*. He came up with the term in honor of Jennifer Lopez, who is never without a man between her publicized breakups. We all know people who fit that description—unable to be alone between relationships and we were trying to dissect why some people are insecure like that. Maybe it's an obsessive need for belonging or touch? I'm actually appreciating my freedom, and the discoveries I've been making along the way. Sadly, I lost my passion for me when I met Jake and focused my thoughts on him. It's nice to get back to knowing what makes me tick again.

The onslaught of calls and e-mails leading up to Ethan's arrival tonight has been a beneficial diversion from my wallowing tendency. It's different dynamic between us since we're both unattached; our free statuses have propelled our friendship to the next level, a special one. Now the moment has arrived. Me along with a couple of other deejays from the station are heading down to see his concert at the Beacon. I'm nervous understandably and curious if he is too. Our plan is to catch up after the show over drinks. His band, Acoustic Division, had been touring Europe; this is one of their first stops in the States. Throughout the years, Ethan would periodically e-mail or call me from the road, filling me in on tour shenanigans, the updates were amusing to say the least. He had invited me and Jake to join them for shows and gatherings multiple times but for the last few years, our attendance record dwindled down to nil. At the time, we were under an exorbitant amount of strain with Jake's promotion at work—one of the many warning signs of our demise.

Hair and makeup, check. Hot outfit and spritz of Dior's, *Addict,* check. A perfectly tart Greyhound on ice to calm me down, check. Was I pining over Ethan when I was with Jake? I cannot lie and say no. I did, unintentionally come to admire him, in a way when you're enamored with a friend you have a special connection with. Kurt pegged it correctly— Ethan and I emotionally cheated. We are human and even ones with sound natures can plead guilty to that. I look at the mirror and touch my neck where the love bite was, it has faded down to a tiny light apricot circle. I can't help tittering as I recall whatever I can from that hilarious night. It was nice having my inner wild child albeit drug enhanced, make my decisions for me since she hadn't made an appearance in a while. I repressed the carefree girl I once was, she ran away when Jake proposed. The thought of being legally bound to a cocaine addict made me grow up swiftly. Ethan had mentioned that he was disappointed I couldn't attend his gatherings the past couple of years. I explained the real reason—a 190 pound monkey on my back going bananas at that time. He was glad to know it wasn't him personally and Jake was the culprit. Now the wait is over and anticipation has me skittish in regards to getting intimate with him. Will he be able to tell it's been a long time for me? Drinking, there needs to be lots of drinking for me tonight, so I can chill out. My phone is ringing.

"Hey Claire, your chariot is here, are you ready to skedaddle?"

"Yes Kurt, I'm coming down now."

I walk to the car and see Jim, our IT friend at the station is holding the door open and Mandy, Kurt and Jim's girlfriend, Haley have their arms out to hug me. Our car ride is filled with guffaws from Kurt's crazy antics and Jim's bottle of *Cristal* he generously passes around. When the car pulls up to the Beacon, my nerves start tickling again. We pass through security with our all access passes. I forgot how cool the corridor looks backstage, the smell of rock royalty that's walked the same hall we are presently. I stumbled over my feet when I see Brett, the bassist, he immediately runs up and lifts me with his arms hugging my thighs.

"Claire, it's great to see you. You know we wouldn't be here without you guys."

I give him a kiss on his cheek. The band didn't need me or the station to get them here; only thing we did was play their music on heavy rotation.

"Come with me, there's someone you've got to see." He leads me by the hand walking a few doors down, I see the band's dressing room and I clench up. To my surprise he walks right past. We stop at the press lounge room and I see Ryder Wynn, a famous singer who I got to know through Sandra; they shared classes at Fordham University.

"Hi Ryder, what a nice surprise. How's life been treating you, mama?"

"Doing great Ms. WLDM, still a strawberry blonde knockout, chica. Brett invited me out the reunion party later, so I flew in. I contacted Sandra to meet up this week, please join us if you can."

As we caught up over drinks, I feel warm hands cup my eyes and a whisper in my ear.

"Guess who?"

Just by his sultry voice and touch, I know it's him. Despite the guitarist callous trademark, his fingers are ultra-smooth and soft to the touch.

"Han Solo?" He grabs my shoulders turning me around and all I can see is the whites of his smile and shiny specs of his grey blue eyes. I glance at him, unable to say anything. I don't want the whole room to know how I feel at this moment. He hugs me close and then grabs Ryder for a group hug. Brett joins in and he whisks Ryder away to meet some of his friends. It's just me and Ethan in the room alone with ten minutes to spare till the curtain drops. He grabs my hand and I can feel a slight shake in his hold assuring me he's as nervous as I am.

"You look stunning, more so than the last time I saw you. The thirties suit you well."

"Thank you, looking as good as ever, I like the scuff. It's good to be here with you and the rest tonight."

I see beads of sweat on his forehead as he stands close. We're both aware of the feelings we have for each other, but the ice still needs to be broken. Jeff Buckley's "Hallelujah" is playing in the background as we stand there. All the fantasies my subconscious has allured me with these past months, have starred Ethan. Now his hand is caressing my arm and it's real. His clamminess is comforting, proving I'm not the only one who's excited. I look up at him and lean in with my hand on his shoulder.

"I can't wait to see you after the show. You now have a date with the audience and I won't hold you up. Shall we?"

He put his head to mine and kisses me on my forehead. We walk to the stage holding each other's waists and I could see the onlookers smiling at us as we passed. It's safe to say, the cat is officially out of the bag. He leaves me on the side of the stage with the rest of the privileged ones and I've never felt more alive. The crowd roars as he walks onto the stage behind a curtain illuminated by candles and red lights. As soon as the first note is played, the audience screams. After a few minutes the curtain drops and the faces are lit up by the stage lights. Ethan's exceptional voice echoes the theatre. You can feel the band's *consummation of passionate souls*, as a reviewer of theirs once said, describing their performance. The stimulated cries faded out for me; I only hear the melodious sounds of the music that puts me into a hypnotic trance.

Kurt looks over to me. "How sick do they sound? Man, they're on fire. They haven't rocked this good since the Garden two years ago. We need to have them on our shows again, ASAP."

I wink in agreement. Two hours felt like two minutes, the show ended after three encores and it slipped its way into my top five list of best concerts. We walk back to the dressing rooms and Brett raises his voice.

"Who's ready for an epic after-party?"

The crowd shouts back. "Yes!"

I look around the gobs of people for Ethan. Where was he? Dylan, one of my former co-workers, is standing to the side of me; I tap his shoulder.

"Lovely Éclair, how's the voice of reason?"

"Stellar Mr. Dylan... and you?"

"Been okay... I need a drink. Come with... I'll get you one. What would like?"

"I'm good thanks, saving my reserves for later."

"Wish I had your willpower, I'll always be an alcoholic."

We chuckle as Ryder joins us. "There you are... Ethan's looking for you."

"Where is he? Why isn't he back here?"

"He had to handle some business with their manager. There's another party happening by the stage so come with."

"Sorry Dylan, I gotta bounce... let's catch up another time."

He hugs us both and says he'll email soon. I walk with Ryder through a mass of imbibed people. I see Ethan in the distance. He looks even hotter than before the show, seems the rock and roll workout does wonders for one's sex appeal.

"Finally, I was about to have them loud speaker your name."

"I was at the other party... didn't realize there was another one. Would it be rude of me to take you away from this so we can hear each other or is your heart set on staying?"

He rubs my back. "I was just about to ask you the same thing. Let's bounce, I know the perfect place."

We say our goodbyes to our group of friends and Kurt gives me a wink. Holding each other, we keep bumping into everyone we pass, delaying our exit.

"Hop on my back, darlin'... I'll get us out of here."

I hold on tight as Ethan grabs two bottles of wine while clutching his arms around my legs, maneuvering swiftly as we head to his car service outside. His driver opens the door and takes the bottles for safe keeping. Now that infamous tension of ours is on overdrive, suffocating and tantalizing me at the same time. I pretend to look out the window as I glance instead from the side of my eye at Ethan who's doing the same thing. We simultaneously edge closer to each other. He holds my face and neck as he leans in to kiss me. This is it. All the dreams that woke me up from his touch have led up to this moment. It's more sensual than I imagined. The car stops. We come up for air noticing The Plaza's awning staring brightly at us. The driver opens the door, telling us he'll have the wine and our belongings brought up to us. We can't contain ourselves as we stumble up the stairs enthralled in our lip-lock, bumping into the elevator doors, making out in front of everyone.

We get off the elevator and he gently pulls his face away from mine.

"When did you start liking me?"

"When I saw you the last time... when Jake and I were falling apart. How about you?"

"I liked you from the moment we met. It's weird, because I loved Stella... then Inez but you just blew my mind... total package. I didn't want to mess up your happiness at the time by saying anything. The timing was awful."

"Oh Ethan, I didn't realize. I wish you would have said something sooner... but I understand why you didn't. Look at us now... who would've thought?"

He grabs me and we slither against the wall towards his room, osculating each other's faces off. After hearing his confession, I am even more attracted to him. Ethan will be my third lover—love. He tries to get the card in the slot as he's pinned up against me. All I hear is *click* and the door doesn't open. Repeat.

"This card isn't working... why now of all times? Let me try again. Nothing... just give me a second and I'll get a new one... don't move, please."

I hold onto him. "Let me try." I take the card while he holds me from behind, licking the side of my neck. I'm about to burst. I put the card in the slot and no go. My knees buckle and he prevents us from colliding on the floor, in a giggling fit.

"Alright... one more time."

I slide the card in and the light glows green. Wait no more. I turn my cheek against his to catch his eye as we go in, the door closes gently behind us.

CHAPTER 12 / *MENTAL HEALTH DAY(S)*

Hmm... was I dreaming? I open my eyes and see I'm in a hotel room, lying in the most comfortable bed with the silkiest sheets. I look to the left of me and there's my songbird, sound asleep, adorned with a week-old beard and his breaths are rhythmic. No dream at all. The sun peeks through the side of the curtain, illuminating the clock to the right of me—8:36 AM SUN. I don't want to leave here anytime soon. I'm going to call in sick tomorrow, way overdue for a mental health day. When was the last time I called in? Two years ago? I deserve this. I'm famished and need to refuel. I quietly get out of bed and tip-toe towards the bathroom, finding a plush robe to wrap myself in. I rummage around till I find my blackberry and write in sick with an indefinite return date. I'm glad I made a chock full of backup discs so all the guys have to do is run them and do basic announcements. I carefully open the cabinet drawers to not disturb Mr. Sleepy Head for the menu. Blueberry pancakes, eggs, Canadian bacon, toast, seasonal fruit, more bacon, coffee...loads of coffee, water...a trough of water and what else? As I call and order room service, I hear sheets ruffling behind me. I turn around and he's blearily smiling at me.

"If you think we're done, you are sorely mistaken... please come back to bed."

"I just ordered us breakfast, figured we need the energy for the long haul. They're bringing up the whole menu plus extra bacon and sausage... and oh wait, what did you want to eat?"

"Just you." He rasps.

"Delivered. Just give me a minute to freshen up."

"Me too... I'm right behind you." And he is, all 6'3" of his fine sculpted naked body. We take a quick shower together and brush our teeth making funny faces at each other. He unravels my towel and I'm intoxicated all over again. Just as we were about to get busy, we hear a knock at the door, I quickly put my robe back on to get the food. I can tell from the bell hop's expression, he knows our suite is soaked in sin as he grins appreciatively from my generous tip. I set the cart to the side and resume where we left off. I can honestly say the sex was well worth the wait of eating breakfast—Ethan is an exceptional lover. He rubs my arm as we feed each other.

"That was mind-blowingly off the charts by the way. I had a strong feeling you'd be the best I've ever had."

After that compliment, I grab him for round six.

"It's official. You're definitely the best I've ever had, is it just me or does each time reach new heights?"

I look for a response as he's on his back looking up at the ceiling panting, leaving me concerned because he's not speaking.

"You okay, sweetie? Do you need water or something? Please talk to me. "

He looks at me breathless. "I need a brief intermission... whatever you want to call it. I'm not in this galaxy anymore..."

"Watch out, you keep talking like that… you'll never return to earth again. How about we get dressed and go outside for some air."

He stares at me with his steely blues, stroking my hair away from my face.

"I just want to stay in here with you. I have lived and breathed this city… we have a lot of lost time to make up and I say we're up for the challenge. We can open a window if you like."

"Well said, rock star but I'm worried about your panting…"

He answers me poignantly with his hypnotic stare, assuring me I am speaking nonsensically. For the next forty-eight hours we kept to Ethan's challenge, sore and muscle-fevered to the third degree. During this time my blackberry blew up with questions about the radio set and the like. I would intermittently check when we came up for air, happily ignoring each one. Radio Claire has *the flu and hopes to return in a few days*. Ethan's manager left irate messages about cancelling two promotional interviews indefinitely. By the time Wednesday rolled around, we checked out of the Plaza and stayed at my place by the beach through the weekend, entwined. Probably the happiest week of my life—love, movies on demand, and takeout with no travel required. I would have never thought it was possible to be this content without leaving the house; now I'm a believer. The perfect week was sadly coming to an end when Ethan's concerts in Boston showed up on the calendar. He said I had to join him over the weekend and wouldn't take no for an answer. I accepted based on the contingency of returning Monday morning for my show. He arranged a car service for us, so we could rest instead of dealing with security and a loud airport. The two nights in Boston flew by and we were back to my harsh reality. I had the car drop off Ethan at his sublet on my way to the station. He had over a week's worth of sleep to catch up on while I couldn't have been more energized. Looking back, I think I was in a sleep haze post bombing— now I am fully awake. I got to the station around 5:30 AM and preloaded all the songs in my head for the set. I figured the guys could use a break since they steered the vessel without a captain for a week. Shane and Jared proved to be considerate counterparts, leaving my desk as clean and organized as I had left it, along with a welcome back Gardenia plant. I tested out the volume on my headphones and heard muffled voices in the hall, the door swings open aggressively and Shane's face brightens when he sees me.

"Clairster, you're alive… thank God. This place sucks without you by the way… did you listen to the show?"

I nodded yes—I'm such a slutty liar. I didn't listen to anything other than mine and Ethan's moans of ecstasy.

"We had so many requests and emails for you from the fans to get better. Do you like the plant? Jose and I thought you would like it."

"I love it, Shane. Thanks so much for everything. Where's Jasta? Or is it now Jose?"

"Yeah, that's his new nickname since he got trashed on Cuervo last weekend… dumb schmuck almost got himself arrested for being a loud mouth with the smokin' bartender at Brother Jimmy's. He's getting breakfast for us and should be in momentarily."

"Sounds like our Jared. Thanks for manning the ship in my absence… you guys did a fabulous job."

"You're very welcome. So how are you feeling? You got the flu, hah? Well you look awesome despite. In fact, you're glowing."

A wry pride washed over my face. "Yeah that flu kicked my ass... I'm feeling much better now. I got in early and loaded the set list so you guys can just sit back and take a breather... you earned it big time."

"Thanks Claire... you didn't have to do that. I'm so glad you did though... I had a rough night with the boys and just want to puff my aches away."

I want to puff the aches in my sore loins away.

"No problem, take it easy. I'm starving... I could eat a house. Do you know what Jared was getting? Maybe I can call in some additions? Get him on the horn buddy... let him know I want challah French toast, spinach omelet and those blueberry crumble muffins they have and what were those things you got from there?"

"Latkes."

"Right... please order a whole bunch of those with apple sauce... the works and coffee, a barrel of coffee. Here, take my credit card."

Shane unblinkingly looks at me stone faced while he's on the phone. "Jose... wait! Don't leave there yet. Claire, or who seems to be posing as Claire, just put in a request for more food than her usual birdseed. You ready for the order? Oh and put it on my card dude, I will pay anytime this lady actually eats something of substance." I gave him the finger with a smile as Shane relayed my order word for word to Jared.

"Where's is my captain? Forgive me, but you're not the girl I know."

"It's me Shanester, just intensified and hungrier than ever. That flu really did a number on me."

More like Ethan literally sucked out every last fat cell

121

my body stored for fuel. No matter how much food we consumed it wasn't enough. Our fuckfest made the New York City Marathon seem like a light jog in the park. Shane looks unconvinced, his eyebrow is arched above his smirk as I'm about to go live. I wink with thumbs up and switch the mic on. Jared comes in with two big bags of pungent smelling food. I cut to the first song and grab the goods to eat. Now both Shane and Jared are gawking at me.

Jared breaks the silence. "I have a confession to make. I don't know if you heard last week but I made an inadvertent mistake on a song title... Blur's "Girls & Boys" and I said, "Boys & Girls." The sad part is, it was written right in front of me and I still screwed up. I'm sorry... prepared for the consequences."

"Innocent mistake dude, it could've happened to anyone so no worries and thanks for telling me. Are you going to eat that chocolate chip cookie?"

I must have struck a chord for them with my newfound chilled out attitude because Shane scratches the back of his head while Jared rolls his sleeves up nodding no. Little did they know, all I cared about was racing home to Ethan for our therapeutic body poetry.

Shane crosses his arms and takes the floor. "I've been observing you for the past hour and I came up with two possibilities for your questionable overly chillaxed attitude. You are either stoned off your ass on the finest leaves around, or you have gotten the finest booty call that you've ever had. Which one is it?"

I forget how clever this chap is, and how shitty an actress I am. I could answer honestly or just play it cool and deny everything.

"Thanks for your theories but it's just repercussions of

being sick and now I feel better. Also more time has passed since the bombing and being away from the rooster call..."

"I call bullshit. It's written all over your face and I can smell it on you. You got a big time dose, didn't you? Please tell us who the lucky guy is. Wait... is it that dude you mentioned from the band?"

"I don't kiss and tell boys, sorry. Let's just say my life has taken an epic turn towards greatness."

Shane nods at Jared. "I knew it, I just knew it. Happy to hear... you were way overdue. So tell us what happened."

That's all I needed was to have these guys know the details of me getting down.

"I plead the fifth boys, so subject change... sorry."

Shane stands up and throws the football at me. "We tell you everything down to the nitty gritty and you can't give us a little something?"

"Well young lads, here's the deal. When a guy describes their indiscretions to a girl, whether she has an attraction or not, hearing the details from the guy will leave her wondering about him, yes, but it will not leave her in a panting dog state. However, the same does not hold true when a girl describes a morsel of *in flagrante delicto*, the guy listening could find her repulsive, and yet in the most warped sense... wonder what she's like in bed suddenly wanting to sleep with her. God forbid if the guy holds the storyteller in high regard. Hellz to the no."

Jared looks at Shane. "Dammit, she's right, Shane. End of discussion."

Shane shoos us off with his arm. "You're both teasing uptight prudes."

"Uptight... yes.   Please think of me as the most uptight nun of them all."

Jared raises his hand in between our giggles. "So remember that girl from the party... Paige?"

Shane's eyebrows rise.   "Not the slaw from my friend's party."

"Yes that one and dude... please don't call her that either. I know that's the lowest of the low in whore speak and she's not."

"Jose, I'm looking out for you like a brother. You can sleep with her, just don't date her. She's not the dating kind if you catch my drift."

I vaguely remember the chick, but her seedy face comes to mind as they continued speaking about her. What the hell would Jared find so appealing about her? He's better suited for a quiet nebbish type. I figured I would let the guys hash it out before I gave my two cents.

"I'm telling you for your own good, don't worry... we'll find you a good girl soon."

"I appreciate that Shane, but I really like her and I'm going to see if I can ride it out."

Listening to him, I realized I shouldn't say anything. He seems to be happy. No matter what kind of advice you try to give a person who is in deep—they will never comprehend what you tell them till they are ready to listen to something other than their own demented logic.

"Okay, just make sure to double bag it."

"Alright Mr. Tactless, tone it down. He obviously likes her and you know as much as I do, when your heart's

124

attached... it's another ballgame."

Jared pumps fists with me. "Thanks Claire, that means a lot. It's been a while since I've been wrapped up with someone... feeling needed again. I missed the attention."

"Absolutely."

Shane gets up to stretch. "I apologize for my insensitivity, I didn't realize... and you're right, that spellbound feeling... nothing beats it. I promise not to talk down about Paige anymore. Now come over here and suck start this Harley so I can also revel in that 'swonderful feeling." Jared spits out his coffee and we all crack up.

I let the guys go home early as I caught up on paperwork and the listeners' suggestions for the show's concept. I jog uptown to Ethan's sublet, opening the door with the key he gave me. I walk in hearing music playing and smell a savory meat dish of some sort. I peek into the dining room and there are lit candles scattered throughout the place. Ethan is sitting in the chair and has on a dark brown fedora hat that compliments his plaid shirt.

"How was your day? I have pork stew in the slow cooker for dinner later. I've missed you."

"You cook as well? I think I've found a keeper. What's this song? I like the beat."

"It's Operatica's "Under the Desert Sky."

I take off my coat and sit on his lap. "I love your hat. Can I borrow it sometime?"

"Anytime... I got a similar one for you. I visited my pal Anton... he owns a cool hat shop downtown. When I showed him your picture, he said you would look great in this. It's in the bedroom."

I attempt to get up for a look but Ethan won't let go of me, kissing me on my neck. He feels his way up my skirt, lifts me up, laying me down on the dining room table. He kneels on the floor. I make eye contact with him knowing the power he currently has over me. After a few moments, he asks if I need a break or want to go outside for some air in my panting state. Touché. We didn't get a wink of sleep as we watched the moon fade out while the sun slowly faded in. The day was upon us, wrapping up our deep conversation as we get ready. He tries to enjoy the breakfast I made but we knew his driver would be calling soon, telling him his car is outside.

"This is getting tougher each time I have to leave for a little, what am I going to do? What are we going to do? I'm in love with you. Why don't we just live together, I know it's sudden but think about it."

"I love you too... you know that. We'll live together, eventually. For now, let's relish the moments we have and work towards having more. The past ten days have been surreal, finally being with you. Despite your tour obligations and a three thousand mile living obstacle, we'll make this work."

"I know... LA isn't my ideal home. The bands stationed there till the next album is finished. The tour is almost over, that'll help. We're finally together... another dream of mine came true."

And there it was, being part of a unit again and not just me, myself, and I. It would be eight months since my demise with Jake and now a little under a fortnight into this new one.

"Claire, I'll take another flight and leave later. I don't want to wait a couple of weeks till we're together again."

"As tempting as that sounds I can hear your agent

now, in a heated rage calling me Yoko. Not appealing my hero, especially when we'll have free reign when I get out there."

We hold each other as we walk down the stoop towards the car. He keeps the door opened and has me wait. He takes out his guitar and strums The Foo Fighters "My Hero." We chuckle between his singing attempts. We kiss goodbye and the car pulls away. I hear his guitar playing for a few blocks till it fades out in the distance. I miss him already.

CHAPTER 13 / *RADIO KILLED THE VIDEO STAR*

"I want to let you guys know, I'll be away for a couple of days after Christmas break. Kurt agreed to cover for me... he's cool so please show him the same courtesy you show me. I promise to bring you back In & Out Burgers."

"Lucky you... going to Cali to see the man, hah? I wish I had a morsel of your life."

"You can't knock the hustler, Salinger. Hey Parker, are you ready to announce the first song on our set?"

He's slumped in his seat, looking tired with a grey balmy tone in his face. I can empathize with him, its nerve racking as hell speaking on-air until it becomes second nature. With the little experience he's had, tough love is in order, like my predecessors gave me—throw the non-swimmer into the deep end of the ocean.

"Buck up little camper, it's your day to rock and you shall. Look at the list and do your best to announce the next set. You need practice and today's the day... make me proud. You're on in sixty seconds."

"I'm not feeling well... can I do this tomorrow?"

"Nope, putting if off won't help, you need practice...

you'll be fine. We're here for you. Get ready." I raise my eyebrows and fingers with three... two... one.

"Hello listeners, I'm Jared, part of the WLDM Morning Crew. The last song, 'My Favorite Game' by The Cardigans, was requested from Jack in Lindenhurst and 'Man on the Run' for Tracy in Merrick. We'll be back with forty minutes commercial-free music on 97.2."

He wasn't bad, a little dry and shaky, lacking personality but his delivery was decent. He screwed up the name of a song title, even after I've reiterated many times to research the artist and title before he types it onto our list.

Shane claps. "Bravo... you almost had it, till forgetting to mention a little known band known as Paul McCartney and Wings and their brilliant song, 'Band on the Run' ... not man. Oh and word to the wise, you might want the listener to know your last name next time. Whoa... dude, are you okay?"

I look over at Jared, he's shaking in his seat hunched over the control board. We run over to him.

"Are you okay? Jared, say something."

"Claire, something's wrong... he's not coherent... what do we do?"

"Call reception, have her call 911 and pull up his insurance on file. Maybe one of the doctors on the 12th floor are available. Let's get him fluids... water... apple juice and a cold wet towel... go!"

I kneel in front of him, wiping his forehead, rubbing his back asking if he's on any medication or if he's been ill. His eyes are closed as he struggles to speak. Shane runs in with beverages and said the doctor's on his way. He holds Jared's head up as I help him drink apple juice. His forehead drips wet ice beads. After he drinks, his eyes open and a hint of peach color coats his face as he holds our hands.

"Jasta, are you feeling a little better? The doctor will be here in a minute. Can you speak?"

"Thank you both... I... "

"Save your breath buddy... no thanks needed. We want to make sure you're okay. Here, drink more juice. Claire, did he say he's ill?"

"No... he didn't. Jared, are you on anything... are you diabetic?"

"Yes... I am. I had a sugar crash..."

"Oh Jared, you poor thing. I'm sorry I pushed you to announce, it's my fault... I stressed you out."

"No... it's not, this happens every once in a while, I skipped breakfast and I know better."

"Shane, can you pass the crackers to me, thanks. You should feel better after eating something. Here... have some water, too."

Shane brings the crackers to him. "Dude, I'm sorry I was teasing you before with your announcement, you know me... I'm an asshole who means well. I'll get you whatever you want, just say the word."

"It's alright Shane, I screwed up so... I should be okay in a few. Claire, how did you know?"

"My old roommate at Columbia... she's Type 1 diabetic and had a similar episode. Are you on shots?"

"Yes. Cursed since I'm fourteen."

The receptionist comes in with the medical assistant. Shane helps Jared into the wheelchair.

"Alright buddy, we'll check on you after the show. Feel better and just text me if you need anything."

"Thanks Shane. Oh Claire, I didn't set up the PSA... did we lag after that commercial break?"

"Look at you... worrying about the set, just feel better. Shane took care of it... we played songs without doing a PSA announcement. So I'll get ripped a new one by Warren... who cares. Just feel better. If the doctor gives the go ahead, we'll take you home with a car service, okay?"

"Thanks Captain, please don't tell the others. I'd rather keep it under wraps... please."

"Of course, amigo. The three of us are family. You have our word... take care and we'll see you later." I let go of his hand teary eyed as the doctor wheels him out.

"Aww shit, Claire... you're gonna make me cry. Please stop... I hate seeing a lady cry."

"I feel really bad for him, he's so young... it's an unforgiving disease."

"Yeah, I know. It's horrible. My heart goes out to him, poor guy. Why didn't he tell us?"

"Put yourself in his shoes, it's not easy. He probably doesn't want people pitying or looking at him differently. You know what we should do... let's help him master announcing."

"Absolutely... he'll be better than me."

* * * * * * * *

For the next couple of weeks, I had him take over Shane's spot announcing. Each time he improved becoming more comfortable with it—now the listeners know his last name. Shane stepped up to the plate by staying with him after the show to coach him. I arranged two half-hour segments of airtime for them so Shane could still reap benefits. This was unheard of at WLDM but I convinced Lana it would work since the ratings were climbing. Each day, Jared's overall attitude became lighter and his performance refined. It feels rewarding, witnessing his advancement overall. I couldn't help imagine if this is how John felt when he sees a patient improve. I confided in Jared that I am in therapy and it solidified our bond.

"Are you guys ready for tonight? All the liquor and food you can squeeze in on a school night."

Shane takes off his new set of specs. "Silly Clarabelle, have I not told you I was born ready?"

"It blows to have a holiday party on a Wednesday night."

"I hear you Jasta, but the good news is we'll have temp coverage till 8:00 AM, which is a doable start time. By the way, Salinger, those glasses do you serious justice."

"Get in line love. Actually, you never have to wait… you have a cut-in-line pass anytime." It's nice to know we're back to our flirtatious selves. Jared reaches for both our hands.

"Can I be the marshmallow fluff in your PB&J sandwich? Please oh please."

Shane throws his signed Derek Jeter baseball at him.

132

"Of course, you fluffernutter."

The Killer's "All These Things That I've Done" finishes as I sing to Jared operatic style.

"You're up, J Dizzle, nail it out of the park."

Shane pitches in. "You can do it, Obi-Wan… use the force, Juke."

He proceeds to do just that. We sing and dance to his half-hour-plus set that featured singles from the Sex Pistols, Tears for Fears, Neil Young, Wilco, Fiona Apple, and Jimi Hendrix. If only the audience could see him behind the mic with his smile from ear to ear and energy resembling sparks— what a sight. He's graduated and I feel like the proudest mom. As the title of Ice Cube's song he just spun, "It Was a Good Day." Shane hands him print outs of emails from listeners who wrote flattering compliments for the "Radio God" that just aired. In honor of his triumph, we did peanut butter and jelly shots at the party. I had arranged with the guys to be in the next morning for 9:00 AM so I could leave earlier to squeeze in a therapy session with John and they could party harder. Everyone looked glam dressed in cocktail dresses and suits, especially the guys who looked handsome, more mature. The spirits were at a volume of eleven and overall it was the best holiday celebration WLDM's ever had. I carpooled with Lana's assistant, Marnee, who lived blocks away from Ethan. We made plans to walk to work together.

The next morning upon our arrival, it resembled a ghost town. Aside from the few temps lingered about, no one was in, not even Lana. Wait, that's not what I think it is, right? No it can't be. Oh God it is. It's a ladies bra on my control board—a black ratty looking bra. Note to slut: spring on a new bra for future play! Frigging amateurs. I get tongs out of the box of gadgets to pick it up and see the size which reads 38B. I know already who this belongs to. It's Nina, one of the intern's on the afternoon show. She has the broadest back I've ever seen on a 5'5" frame. Now the question is who nailed her? It's not Jared, since he's exclusive with Paige these days. It's not Chad, the deejay from the show she works on because he's happily married to a swimsuit model. Stephen for all I know is asexual—he wouldn't know what to do with a naked woman in front of him. It has to be Shane, I just know it. He can command way better play than her, is he kidding? And what the hell would cross his mind to bang her in my studio? I toss the evidence in a bag and throw it in my drawer. Marnee wouldn't understand and most likely overreact by racing to Lana with incriminating evidence. I couldn't help thinking they juiced all over my desk. I need to disinfect ASAP.

"Marnee... do you mind getting me cleaning supplies."

"Sure, what do you need exactly?"

A fucking flame thrower. "Clorox all-purpose cleaner wipes or similar... thanks."

She comes back in a flash with a bucket of cleaning items and asks if I need help, I told her no thanks. This was a job for me alone, I didn't know if a pair of boxers would jump out as well. I wiped everything down feeling skeeved out in the process. I took a quick shower at the gym downstairs and changed into my yoga clothes. When I got back, Jared had already set up and advised Shane was on his way in.

"How are you feeling, Claire? I'm hurting in a bad way. It's cruel we have to work after such a booze fest. My liver fell out on the train."

"I hear you. It is messed up... just so they save a few dollars by having a party mid-week. My head is splitting actually, I need some Excedrin... do you want any?"

He nods no. "I'm already three Aleve in, thanks."

We get visits from interns and deejays from the other shows, gossiping about who made spectacles of themselves and hooked up. Kurt and Jared predict Shane and Nina did and I can't help agreeing with them silently. They ask for my thoughts and I choose the oblivious route.

"I have no idea... I was too pickled to notice. Besides you know me, I don't partake in the peanut gallery." Jared laughs as he handles the request line.

"Great C Note, now I feel like an asshole. But it's so much fun to talk about whom slutted up with whom from the holiday party."

"Aww, Kurt... you don't need me to make you look like an asshole, you're a bona fide yenta and that's why we love you. I just don't want to be involved with idle speculation."

"By the way... how's Ethan?" Kurt smirks devilishly as he asks.

"He's fine. Now you're a top shelf asshole but still lovable. I have to work... smell you later."

During the first set, I visualize Shane and Nina fornicating on my desk. I don't know why it's reeling in my head, like Dan Aykroyd's character suffered from in *Ghostbusters*. Except it isn't as sweet as the Stay Puft Marshmallow Man—it's dark and sordidly erotic. I'm curious of the scenario and the positions they used. Did he take her from behind? Did he put a revised spin on missionary? Maybe she used the reverse cowgirl on him, sprawled out on my desk? Jesus, what is wrong with me and my licentious mind? I'm worse than a guy. Maybe I could ask him if we're ever sloshed at a work function, over some laughs while trying to guess. Considering our past, asking Shane straight out might imply an inappropriate curiosity or jealousy. Who am I kidding? It is improper but the thought of him riding that trollop on my desk is tormenting me. Of all desks, why mine? Was this his *fuck you* salute since I never gave him a chance post make-out? Why couldn't he use Stephen's couch at the other end of the hall or his own desk? When I give him back the bra I will ask him, which in all fairness is a legitimate question, considering I eat here for Christ's sake!

"Claire... are you there?" Oops, Jared's caught me zoning out, apparently ignoring his five IM's.

"Sorry, preoccupied in hangover stupor. Want to tell me what you wrote or do you prefer I read it?"

"No worries... just didn't know if you wanted me to line up the next hour of music, so I put it on autopilot."

"Good thinking... yeah I'm pretty checked out today and like you said, our productivity level is nil. We should order lunch on them since we're here later than normal. Let's order from Ollie's... I could use a fix of banana chicken with fried rice. Figure out what you want and give the order to Marnee."

"Sweet... thanks. Should I get something for Shane?"

"No. That's what he gets for being pathetically late."

"You got it. He should be here roughing it like the rest of us... though he was pretty sauced when I left the party."

Shane walks in looking like swamp ass with his green face and bloodshot eyes.

Jared hands him a water bottle. "Damn dude, you look awful. What happened?"

"I've vomited three times already and I'm finally able to stand. I literally got hammered by Mr. Jack Daniels. I am sorry I'm late... I'll cover for you guys when I get right."

"Shane, I have a question for you. When I left the party, you were doing shots with Nina and Deirdre, so which one did you hook up with? I'm guessing both."

Hmm, maybe Jared will find out the answers to my questions.

"None of your business... we just got really drunk."

Jared smiles at me and leaves to go to the bathroom. This is the perfect time to give him Nina's bra.

"Hey Shane... I have something here that I found. Considering it's sensitive, I put it in a bag."

He looks in the bag. "Oh shit. Does everyone know about this?"

"No, just me. Look, I don't care who you're breaking drawers with, you know that, but I just have to know... um... where exactly did the show take place?"

"Thanks for keeping it under wraps... I swear it wasn't here. Well, we started in here and then ended up on Stephen's couch, then back in here... over there in the corner using the blankets we had in the bin."

Great, now they have to be fumigated.

"So... definitely not on my desk?"

"No... Jesus no. Why would you think that?"

"Because I found her bra on my control board, sprawled over my coffee cup."

"Oh... her bra probably wound up there when I was carrying her around... I flung it off but we didn't do it on your desk, I swear."

I felt better. Yet I still needed to know how they did

it, how many times and… yes I know. I am disgustingly corrupted and have problems. I'm in therapy, so give me a break.

"Good to hear, you may want to get that back to Nina."

"Wait, how did you know it was Nina?"

Oh shit. Me and my big mouth. He should believe my mathematical equation of bra/back measurements, I hope.

"Well, after Jared's comment, I presumed it was one of the two girls he mentioned and when I saw the bra size, I knew it was hers since Deirdre couldn't be more than a 32A."

"I think it's interesting… how out of the whole station, I'm the sleaze that banged a co-worker in the office. No one, not even you, gave me the benefit of the doubt?"

I didn't know what to say. He is right, we summed up it was him in less than five minutes. We all have crosses to bear, especially bad boys and Shane was no exception. No matter how loyal he is when he's someone's boyfriend, he is way too sly when he isn't.

"You should feel complimented. You men love being revered for nailing a chick at the office, come on now. Look, it came down to the process of elimination. I didn't think of you at first but when I went through the list of XY chromosomes here, you were the only one without anything to lose. Don't think anyone targeted you."

"Okay. Please let's keep this episode with Nina on the DL… for her sake at least since she has a boyfriend."

"Yes I know and of course I won't say anything. Decide if you want to confirm with Jared. Hasn't Nina been serious with her boyfriend for a while? Some committed wife she is, hah?"

"He's not, as she put it, ringing her bell in the sex department... hence why she looked to me."

"Still no excuse. She needs to leave the poor sap who doesn't know where her clitoris is and move on. I have no sympathy for deceivers that have their cake and eat it too."

His eyes widen in surprise at my judgment. "That's a little harsh... no slack for the needy, hah? I hear you hun and I agree. I would never date a chick like that because as you know I have no love for cheaters either. Except when I'm free and just want to have fun, the cheaters will do. And boy, oh boy, do they do." He winks.

I reckon in their inebriated state, they screwed at least four times and it started off in typical porn fashion with oral sex and... there truly is no excuse for my X-rated imagination.

Jared rushes in. "Another two hours and we're out of here. The food should be here soon... yay."

"Yay is right, I can't wait to eat. Sorry Shane, we didn't order anything for you, I didn't think you were coming in anytime soon."

Shane holds his stomach and belches. "No problem, I can't eat anything for a while..... I'll just spew it up."

"What shall the last song be, Captain? How about a throwback?"

"Good idea, Parker. Yes, I have the perfect one... Naughty by Nature's "O.P.P." Yes, let's play that." Shane pouts giving me the finger.

The air feels refreshing on my walk to Ethan's spot. I'm indebted to him for letting me stay there while he's away. The withdrawals have set in and he's only been gone nine days. I couldn't wait for tomorrow, boarding the plane, taking me to California. The band has finishing recording and I'm joining him in LA for a long weekend. It's been a couple of years since I visited LA; I couldn't wait to explore it with Ethan. I feel a vibration in my pocket, it's a message from John's office confirming my appointment. He agreed to see me earlier so I didn't have to rush getting to the airport on time. I had talked with Greer about what John suggested, cutting off contact with her and the mere mention of Jake for an indefinite amount of time while I healed. She understood and was supportive. The last time I talked with her, she said Jake was improving; therapy has been helping him. If you would have told me the two of us would have wound up under the care of quacks I would have laughed and cursed whoever predicted such. Never say never. I am living proof that anything can happen and it surely does. I met up with Bianca and Sandra for dinner at Tao. Even though I still wasn't feeling well from the holiday party, I was ready for another fun night. We migrated to The Bar Downstairs at The Andaz Hotel and got properly sloshed on lemon lime vodka concoctions while being hit on by hot business guys—it sure does wonders for a woman's lonely ego.

CHAPTER 14 / "*IF I GOT TO CHOOSE A COAST I GOT TO CHOOSE THE ... [?]*"

Virgin Flight V27 JFK to LAX—this will become one of my favorite commutes, the start to a promising friendship with this nightclub in the sky. That's what happens when you date a rock star; planes become your second home. This West Coast jaunt couldn't have come at a better time since I was overdue for a get out of dodge break. When you tell some people you're LA bound, the usual reaction is *I can't stand LA... so pretentious, plastic and superficial.* While those sentiments are true for most that live there, these reactionaries never mention the exquisite scenery from a hike in the hills or a cruise on the PCH or Mulholland Drive. It's always about the so-called people that epitomize a destination and I beg to differ. I know some genuine cool cats living there that are as real as the stretch lines on their body. I have toyed with moving to California many times in the past few years. The question always remains: will I be happy out there? Part of me feels I would while another part of me is scared I wouldn't be. This of course was before Ethan stepped onto the scene. He's been in LA for three years as his producer's based there. The amusing Virgin American pre-flight safety video comes on, makes me wish all the airlines out there had a clue. Bob Dylan's "Tangled Up in Blue" plays and I press skip on my iPhone, too bleary a song on such a sunlit day. I can hear the engines rev as we prepare to takeoff. I'm going to use this time to write a pros/cons list of living in LA.

Pros –
Unlimited sex with Ethan
Cruising PCH
Mexican food
Unlimited Marijuana... legally!
Griffith Park
Mulholland Drive
Wine EVERYWHERE
Higher quality of produce and flowers
Living in walking distance of Little Dom's
Better weather
Chateau Marmont
Laid back attitude
Music immersion - especially in the Silver Lake district (sweet)
Pacific Ocean

Cons –
Limited sex with Ethan
My Radio Show (this one's a doozie)
No job or shitty one at that (potentially)
Pretentious flakes (this one's going to wind up bothering me)
Slower service (especially pertaining food and annoying wait staff that explain and drag a sentence-long description into a long chapter with useless fillers of their tastes, suggestions and events of the latest date they just went on. Look, if we don't ask, don't tell—PLEASE! We East Coasters appreciate direct concise apropos answers and don't give a hoot about your life story)
2nd Avenue Deli (nothing compares, not even Katz's)
Italian food
Influx of actors and actresses and the likes of all drama idiocy
Traffic (a ten-minute drive that inevitably turns into an hour-and-a-half)
Close proximity to family

"Hmm… unlimited sex with Ethan, that a girl."

I could feel a flush rush to my face. The passenger next to me, an older woman who looks like she's in her fifties is curious.

"Hello… do you always look over at what people are writing? Just curious because it's ballsy and I admire it. My name is Claire, what's yours?"

She smiles, making unblinking eye contact with her sapphire blue gems. She is put together beautifully from head to toe. Her auburn hair is coiffed to French twist perfection. Her attire is a classic skirt suit, ivory-colored with a cinnamon collared shirt accessorized with gold and sapphires scattered on her neck, ears, and wrist. Her shoes are beautifully vintage, two-toned chestnut and ivory high-heeled stilettos. If she were a man she'd be known as a Dapper Dan. I wouldn't be surprised to hear she's a former model, a classic beauty with gams that would have any leg man do back flips just to touch them.

"My name is Dale. It's nice to meet you. I hope you don't think I was eavesdropping; what caught my eye was the zebra print pen you're writing with. Of course as I leaned in for a finer look, I noticed what you had written and I'm a big fan of that as well, so I figured we'd get along. But seriously where did you get that fabulous pen?"

She has completely redeemed herself. I hold the pen out to her for her to hold.

"I got the pen as a gift a few years ago... I think from J Crew or Anthropology. It's nice to meet you Dale... great name by the way. Are you from New York or LA?"

"I'm from Valley Stream, NY, back when it was an affluent village. And you?"

"Garden City... still chock full of arrogant pricks. Are you visiting or..."

She smiles. "Yes, my daughter. I make a couple of trips a year to see her. Let me guess, you're visiting this Ethan character."

"Good guess."

She puts my pen back on the tray. "Can I ask you a personal question?"

I think the formality flew out the window a hundred miles back.

"Why not?"

"Great. Does he satisfy you in bed? I hope you don't mind my frankness, it's just how I am… so please don't take offense."

My eyebrows rise up. Confessing my moments of O status on a plane with the guy staring at me from the window seat next to Dale, waiting for an answer doesn't help my reluctance.

I lean in to whisper. "Oh yes, tenfold I'm grateful to say. I don't mind your candidness… let's just keep our voice down so no one else hears, with the babies on board and all."

She looks around and grins at me. "Of course… good thinking. If you get along with him outside the bedroom too, then you need to marry this guy. It's hard to find a man who can hold a good conversation and ring your bell in the sack at the same time."

Now the window seat guy is sweaty.

"I'm optimistic for whatever the future holds… we're still new so…" I motion to the peepshow viewer and Dale turns towards him.

"Excuse me sir, we don't appreciate you prying in our sensitive conversation. How about being a nice gentleman by putting your earphones on and watch Brooke Burke on *Dancing With The Stars*… you can salivate over her as much as you want. Thanks."

The guy immediately followed her instructions and settled for

Jennifer Aniston and Brooklyn Decker in *Just Go With It*. I revered this new acquaintance sitting next to me.

"Okay darling, now where were we? How long have you been going out with him?"

I brought her up to speed with the whole situation, even Jake got thrown in. She's a great listener, anytime she added commentary it is genius—truly sound advice. She told me how she was married for a second time to the love of her life. Her first husband tragically died when they were in their mid-thirties. She met her second husband when she hired him as the attorney to handle the estate affairs after her first husband's death. Towards the end of her case, they both found themselves smitten and the rest is history. Over Colorado, there is severe turbulence; we both nervously keep each other amused by talking. I enjoy listening to her speak, her voice has a rich melodious tonal quality. She comically compares men's lovemaking styles by their nationality. She swears by the French.

"If you can get past the fact that most are bi-sexual freaks... they're magnificent in bed."

"Full-bred Irish Men usually have small willies and don't like kissing you south of the border... such a travesty." Half-breeds were a different category, revealing she is Irish and Italian.

"They're usually decent, though a couple also fell short on the meter stick."

Luckily her current husband, Jackson, is French and Irish—same as Jake. We both agree those players are blessed and know what they're doing. She warns me against Germans being cold. The English, Italians, Spaniards, Eastern Europeans, Russians, and Arabians have her seal of approval. I tell her Ethan is Russian and English and she solidifies he's a keeper. I ask if religion plays a factor and she says yes. Jewish, Jesuit's, and Buddhists rated very high in her black book. Catholics were in the median to high grade and anything Orthodox, except for Greek fared poorly. I point out how I heard so many rumors of the Catholic school girl sluts from my guy friends back in high school.

"We're talking about the men, Claire... women are another ballgame."

She's right, dammit. Her experience with sixty-two men has me convinced. Dale offers me an apple cranberry muffin she baked for the plane ride.

"So you're on the fence about moving? I say, just do it... do it before you're too old and afraid. I was fortunate enough to live in different countries and states before coming back to my native stomping ground."

"Dale, these muffins are legit. I want the recipe. Out of curiosity, how long did you last, being away from New York?"

"Glad you like them, I'll mail it to you. I lasted fifteen years. After my first husband, Jean-Marc died, I got homesick. When I was with him, it made the experience significant. When he died unexpectedly in a plane crash, I was lost. Even though my home in Monte Carlo was comfortable, I couldn't help thinking about him and our good times together. Blame it on painful reminders but as soon as I left... the life we shared together stayed there." She has tears swelling in her eyes.

"Dale, if it's too difficult to talk about, I understand."

She grabs my hand to hold. "I'm fine... just tickles the emotions. Where was I? Right, the plane was his friend Barrett's... they served in the Air Force together. Their friend died in Johannesburg of a heart attack and they flew in for the service. I was seven months pregnant with our second child

146

and wasn't cleared to go. Barrett had flown us many times and was a phenomenal pilot. It was determined that engine failure is what caused the plane to go down."

"I am so sorry to hear. You are the bravest woman I have ever met, such tragedy and look at how you prevailed."

Dale lost her husband while she was seven months pregnant and I thought I had it rough.

"I had no choice... I had a three-year old at home and one on the way. Kids remarkably give you a strength you never knew existed. It was a tough time and luckily my sister and mother helped me through it... another reason why I moved back. Not to change the subject, but I'm curious... you had mentioned the difficulties with your previous relationship, what exactly happened?"

Without hesitation I told her everything. By the end of my tale, she looks at me like a mother about to warn her daughter from right and wrong.

"You did the right thing, Claire. Don't ever doubt yourself on that painful decision. Love and marriage are enough of a roller coaster without having additional mechanical difficulties. We're both brave souls."

"Well, you've given me hope. You're an inspiration... I'm glad we met."

"Claire, I can't believe we're almost landing... let's exchange emails so I can keep in touch with you. Would that be okay?" She puts her glasses on.

"I would love that."

"Great, let's use that lovely pen of yours and write it down... I'm an old school chick and don't believe in icalls... blackballs... whatever they're called." We giggle exchanging handwritten contact information.

"I would like for you to have this pen, Dale. Please keep it as remembrance of our delightful flight conversation."

"Oh I couldn't, since it was a gift. Thanks for the gesture though, that alone, is cherished."

"I insist, I hardly use it and have plenty of funky pens to last me two lifetimes. I love letters so if you feel inclined to write, I promise to reciprocate. You have my information and if by chance I move next year, I'll write you my new details."

Dale takes my hand and holds it for the rest of the flight. We talk about more of her life experiences and how she's always lived by the existentialist code. After we land, we walk off the plane through the terminal where she sees her daughter waiting. Dale introduces us and she looks like Dale's younger twin. I call Ethan to meet me outside as I walk out with them. I hear my name being called, I turn around and it's him. He picks me up holding me tight. I motion to the ladies and introduce them all.

Dale leans in to my ear. "He's a fine looking gentleman." I nod and kiss her cheek.

She then leans in to his ear. "She's a gem, you're very lucky. My compliments to you being blessed and clued in… a rare breed."

He looks bewildered but smiles thanking her nonetheless. I whisper to him, saying he's about to have a good laugh when I explain what she means. We walk Dale and her daughter to their car and say our goodbyes. Ethan has my luggage rolling in his left hand while his right one was around my waist as I tell him what Dale meant.

"I think we need to make her proud gorgeous, by bestowing my blessings and clued in genius onto… in you. I'm so glad you're here… I've missed you awful."

"The distance is getting to me." I hold and lean on his arm as he drives us to his apartment in his light blue 1972 Ford Mustang convertible. I forgot how brightly golden the sun shone in the West—another pro to add to the list. We caught dinner at Little Dom's that night and it was as good as I remembered. Afterwards we strolled down North Vermont Avenue, hearing Marty and Elayne tearing up the Dresden lounge through the opened door entrance.

"Is this something you could get used to doing? Strolling down with me on various streets in the greater LA area?"

"Of course it is… just as long as we can stroll down some of my favorite streets in the NYC area, too."

"That goes without saying. If I had my way, I'd live there permanently. It's the nature of the record-making beast unfortunately. The good news is, I pushed to mix and record at the Record Plant and the producers finally agreed. That will have me East for at least two months, if not more. I want to marry you. I asked you that night in New York and I meant every word I said. You didn't give me an answer. I want you to be happy and I understand if you don't want to sacrifice your show for me. Worst case, we can try to shuffle between both cities."

"I love you… especially that you understand me. We're headed towards marriage… definitely. I just want it to be right because you know the catastrophe that happened with my last effort. I am moving on, you have helped me incredibly with that. It's just going to take some time, but I'm getting there. The heavy hitter is giving up my show. I know I can't sit at home, twiddling my thumbs like Suzie Homemaker. That's my conflict. I hope you can understand by being patient with me while I work it out."

"I do understand. If you were to propose this to me, I would say the same thing. I love what I do... I know you love what you do and that's important for both of us. I don't expect you to sacrifice your livelihood for me. It's not fair to you or anyone for that matter. I'm just asking to explore the possibilities. We can use our connections to see what options we have so it works. I'm sorry for throwing a monkey wrench in your progress. The way you're dealing with the aftermath of what you went through, I'm in awe, babe."

"You don't know what it means to me, your willingness to compromise. I will put the feelers out... see what I can work out with the station. I hate sounding selfish... it's not my intent. I'm scared to lose you and everything I worked so hard for."

"It's me who's being selfish... my living situation that's the inconvenience. It's crazy, last year you weren't an option and then seven weeks ago, my life got turned upside down when you suddenly were. I've never been happier, knowing I am finally with you after all this time. Just bear with me, we'll make this work... whatever it takes."

We make-out on Hollywood Blvd. I didn't care about the public display of affection because I couldn't help myself. On our walk back home I thought about how years ago, I would never throw in the towel moving three thousand miles for a guy after just six weeks. Now I'm seriously considering it because he's not just a guy, he's everything. He affects me in ways I never imagined—his likes, opinions, style, mannerisms, how he talks—especially about something he's passionate about, and how he makes me feel. He's a captivating impetus like no other. I've never met anyone like him and that's what scares me with guardedness. Am I in his league? Will he feel as strongly for me as he does now seven years down the road—loving me, no matter what? Why can't I just get married and go with the now? Why do I care so much about tomorrow? I sent Lana an email after Ethan fell asleep, asking her what my options were with the station and her connections around here. I needed to pray. The last time I prayed was the day I found out about Jake's attempted suicide. I also prayed for forgiveness for not praying on a regular basis. It's not that I don't want to pray regularly, I usually fall asleep before I have a chance. Sad excuse but true.

Forgive me Father for I have sinned. It's been a long time since my last confession and I hope and pray that you hope and pray for a troubled soul like me. Please help give me the strength to make this work with Ethan, if it's meant to be. Please give me signs if it's not and thanks for forgiving my inconsistent communication with you.

* * * * * * * *

While Ethan worked on his record, I explored hidden treasures at Matador Beach, nestled next to Malibu, cruising around the winding roads towards the valley. I stopped at some fruit stands en route to find the sweetest strawberries I had ever tasted. My friend from the station, Kamden, lives nearby in Malibu; we made plans to meet. As a free-lance writer, she has time on her hands to peruse parameters and wander with me. I drive to her abode and she's outside by her stoop. She's always had great hair, waves of chestnut and caramel swirls down to the middle of her back. Her skin is tanner than I remember, seems California agrees with her. I park in her driveway and she drives us around, acquainting me with all the splendors of surrounding neighborhoods.

"I know you'll like it here, especially for the better weather. The only thing is you will miss New York. I like having the break from the hustle and bustle but sometimes I crave it. I have some friends at KROQ... I'll put in a good word. I don't think you'll have a problem finding a job out here. I write a lot of reviews for them, they love me there... they'll lead you in the right direction."

"That would be awesome Kam, thanks. I'll probably

wind up liking it out here... Ethan alone guarantees that. I love my show though. I've worked so hard from the ground up and look where it is now. It's the only thing in my life I didn't fuck up. To have to give that up will crush me."

"I can relate... it's not just you. I had a similar issue and it worked out. Don't get me wrong, it was grating as fuck but we did the long distance for a year and it worked out. You both need to be happy. No one is any good to someone if they're miserable. "

"You were always a smart cookie. Hmm... speaking of which, let's get those carnitas tostadas you were raving about."

"Done!"

We finished lunch and visited the Getty Villa in Malibu. Compared to the Getty in the hills, this one was far more intimate then its grandiose relative. Her boyfriend met us at their apartment and they followed me in their car driving back to Silver Lake to meet the guys at the recording studio. We all went to Mexico City Restaurant for dinner. This would be the third time I'm eating Mexican food and I have only been here eighteen hours. One by one, our friends leave to go home.

"How do you feel about a drink at the Chateau? Some of the guys were heading over there for a friend's birthday thing. It'll be fun."

"Brilliant idea, leader... let's go."

We enjoyed a few rounds and then separated from the others to take a tour of the hotel. We found a door that was unlocked leading into a lounge-like room with a couch and large framed mirrors. It had some spots under renovation. Ethan locks the door behind us. The room is dark with big arch windows, faint lights from outside subtlety highlighting the walls. We look out at the view holding each other. I lead him to sit on the sill. I place our jackets under my knees as I unbuckle his pants, straddling him. While in our throws of titillation, I see people out the window walking on the lowly lit street. One of them, an older man looks up and doesn't move an inch. He stands there staring at me and our display of sweltering climax.

* * * * * * * *

It's 7:20 AM, 10:20 AM my time and I could sleep in all day. I hear Ethan talking on the balcony about pending renovations for the communal gym with his neighbor. At the moment you would never guess he's a successful singer in a famous rock band in his boxers. His neighbor is attractive and her body language is apparent as she writhes around in her black boy shorts and tank. Ethan sees me through the window and comes into the kitchen.

"Honey… you sure you don't want to throw on a t-shirt and cover up out there? You may draw unwanted attention to rabid felines in the building."

"Ooh, I love that your jealous right now, it's such a turn-on. Rest assured, love… I only have eyes for you. You do realize the fillies at this complex are all over fifty, even though they look thirty. Besides… out here, everyone hangs out in their skivvies. I got some chocolate almond croissants for you. They're in the oven on warm. Coffee should be done in a minute."

"You're the best. The only thing I could think of as a perfect accoutrement is Nutella… do you have any?"

He smirks muffling under his breath *tsk tsk*. "In the cabinet to the right. Woman, how could you ask such a thing? That puppy is always stocked, always."

I knew that but I liked keeping him on his toes. "Are

153

you in the studio today?"

"Nope... not till you go back. I wanted us to have time to spend together... so whatever you want to do."

"Surprise me."

"Okay, let's finish breakfast and get ready."

My day with Ethan led us hiking up to Griffith Park Observatory. I hadn't been to a planetarium show in a while and it wound up being a relaxing pit stop for us. We had both fallen asleep and were awakened after the show had ended by a kind usher who assured us it happens all the time. We continued walking along some steep hills. The views were beyond breathtaking, compliments of the Pacific Ocean, sun, and mansions scattered throughout each cliffside. The picturesque scenery had a calming effect on an alarming excursion, with no compass, cell phone reception or trail marks to guide us. We had a great conversation, surprisingly learning things we had never known previously about each other, like what our greatest fears are and what other occupations we would do. His greatest fear is to be murdered and he would be a physical therapist if he wasn't a musician. I told him my greatest fear is to become deaf and the only other job I could see myself doing would be a high school music teacher. We discovered we're both ambidextrous, and aren't fans of the overrated Magnolia and Georgetown Bakeries. After an hour or so along the trail, Ethan secured us to familiar ground. Enamored with the weather and sunset, we decided to pick up wine, hot sandwiches, and chocolate covered strawberries from the local market nearby. He had brought extra sweatshirts for us in his backpack; I guess he knew we'd wind up outside that chilly night and I'm glad he thought ahead. If I were to die at this moment, while holding each other on our flannel blanket underneath the stars shimmering on us, I would be happy. Simple things like noshing and drinking in the middle of nowhere, with a few scattered couples sharing the great space with us would leave a significant impression.

The long weekend in LA went by quickly, even while we were standing still. I have a big decision to make. We said our goodbyes outside of LAX and it was a bit more emotional than I bargained for. Ethan would be back in New York in a couple of weeks—helping lessen the blow of our time apart. I didn't think I could feel safe again in the arms of another but I was wrong. One less fear to contend with. The flight back didn't leave me sitting next to a knowledgeable mother figure. This time the music and reminiscent tid-bits of the past few days did all the entertaining. When I got home from JFK, I was too spent to shower or brush my teeth. I collapsed on my bed, engulfed in a sleep trance for the next ten hours. When I awoke, I remembered my dream from earlier. I was standing alone on a train platform and the sun was beaming down. Two trains across from each other with no bound destination scrolled across the message boards. Two conductors, whose faces appeared blurred at first till I got closer, realizing it was static, white noise covering their faces. They stuck their heads out of the window of each train. The one to the right shouted: *Come on aboard… don't be afraid!* I shouted back: *Where are you going?* He wouldn't answer. The one to the left of me bellowed: *What are you afraid of? It's just a train ride, get on!* I asked him which direction his train was headed. No reply. No matter how many times I asked. I couldn't choose which one to board while feverishly looking in the windows of each train, to see if there were any passengers or signs with a destination. I found nothing. The bells were ringing as the doors closed and in an instant, the scene within the dream had vanished. My cell phone had rung. It was Ethan, leaving a fourth message checking if I had arrived home safe.

CHAPTER 15 / *THE BRIDGE*

Ethan generously arranged with his friend to extend his sublet agreement so we had another option in New York and for me to use during the week for work instead of commuting. He lucked out with this crazy condominium deal from his producer's son Patrick, who had relocated for a business project in Hong Kong with an indefinite return date. I spruced it up with additional artwork that didn't need hanging, along with plants and flowers. I had Fez and Sandra over often for dinner and sleep-overs when the loneliness set in from Ethan's absence. Skype helped, but it still didn't fill the void we were both feeling. At work, the guys were keeping my spirits up with their stories. Jared finally saw the light by dumping Paige for a nice girl named Taran, a friend of the interns who works on Stephen's show. Shane had his hands full with a new chick on the scene named Gwen. While he was deliberating if she was dating material, he kept up his sordid relations with Nina. As he put it mildly, "If you're gonna be intimate with two women at once on separate occasions, you have to do it while you're young and the erections are reliable." We should all have his problems. Sandra is still going strong with Tomasz and Fez is getting hot and heavy with this guy Hans he used to work with. Fez had a life-size cardboard cutout of Ethan made from his advertising friend's hookup at work. When I had people over, they would feel around the crotch area and have fun with it. I would kiss it while Skyping with Ethan, It was such a hit with him, he had one made of me. We had a few more weeks till our reunion, his band was almost finished with their album, and our planned visits kept us going in the interim. In a strange way, I was enjoying some alone time, catching up on dailies and focusing on therapy. I also had an itch again to get back into running again. I felt stronger physically and up for the challenge, happy the winter was behind us. My last run was a little over a year ago, I was at eight to ten miles; I used to run across the Williamsburg and Brooklyn Bridges when I was living in the city. This would be good for me, getting me out of the house after work instead of having time to dwell on Ethan reminders. I push play on my iPhone and start breaking in my new pair of Nike's. After twenty minutes I'm already out of breath, I downshifted to fast walking since my legs were hurting. I'm a few blocks away from the Williamsburg Bridge but had to save reserves for the couple of miles back to the apartment. I remember this same scenario, when I first ran a few years ago building stamina. I skip the bridge and jog back to the apartment to shower and get ready for my appointment with John.

"How are you, Claire... how was your week? Anything you want to address from last week's session?"

"I want to thank you again for helping me with my breakdown last week. It's painful going back to the times with Jake... I appreciate the support."

"Of course, anytime. You have made a vast progress by expressing your feeling without thinking, kind of like free flow writing... it helps when you don't have to censor yourself."

"Not to get off the subject, but my latest dilemma is getting my running score back to where it was. I used to pull almost ten miles effortlessly. When I ran this morning, I almost dropped dead after two and it's bumming me out... a stinging reminder of how I let myself fall abandoned."

He nods as he writes in his notebook. "Well this is a common problem. It's happened to me a few times… I used to play hockey in college and I keep up on a league here in the city. You had to see me after a year's hiatus… I was awful and in pain. After a month or so I got my endurance back, so stick with it. I think it's great you've taking it up again."

"I know… I just need patience."

John is twirling his pen with one hand looking out the window. "May I ask how are things going with your boyfriend? Last time you mentioned, the long distance was burdensome. Any other thoughts?"

I don't know what you call it, but it's awkward talking to John about Ethan. It's obvious we have an attraction towards each other. Now that I'm committed to someone, the chances of it going anywhere are low but that vibe echoes softly in this room. Over the past couple of months I've noticed random comments from him. Maybe it's nothing, or maybe these signs are meant to be read as more.

1st clue: Mirroring. He mirrors my gestures, phrases, and views. Imitation really is the greatest form of flattery.

2nd clue: The way he holds my arm when he greets me. He caresses the side of my bicep with a gentle hold. Maybe he's just a physical person and it's not the fact he wants to bed me.

3rd clue: His quiet gaze. The way he looks at me sometimes without saying anything leaves me wondering about what's going on behind his eyes.

4th clue: He always manages to talk about my show and the mutual bands we like, something I never tire of conversing about. It's an endearing subtle gesture, yet leaves a heavy impression.

I wish I could address this with him so I could tackle the slight betrayal I feel towards Ethan by enjoying this bi-weekly flirtation. I had narrowed down to two visits a month, helping simmer down the mounted tension of frequent visits. If I wasn't with Ethan, this would be the guy for me. He's smart and has that nerdy sex appeal that turns me on. He's a character with sound ethos yet has that fetching carousal edge behind his light brown eyes. Crazy right? I'm with the ultimate boyfriend and I have a slight attraction for another. How could I bring this up?

"Claire, you look like you're in deep thought, you said things were well but the distance is a snag."

"Sorry, momentary brain freeze. Yes, maintaining a long distance relationship is harder than I thought. We're doing the best we can with the situation. I won't lie, my insecurity levels have increased but I'm working through it. I want to bring up what one of the interns addressed the other day. Scott is smitten with his girlfriend but he has a crush on Amanda, this nice chick that waters our plants at the station. It's natural he would be attracted, right? I ask because this other intern from another show brought it up and was adamant that Scott is in the wrong having an attraction towards Amanda. I said it wasn't wrong provided it didn't get physical. What do you think?"

"Interesting... well I see your point about it not being wrong if boundaries are sustained, but the question is, how significant is the crush? If it's mild flirtation, then that's par for the course and relatively harmless. If his attraction is substantial, then the threat of an emotional affair can morph and that can be more significant than the physical act itself."

Oh dear. "How would he know the difference? The degree of the crush I mean."

"Good question. Well how often does he think about

her?"

Honestly, I only think about John when I see him and well anytime I play Arctic Monkeys, dammit.

"I think he mentioned only when she comes in… like twice a week."

John looks out the window for a moment, and then looks at me as if his cleverness has figured out the game I'm playing. "That should be safe. However… if he thinks about her more often or if certain things keep reminding him of her… then it becomes questionable. How come this has piqued your curiosity?"

"I can relate… been there before, and find it fascinating that when it happens to someone, they usually don't have the nerve to acknowledge it. In Shane's case, I don't know if I agree with your point entirely. He sees Amanda a couple of times a week, so how can he not possibly think of her when she brings up tulips, her favorite flowers she told him in passing at one point. Isn't that just typical sense memory or nostalgia-esque?"

"You mean Scott, right? (I nod yes embarrassingly.) Yes, that would apply if the said person didn't have a somewhat physical or emotional attraction for the person they are being nostalgic with. You clearly can see that difference right?"

Yes but I didn't want to admit defeat. "I will let Scott know he may have a problem and to come see you."

"Absolutely, I'd be glad to help. Those feelings though… they do happen from time to time."

I tried reading his face, but he kept his head down writing in his notebook. "I have a dilemma John, a pressing decision to make. Do I move out West to live with Ethan,

160

leaving a job I love or possibly sabotage our relationship? I don't know what to do."

"That's a huge decision to make. Without sounding selfish, who am I going to listen to in the mornings? Hopefully that's all you need to sway your decision to stay put."

Now if that's not blatantly flirting, I don't know what is. "You're too kind. It hasn't been easy to decide. I'm at a crossroads and just wish someone could tell me what's the best choice to make."

"Okay, let's work on this, to help you figure out your current obstacle. The first thing you have to answer honestly is, what will make Claire happiest? Then, we take it from there."

"To have Ethan here while I work at my show... that would be ideal. Unfortunately, it's not a choice on the menu due to his band commitments with their LA-based producer. The next best thing would be to maybe do a bi-coastal arrangement, some time here and there. I am trying to arrange that with my job."

"Sounds like that could work. If I may speak freely, I think there's another underlying issue that may be bugging you as well. Understandably, giving up a job you love is reason enough to not want to compromise, but maybe it's the thought of... surrendering completely."

"Yes. Yes it is. My last effort surrendering didn't last and I'm scared. I love what I do, having control of something great, it's become part of my salvation. It was a positive distraction when I was enduring problems with Jake. At work there is never a façade... well maybe a little one when my boss creeps up on me (we both laugh). I have freedom there, calling the shots on my own work of art."

He stands up to stretch. "Are you fearful you may need that so-called distraction now, as well? Let me elaborate... from what you described about your job... that was your release from the painful truth of what you were living with Jake. My question is do you still feel you need that same security blanket?"

"I don't know. He's stable and we do love each other. I don't feel I need it as much, like I did with Jake. It's just now, I have worked so hard to get where I am. I don't want to lose it."

"Understandably and it's perfectly normal to feel that way, so don't doubt that or feel guilty about it. Besides your ambition, I think it's a conjunction of trust issues too. Considering the pain you were caused and experienced, it's very likely an outcome. Keep in mind, trust is often mistaken as a proposition but it's not... it's a matter of degree. We can work on this by helping you restore a healthier trust level."

"That's a bold statement. I see where you're coming from but in regards to Ethan, I do trust him, our level of intimacy alone proves that. Listening to you, I realized something. It's not Ethan I'm untrustworthy of. It's me. That's what terrifies me. I can't predict how I'll feel in five years or ten. To give up one of my most cherished resources of security for another person is huge."

"Yes it is. It's brave to acknowledge a revelation like that. How do you feel?

"Like a weight has been lifted. Yet, still alarmed... scared not only I'm my worst enemy but not being able to control myself."

"Control yourself of what?"

"My actions. Ones that lean towards the negative sides like not moving and possibly losing a relationship. Or

162

my instincts... thoughts that get out of control at times."

"Claire, no one has complete control all the time of those things. Your experience of heartbreak has left you doubting your instincts and that happens, symptoms like that are common. We're working on that. What thoughts are concerning you? In reference to your question about moving or not, I'm not here to tell you choice A or B is the right one to make. Only you know what the right one is. I can only help you trust and feel secure in your decision."

"I know... it's up to me. I'm struggling with which way to take at the fork in the road."

"That's understandable. Let's tackle that struggle you're having and pinpoint what thoughts you're unsure of as you mentioned before. What are some of them?"

"Just typical doubts I think about... like what if I fail again in a relationship? And trusting my intuition, believing I've made the right choice personally and professionally. Trust, there's that word again."

He smiles. "It's a heavy-hitting word for sure. Real quick, I see you don't have more sessions scheduled. Will you be back to meet in two weeks?"

"I'm taking a time-out for a month. I leave for LA in a few hours... then Ethan's visiting me. I will be back as soon as things simmer down."

"That's nice to hear for you. Considering we used to meet once a week, it's crucial to keep up the ongoing momentum without lapses for long periods of time. I was concerned you weren't coming back for treatment, considering how well your improvements have been."

"John, why would you think I wouldn't come back? I didn't mean to give that impression."

"Of course, sorry I presumed incorrectly. One month from now it is. May I ask you a personal question?"

Here it is, the moment of truth: will you run away with me?

"I thought all of your questions were personal."

He grins. "Do you see yourself marrying Ethan?"

It would not be today. Coincidentally, why is he asking this? Is he concerned for my wellbeing or trolling for information to quench his own curiosity?

"I can see myself married to him, yes."

He touches the arm of his chair looking down. "That answer… honest answer is imperative to your decision… I hope that helps."

John didn't make eye contact with me as we said goodbye.

* * * * * * *

It's Saturday, 6:30 AM. Birds and construction noise have awakened me. I should use this time to go running. Once I'm up, I unable to fall back asleep. I get myself together and jog downtown, picking up the pace every couple of blocks making my way towards the Brooklyn Bridge. From Ethan's, it's roughly two-and-a-half miles. My goal is to run over it without walking, then back to the apartment. It's a far-fetched accomplishment but I'm determined. I am still revved up by what John stressed in regards to my trust issues. Is this another wound from Jake I'm to suffer from? I feel like venom is streaming through my veins, seeking vengeance for another one of his curses. I'm already doused with sweat only fifteen minutes in, mixing with the cool breeze of February. Chinatown's approaching and it's the most challenging part of the run. There are a million people walking on the sidewalks; you have to daringly sprint on a street lane just to keep up momentum. As I breeze by for dear life, I continue down the congested streets leading me to the Bridge. I see many people walking, taking pictures, stopping to buy fruit, or wandering aimlessly. I forgot to bring my iPhone with me foolishly, running without tunes is tough. In some warped way, I could use a break from the soundtrack of my life, to reset myself from the continuous melody since as long as I can remember. Just hearing my feet hit the pavement mixed with sideline conversations and city sounds is music to my ears. I approach the bridge, already gaining decent speed and unlike yesterday, my feet and legs feel weightless. The view is as serene as I remembered; it's been way too long. There are mounds of foot traffic and cyclists trying to go around the middle divider. Upon slowing down, I notice a mother and daughter fighting off to the side while another kid, a boy whom I presume is also hers, is crying on the ground about eight feet away. I walk over to him and grab his hand leading him towards his mom.

"Is everything okay? He's yours, right? He was close to the rail… just making sure he's safe." She nods and takes him by the hand thanking me.

I run again on the path, passing the special spot where I used to stare out and meditate. Touchdown, the end of part one. I circle back the other way and the wind is blowing fierce, no tail-wind advantage on my way home. I feel discomfort on my side like something is rubbing against my hip. I put my hand in my windbreaker pocket and feel a stone-like piece with a chain attached to it. I stop abruptly. It's the necklace Jake had given me. A jade stone necklace he had made when he went to China for business. One of my favorite pieces, it's unique with a raw dark green color, horizontally oval shaped with clasps at the sides, attached to a silver chain. He had said it was tough deciding what he could bring me back as a gift. While he was at the local souvenir shop, he noticed an old jewelry store outside and went in to see what they had. He met with the owner, who helped him design a cut-to-order piece from the stones displayed. It had taken the jeweler the rest of that afternoon to create. I remember when I opened the box and saw it—I was an emotional mess by this handcrafted one-of-a-kind gift. I forgot I put it in this jacket, well over a year ago. I thought I had lost it. I know I'm supposed to rid myself of anything Jake. I could fling this off into the Hudson and never look back. I'll never have the nerve though, no matter how much it reminds me of him. There were extraordinary times too, not just dark ones. I stand in the middle of the path, people transporting around me with cement attached to my feet. I admire the view while flickers of dating-a-rockstar insecurities whirl around my head. The boats are distracting me from pressing decisions that need to be made. My stomach is growling at tiger level. I can make it to Delimarie, their sandwiches are worth it. I hold the piece of jade in my hand while I run back. It gave me a boost because I was comfortable running steadily fast. I cut through Chambers street and sparkles from a small jewelry shop catch my eye. I break to look at the window display of their pristine green items and notice a piece sort of like mine. There's a handwritten quote on a note card in back of it.

"You must get a piece of jade and keep it close. Then your blood will go into the stone, and the stone will get into your blood. The blood will then become your stone, and you will stop bleeding."

CHAPTER 16 / *SACRAMENT OF PENANCE*

The graveyard shift. I repeat the graveyard shift. Every year like clockwork I get stuck covering the wee hours show while Stephen Jones, the regular deejay is on vacation. The coverage is rotated but it's still jarring when you're tagged it. Working a double header, starting at 1:30 AM and ending roughly around 11:30 AM, just-give-me-a-gun-right-now. My sleep pattern will be screwed up, succumbing to erratic cat naps that extrapolate the disgruntled bitch within me. The only saving grace is using preset show discs with little announcements. Jared and Shane agreed to help me out in my red-eye misery. It's a good thing Ethan is stuck promoting in the Midwest this week, since this schedule would limit our time together. Where is my jacket? More like fisherman's gear, it's a friggin' monsoon out there. I have a twenty-three block walk to the station, I could easily slip on the 1 or 2 train but I hate riding the subway. In my whole existence living in New York, I have only ridden the silver slug-way three times. Keep in mind I'm thirty-one years old so you do the math. I'd rather be a drowned rat than ride that cumbersome transport. Background music to start my water ski adventure is on, conveniently playing Led Zeppelin's "Fool in the Rain." I ran to the station in under eleven minutes, not bad if I say so myself. Unfortunately, I can confirm some fallen soldiers along the way. The most vivid one that comes to mind is when my lightning foot clipped this delivery dude in his lower calf. He yelled falling to his knees, and the whites of his eyes glowed as I flew passed him screaming apologies—survival of the fittest, brother. Water is weeping loudly behind me, leaving an offensive trail down the hall. New York is not known for glass cutting rain like you find in the South but tonight the gods are angry, probably chilling out at a bagel shop in the Village toying with us locals over a glass ball. I'm already tired and we haven't begun yet. This is not good. I need happy thoughts, yes let me think about my adoring boyfriend, less than a fortnight till I see him. Wait, is this a foam contraption? We have a foam contraption on our coffee machine now. Correction, a new espresso cappuccino coffee maker, oh my. This is a big deal for this archaic establishment; I hope this fancy contraption tastes as good as it looks. Now how do I work this puppy?

"Hmm… what's that delicious smell, Captain?"

"That would be my mixed brew of Hazelnut cappuccino compliments of this baby. You need to try this… it's way better than Starfucks."

Shane doubts me with a poignant smirk. "You're joking, right? Better than Starmegabucks?"

I show him how to work the new fixture. We walk to Stephen's studio, which is on the other side of the hall from mine. It's smaller and dingier than my space and in dire need of a brightening paint job. I lucked out with the deejays who share our studio. We demanded from management a peaceful updated scene a couple of years ago and they delivered. Stephen's crew is the most bedraggled looking creatures I've ever met. They stroll in with their Birkenstocks and nomadic hippy appearances of not combing their hair, let alone taking a much needed daily shower. It's as if they arrived on the Berkeley bus from hell. Sadly, Stephen is a rehabilitated pot user—my condolences to him. You would think being on the wagon would have improved his sloppy, smelly work environment that resembles a homeless shelter. Don't get me wrong, I have nothing against vagabonds, but I do have an issue tolerating any cretin that makes over 150K a year and looks like a vagrant on purpose; now that's just stupid. Jared strolls in completely drenched with no umbrella or rain gear.

"Let me guess, you rescued a dog that fell into the Hudson River? Dude, seriously... here's fifty dollars, go get yourself some wellies and a poncho."

Jared's mouth drops as he looks at Shane with fire streaming out of his eyes. "Fuck you, Salinger... you patronizing bitch!"

Shane and I laugh. "What happened buddy?" I ask.

"I was out with Taran before the downpour. She didn't have an umbrella because nobody knew it was going to be Noah's fucking Ark out there, so I gave her mine. When I left her, I dashed to not one... but four Duane Reade's and none of them had any umbrellas or as you put it asshole, ponchos. By the time I hit the fourth spot I was already soaked so I gave up. I was able to buy underwear, socks, towels, and a sweat suit instead."

Shane claps and whistles while I shout. "Bravo, Maestro!"

Jared cracks up, trying to take a bow where instead he falls into his chair. It's times like this I treasure most with these two characters.

"Parker, go dry off... change and make yourself a cappuccino, espresso-macchiato, whatever oh oh you're feeling."

"Very funny Captain... but I'm not going back out in the ocean."

"You don't have to, seems the station got the guinea hookup."

His face brightens up as he dashes to the kitchen while we set up the show. We decide to make Jared a spectator the first segment since it's half the work my show consists of. Besides, he deserves a much needed break. He's been exceptional these past few weeks with no botch ups. Just knowing he's here in case Shane or I need coverage while we snooze is clutch. One thing's apparent—we are lacking our loquacious energy. We're already bleary-eyed but café coherent, let's hope these brews last for another eight hours. Shane, of course, is the first to use his snoring pass two hours in. I'm next with under an hour left and the guys obligingly steer the ship as I crash on the cot Ed lent us.

"Clairster…" I feel tapping on my shoulder and wake to Jared standing over me.

"Hey… how long did I knock out for? Go rest, I'll take over."

"No need… we're already a half hour in your show, Shane is out getting us breakfast."

"You guys are the best. One night down… four more of hell to go."

I check my blackberry that has not one but three sweet messages with pictures attached of Ethan's tour bus scene. He stopped by the Pitchfork Pie Stand in Iowa and took a shot with Brett emulating the *American Gothic* painting. Brett wore the bonnet posing as the woman.

The next few days and nights bled into another quickly with minor trials and tribulations that only lack of sleep can bring. Did I fall victim again by falling asleep on air along with my snoring amigos? Hell yes, guilty as charged. The good news is we made it. Here we were at the last night of this insane assignment. I arrive a few minutes late from oversleeping, and the guys kindly had Stephen's show ready to roll. After I finish announcing, I think back to the dream I had earlier about Greer and Jake. It consisted of them having me over for dinner, assuring me all was well with Jake. It appeared awkward at first, but the tension wore off after a few dream minutes. Then all of a sudden, it went south with Jake raising his voice, belittling me with *Quitter. You are nothing but a quitter. You quit on us and you have to live with that, Miss Selfish.* He repeated those words a few times before I woke up in a cold sweat. I had slept through my alarm which rarely happens. Where did this dream come from? Maybe it's a sign I should reach out to him? Ethan had suggested I make peace with him and he's right. Our statute of limitations to clear the air is almost at its due date. My mom had said if Jake didn't want to talk with me, then I should confess to a priest or whomever I felt most comfortable talking to. I have no ambition visiting a priest for the so-called penitential grill since well, I don't find a man of the cloak comforting for my debased mind let alone comfortable confessing to one of them. My examinations of conscience with John are effective acts of contrition.

"How are you doing over there? Need a nap or is there something you want to address?"

"I'm good Shaney, just thinking about this dream I had... it gave me the heebie-jeebies. How are you two?"

"Strikes and gutters... strikes and gutters."

The three of us chuckle after Shane quotes *The Big Lebowski*, that movie is chock full of one-liners that can put the Devil himself in a giggling weed-induced fit.

"What was the deciding factor that had sprung you with Jake?"

"Interesting segue, Shane Vader. I would have to say it was halfway into the semester. We were in a Biology class together, paired up as lab partners... he sat across from me. He had this charm about him and I liked his style. Considering how intelligent he is, he never had a shred of arrogance and that rated high in my book. He wore his jeans well and had these cool bohemian-esque t-shirts and hoodies you couldn't find at The Gap. It made him a bad-ass anomaly, standing out by not following the fashion herd. What about you? What did Alyssa do that hit you upside the head?"

He takes his glasses off and rubs his eyes for a moment. "We worked together at the Georgetown Library and I knew from the second I met her. She had this confidence about her when she walked into a room. Her... *what you see is what you get* quality and how she could make such a simple ensemble without makeup look hot. Crazy, right?"

"Not crazy at all, my friend. Jastology... what say ye?"

He clears his throat. "We were next-door neighbors, so I got to know her before we dated. I'd have to say it was her infectious laugh... kindness and our chemistry that lured me in. I grew up with a lot of bitchy girls in high school and she was a welcoming relief. If you would have told me she'd break-up with me for needing to explore her options, I wouldn't have believed it. She ripped my heart out." He put his head down.

"It's alright buddy...she's just another heart-breaking bitch that will suffer, I promise you. Mine dropped me for the same reason. I wish I could tell them both they'll never find anyone better... ever." Shane bemoaned.

I knew I was out of their equation since I was the

dumper and I'm sure at some level I was also considered a "heart-breaking bitch" in their eyes and I'm okay with that. I wouldn't wish what happened to me on a snake. My ineptness at handling it had its own stigma attached to it. I switch the rest of the show to autopilot for us to chill out. We lounge on pillows and blankets on the floor in a circle. The only thing missing is a fire pit with marshmallows and sticks. Shane's staring at me, as if he was expecting words of some caliber to roll out.

"Claire… what happened that night between you and Jake?" Brave Shane strikes again.

I take a deep breath. "Jake is a cocaine addict. It started about a year after we met… he was in his first year at law school. His schedule was overloaded since he was also working a part-time job. His friend, Lance, had hooked him up with uppers to… as he called it, *get through the first year.* Then he graduated to white lines a week after. I didn't approve but Jake always managed somehow to get his way. I was so young back then… naïve, feeling invincible along with him. I even tried it a few times. It caused me to stay awake for days on end, so I lost the desire for it quickly. I honestly thought when his work load lessened he would get over the phase. He didn't. He graduated top of his class and landed an Associate position at a prestigious law firm. Our lives took a 360 turn from preppy innocents to life in the fast lane. Sprawling apartment in the West Village his firm hooked him up with. At first, I couldn't have been happier… with my on-air career morphing and Jake's love and success surrounding me. He was heavily using at that time but I didn't realize it till the nose bleeds and shortness of breaths showed up frequently. He also became intolerably aggressive… short fused. After four years together, I asked him to stop using and come clean. He agreed and quit cold turkey. I was so proud of him. It didn't last long though. His sobriety and our roller coaster ride lost its breaks from then on. I loved him so much that I chose to put up with it. Worst mistake I made looking back. I broke off with him a few times within the last few years we were together… when his habit became even more burdensome, especially on his health. Every time I left, he would stop… get back on the wagon and stupidly I'd run back to him. We were engaged for three years. I kept stalling the wedding because of my conflict. He kept pushing the issue everyday… *Let's just elope and get it over with*, but I always said no in a way he would blindly understand. I know this didn't help his condition, that sense of rejection was killing him inside a little each time. I didn't mean to reject him but it's what it was looking back on it. See, I never grew up with any type of substance addiction; it was foreign to me. I couldn't take the suffocation it was causing us both. What's so sad is, had it not been for his problem we would have been married now with kids. I give him credit though… sticking with me despite, never once lying to me about his falling off the wagon. He was honest with me, even when I didn't appreciate it. A year before I finally left him, he was being treated for heart problems… directly caused by his usage and that was the start of the end for us. I couldn't stomach the fact that he'd be dead within the next five years if he kept it up. The son of bitch wouldn't desist and that's what hurt the most. Didn't he fucking realize that I couldn't see the love of my life dying like that? Didn't he understand what effect that had on me… dealing with it? He's a Rhodes Scholar that was stupidly clueless to that revelation."

Jared hands me tissues to dry my eyes and asks if I want anything. I just want to finish.

"The night of the bombing was Sandra's birthday party. It was in the City at her ex-boyfriend's apartment in Soho. Bianca joined me that evening… Jake had to work late and planned to meet us later. The shin-dig was awesome… Sandra went all out with the music, food, and fun gadgets like night vision goggles and fake mustaches for us to wear. I was outside on the balcony catching up with some friends from high school that I hadn't seen in over ten years. One in particular was my old friend Max. When we saw each other, we immediately picked up our friendly rapport like we were sitting in English class again. I didn't realize at the time Jake was watching us from inside the apartment... for I guess what would have been a few minutes or so. However long it was, he didn't like what he saw. It was just two friends catching up. What Jake supposedly witnessed was a physical chemistry between me and Max or as he aptly put it... *your body language said otherwise.* This further fueled his cocaine edginess... presumably he had just done lines with his work friends. Jake had it all wrong, Max and I weren't flirting... we hugged because he had told me of his recent engagement. Had Jake known Max's fiancé was getting us all a drink with Sandra... maybe it would've prevented his rage within. I caught his eye as he was walking towards us and immediately I knew he wasn't right. I excused myself from Max and the rest to avoid a scene and ran over to Jake, leading him back inside. I knew my cronies would understand since Sandra winked at me as she joined the group to entertain them with my abrupt exit. Jake was strung out. He angrily confronted me with paranoia... *Who is that fucking guy all over you? I saw you both flirting... why are you doing this to me?* I explained to him what I just told you and he doubted me. I tried coaxing him to calm down and have a drink but he was too charged up. I begged him to tell me what was wrong since his jealousy wasn't warranted... his wiry countenance startled me. I asked him how much coke he did and he wouldn't answer. He kept groping and yelling at me... after a few minutes of trying to make him stop, one of my friends pulled him away. I told him to leave. I couldn't take him like that anymore. He then pleaded with me to go home with him... I was adamant saying no. He finally left after a few minutes shouting at me while he walked out... *Do you have a clue how deeply I love you? I don't think you ever will.* Before I could answer, he was gone. I went to the liquor cabinet and poured myself a couple of shots since I was stressed out. I joined the group outside apologizing for the scene. Bianca whispered in my ear *It's gonna be okay.* My friends were supportive that night making me laugh, enjoying the merriment of Sandra's celebration. Bianca kept feeding me vodka and cranz. I'm hazy on how the party ended... but remember walking up the stoop outside my place with Bianca who was sleeping over. We get inside the apartment and see all the lights were on, squinting from its brightness. I yelled out to Jake, but there was no answer. I clumsily fell while helping Bianca put sheets on the pull-out bed. I crawled to my room and when I opened the door... I."

"Claire, are you okay? Here's some tissues... can I get you anything?" I nod no to Jared as I wipe my face. Shane reaches over and pats me on the back.

"I... saw Jake on the floor face up with his mouth open and eyes closed. He looked like a grey ghost. Normally he had the warmest color to him but not then. I crept towards him calling out his name but he wouldn't respond. He wouldn't wake up. I put my hands on his face and chest. He was ice cold. I...I... screamed and Bianca came running in. I broke down from shock, feeling like I was submerged underwater and all was silent except hearing Bianca crying over the phone *he's barely breathing... hardly any pulse... please hurry the address is...* I couldn't stop crying. Bianca tried resuscitating him with CPR. I didn't move. Somehow, we wound up in an ambulance on the way to the hospital. I don't remember the paramedics arriving. I could see the doctors using the heart pads to revive him and the loud shouts of *CLEAR!... BOOM. CLEAR!... BOOM.* After they revived him, he was barely conscience. He looked like a science project gone awry. He had two set of IV's in his hands... tubes out of his mouth and heart monitors etched over his whole chest, wired to a machine that annoyingly beeped every other second. Bianca was Mother Teresa that night. She handled every detail down to filling out forms and consoling Jake's family when they arrived. I was a wet statue. Greer sat alongside with me sobbing for a while. At some point, the doctor advised us to go home and come back later that evening. Bianca brought me back to her house on the Island. I couldn't go back to the scene of the nightmare. I felt like I had already lost him, that he died and this was my mourning period. Bianca asked what I was going to do... leave him for good or stay with him while committing myself to a mental ward. I knew it was over but I couldn't tell him in his fragile state. I didn't go back to the hospital that evening... I was weak from vomiting. I checked in with Greer, she was there for the both of us. He called me that night and Bianca said I was asleep... I wasn't. I couldn't talk to him. I called him the next morning and he sounded awful. He kept pleading for me to visit him so he could apologize and see me in person. I didn't feel well and he understood that I wasn't able. I finally went in the next evening. Sandra came for moral support. She waited outside while I was in his room. I remember the sickening smell in his room... I almost vomited again. The color in his face came back slightly but he still looked clammy. The doctor went over his prognosis with us... explaining he had suffered a mild heart attack and needed to undergo further tests to rule out surgery. His heart had sustained large amounts of scar tissue, trauma, and weakened over the years with his usage. I was surprisingly calm as the doctor relayed it to us, unable to look at Jake. I tried breaking the tension-filled silence with some idle banter about how shitty he looked. Instead of smiling, he teared up instead. I cajoled him with the old *Don't beat yourself up... be thankful for the second chance you've been given.* He kept reiterating... *I am sorrier than you'll ever know. I never meant to hurt you or put us through this. I regret this problem... there's no excuse. Please forgive me.* I assured him I had but it didn't change my mind to stay with him anymore. I pretended that everything was okay. This lasted for the next week while he was in and out of procedures. I was the perfect fiancé standing by her sick loved one. Little did anyone know except for Bianca, I was worthy of winning an Oscar. I don't know how I did it since I'm useless under pretense but there I was... numb as the great pretender. One night after everyone had left our apartment, he pulled me close to him. I don't know why, but I felt it was my moment to address the inevitable. I explained that I loved him with all my

177

heart but it wasn't the same after that night. We had domino-effect problems and ill communication for well over a year and he agreed. He was more stable than I had anticipated as he listened to me rationalize our permanent break. It was probably the pain killers... it aided my task greatly. He understood for the most part but kept insisting I needed to give him one last chance, which would be *unlike any of the other chances you've given me.* I was proud to finally stand my ground. I had heard his empty promises so many times before. I took off my engagement ring and put it on the table next to him. Guys... we'd need a few more hours to go into specifics of our conversation that night but the summary is this: we went through hell and we're both in therapy now. He's also in a drug rehabilitation program. We didn't leave off with the usual *Well let's see where we're at in a year,* due to my resistance. If you were to ask me how I lost courage to stick it out, I still wouldn't be able to answer that question. The hardest part of this... wasn't losing the battle with Jake. No. It's forgiving myself for not be able to stay with him. The guilt, the embarrassment, and all the other shitty analogies you can add to it. That's what ripped my heart. For us to continue together as a couple, it would have to be conditional. Jake and I knew we could never succumb to that. That's the end of my story."

Shane and Jared's eyes are wet with sadness. Judging by their long turned down faces, I don't think I'm known as a heartbreaking bitch now. The guys didn't say anything and I didn't mind. I felt relieved telling them.

Jared breaks the seriousness. "The show's been over for like ten minutes and we didn't do the last public announcement."

I joke with them that my ass is already on Warren's serving platter, this was the cherry on the cake. We set up my show and our energy went into overdrive. I proceeded to spin one of the best shows of my career that morning. The song list included some notable greats like Led Zeppelin's "The Rain Song," Stephen Fretwell's "Play," Julian Plenti's "Skyscraper," The Foo Fighter's "Pretender," The Pretender's two play "Message of Love" and "Talk of the Town." I ended with Sting's "Valpariso."

"Let's get out of here fellas. Keep the faith, your true North's are waiting for you."

Jared chokes up and Shane puts his arms around our shoulders. "I know you don't need my two cents... but I'm proud of you. I would have done the same thing. Your story isn't over yet... you'll make peace with him. I know it. Just out of curiosity... what's his last name?"

"Raleston."

We walk outside into the warm glaring sunshine that remarkably feels soothing on my face.

CHAPTER 17 / *SPRING AWAKENINGS, FLOWERS IN BLOOM, A WEDDING, AND A FUNERAL?*

Ethan is tickling me as we snuggle. I am savoring our last few days before he has to go back to LA. He's already booked me airline tickets for his shows in couple of weeks in Chicago and Toronto. I could get used to this rock star life.

"What are you thinking about, darlin'? You look quite pensive for someone that had two orgasms last night."

"Actually it was three. Remember the one by the piano that started it off?"

"Oh yeah, silly me. Ready for number four?"

"You spoil me. Sex with you is equivalent to gorging in Wonkaland, except the difference is you're more addicting than any candy out there. You're a drug... I'm druggin' on Ethan."

He laughs. "It's you. You bring it out in me. To be compared to Wonkaland, Jeez... I'm touched by that sentiment. Speaking of which, I could go for some chocolate right now. I'll go heat it down and we can pour it all over each other and... I'll be right back."

Oh I am so burning in hell for all the sin I'm consumed with, I just know it. I thought Jake corrupted me, I was wrong. I wasn't fully aware of the depths of levels or as specified in Dante's *Divine Comedy*—three *canticas* of *Purgatorio, Inferno,* and *Paradiso*. I now understand what that allegorical work of art really means. With Ethan, I'm stuck between purgatory and hell, specifically the Sixth and Seventh Terrace circles of Lust and Gluttony. At this rate with the amount of carnal frolicking, I'm not making it to heaven, no way. I will die a slow painful death in the Devil's home, and I'm dragging Ethan along if he is doesn't make it there before me. After we got out of bed, we see the mess we made of chocolate, cool whip, bananas, and hot sauce which stained the sheets. We cracked up deciding to launder or throw them away. We really are doomed. After we shower and get dressed, Ethan reiterates his question from before.

"Seriously, what were you thinking about before our romp feast?"

"Not much, just about moving and some other things like your upcoming shows."

Ethan answers his phone as I tidy up the apartment.

"Alan said all the shows at the Oracle Theatre and Hollywood Bowl sold out within a few hours... I can't believe it."

"Such a milestone... I'm so happy for you. You've all worked so hard. Enjoy every second of it."

"You have a lot to do with it. Your love and support. In case I stupidly forget to tell you, my muse, just kick me in the ass, okay?"

I nod yes and we hold each other. "Sorry babe, where were we before the call? Right, what other things have been playing on your mind? Jake? The repercussions of us being together?"

"Yes… I was thinking about those things too. I heard from Greer that Jake is doing better and he now knows we're an item. She let on he wasn't thrilled obviously and has issues with it. I want him to move on like I did, and if he can have a slice of the happiness I have now with you, well that would be great for him. I wish him the best… but it's not my concern anymore."

"With what he put you through and how you kept it together like you did, you're strong… that's one of the many things I love about you."

"What would be top of the list of what you love about me?"

He comes over and pulls me onto his lap. "Where do I begin? Well, your kindness for one, you have an innate knack to always put me in a great mood. Your eyes… the most gorgeous set of emerald gems I'll ever look into. Your philosophy… soft skin… sexual appetite."

"Well I've melted. What you are holding now is just my body, my soul has been floored. My list is similar, except I think my skin is much softer than yours. (He tickles me.) I'll tell you what I also cherish. I never hear that uncontrollable voice in my head that screeches on autopilot like it did with you-know-who. I never hear it when I'm with you."

"Feedback. That obnoxious sound that lingers until someone turns the switch off or unplugs the instrument that's causing it."

"Exactly."

The problem therein lies when you can't pull the cord on it. I already felt like I was living a new life, even while still being on the road to recovery. Each day, I am ridding layers of the what-if guilt by not giving Jake another chance. After a run in the park, Ethan and I took a Zen break by lying on a bench in Washington Square Park. We read *The New York Times* and played the crossword puzzle together. I turn to a page in the Obituary section. There were at least ten names of the recently deceased, one stood out like a neon flashing sign straight out of Vegas.

Black Celebration Funeral Services for Claire Convezionale, are being held At the Long Overdue Funeral Home located at 1972 Reverie Drive, New York, NY 10012."

A funeral? Yes, I can confirm there was one. A beautiful ceremony with the most touching eulogy I've ever had the pleasure of hearing. Funny thing is, I didn't cry like Snoopy at this ceremony. Relief and happiness were the best adjectives to describe what actually washed over me. It seems the imminent death and burial of the world of maybes and what-ifs had tragically died with Claire. She had been blessed this year with the consolidation of something profoundly deep and emotional, that connected her with more closeness to people she loved. Before her demise, she had eagerly given birth to her latest discoveries which left her no longer fighting against challenges she had struggled with so many years that left her perplexed. No more. The proof was she had been observed days before her death as being "much more jubilant and stable" within herself and the people she shared her life with. Claire was noted saying days prior to her demise. "I guess the understanding and encouragement I have from my loved ones reminding me of options I'm fortunate to have. I never thought I would play against the cliché card by unexpectedly falling in love with an old friend. An extraordinary destiny force when and how it happens. I started the New Year with the ultimate question, contemplating who I would like to be proceeding forward. The person I have always been, up until now or the person I always hoped that one day I could become. Not that I've been too shabby thus far, but there is always room for improvement. What I discovered in my latest analysis of my relationships in general, is there were a few snags that needed mending since they were causing static on my radio show called life. Non-melodious tunes that coerced unhappy callers to request songs lacking key changes and beautiful harmonies. What helped me start the enhanced version of myself was finally finding a way to forgive the what if's. What if's doesn't need explaining or excusing, they just need to be realistically recognized

183

and addressed. Denial in all forms is the Anti-Christ, plain and simple. Nor will you ever benefit from concluding that it's too late for anything to alter, take it from me. At this moment, I have a sincere sense of belonging while I am about to embark on yet another journey, focus shifting towards a new adventure, romance, and the exploration of dreams—that I will make reality. I am constructively resolving issues that have been a source of discomfort for years, and rather than beating myself up, I absolved being patient for the healed side of me to emerge. I realized it isn't my life or the people around me that needs tweaking, nuh-uh... it's me."

The old Claire Convenzionale was laid to her final sleep surrounded by her soul mate, family and friends—adorned with music and flowers. May she forever rest in eternal and melodious peace."

"Claire... darlin'... where were you? Are you lost in reverie again? Do tell... you were daydreaming about me, weren't you?" I stroke Ethan's hair and playfully pinch his nose.

"Do you remember my friend Bass, who first toured with the group as our tuner?"

"Yes... how is he?"

"Well, he's getting married next month... I want us to go the wedding."

"I'd love to... where is it?"

He hands me the Arts section of the *Times*. "It's in San Diego... you can take some time off, right?" I guess my high-eyebrow look told him I need convincing.

"Please... my angel. I know I've been asking a lot of you... taking time off but please..."

I have been taking more time off than usual but I feel I've earned it for all the years I didn't. This came at a good time since I could also go on interviews with the stations Lana and I had reached out to.

"I think I can pull some strings." He smiles, rubbing my calves.

Shortly thereafter we went to Whole Foods and picked up groceries for our get together with Sandra and Tomasz. We had everything covered but dessert, which they are bringing. We grilled meats on the barbecue and I put the finishing touches on the side dishes as they arrived. To my surprise, Tomasz chose two desserts, assorted macaroons from Bouchon Bakery and a devil's food chocolate cake from Balthazar Bakery; Ethan and I are impressed. The wine flows while a medley of LA band tunes from The Doors, Beck, Spoon, The Beach Boys, Van Halen, and Red Hot Chili Peppers played on Ethan's Ipod.

Tomasz motions for my attention. "Claire, I was listening to your show the other day... great job, especially on that free flow portion. I haven't heard Beastie Boys 'Get It Together' on a radio in years and that great song by Neneh Cherry... I forget the name. I like what you're doing these days. What's the inspiration?"

"Thanks... I usually play my favorite tunes, along with the audiences' request. As for inspiration, well he's sitting right there. I like rotating classics you haven't heard in a while. I basically have carte blanche on the formatting concept, I lucked out. That Neneh song you're thinking of is a cover, 'I've Got You Under My Skin' by Cole Porter. That version is featured on the album *Red Hot and Blue*."

Ethan glances at me with an expression I hadn't seen on him before. It's as if he has the weight of the world on his shoulders and his slate grey eyes look heavy. He did something similar the last time I talked about my show with a friend. It may be a harsh reminder for him, knowing how much I love my job and him being the culprit of me possibly leaving it.

"My compliments to the chefs, I don't know who cooked what but everything is delicious... right, T?" Sandra says as Tomasz nods yes.

"Thanks, I manned the grill while Claire took care of the sides."

After we ate dessert and cleared up, Tomasz was in the mood to soak in the hot tub and wanted us all to join him. I don't know how he persuaded us with his crazy idea but we soon found ourselves in our skivvies jumping in after him. That was another perk of Ethan's friend's two bedroom sublet. Not only did it have a decent size terrace, the six person hot tub was installed recently. Sandra refills our glasses with wine and I already feel giddy. The guys tell us funny stories about their partying pasts. I whisper in Ethan's ear, warning him that Tomasz is the epitome of wanton-prone-to-pander and to ignore half of what he says. Sandra kissed her cowboy affectionately after each debauched story he told. I don't know if it's my buzz playing tricks on me but I could swear Tomasz is glancing at me a little too often. It disturbs me as opposed to feeling complimented, considering I've had this guy's tongue in my mouth.

Tomasz claps his hands to get our attention. "So I have an idea, why don't we have a foursome?"

I'm speechless and Sandra's eyes widen as she stares at me in embarrassment.

Ethan clenches his arms around me tightly. "No thanks dude, we're good. Why don't we dry off and I'll make a fire on the charcoals and we'll hang out."

That infamous elephant is in the room.

"I didn't mean to offend. I just figured, you being a rock star and all... it comes with the territory."

"I'm not offended… and yeah, it's understandable to think that but I think the ladies may feel uncomfortable… so with that, come help me with the grill."

Tomasz is red and apologizes for his insensitivity. We get out of the tub and Sandra grabs me to join her in the bathroom. I uncontrollably laugh while she holds my hand leading us to the bathroom.

"Why are you laughing? I'm so embarrassed. What the fuck am I going to do with him? He has no off button… I can't control him. Are you okay?"

I'm kneeling over in pain from giggling, Sandra cackles at the sight of me.

"Okay, I'm officially drunk. Look, we're all freaks but Jesus… he's balls out crazy. You have a felon on your hands, Sandra Dee. I hope you're using condoms."

"I know… I don't know what to do with him. I'll spare you the details of where he had me hanging from the other night. He got pissed… (laughs) because I couldn't reach around… (laughs) to his… (laughs) ass… (laughs) to stick my fingers (laughs) in… "

We bust out in giggling fits, gasping for air.

"Ladies, are you okay in there? Ethan asks in a comical tone.

"We're okay babe, we'll be right out."

We calm down and walk out onto the terrace.

Ethan motions to me. "Come here love, nothing to be afraid of… it's safe here. Tomasz was just feeling a little randier than usual. He just finished telling me about that hysterical morning after Shane's party."

187

I roll myself into Ethan's embrace. I wasn't worried about the details, since I had relayed the story to him a while ago omitting my details with Shane. The guys bring out chairs from inside for us to sit. I rest on Ethan's lap as we feed each other another round of dessert. I lean into his ear. "You do realize we'll have to deal with more foursome requests with Left Coast zealots if I move there."

He rubs my neck and puts a piece of cake in my mouth. "True, it is where I lost my cherry to more than one in bed. Ahh…oh… those were those the days."

I put a big piece of cake in his mouth in a jealous frenzy. He muffles through bites.

"Word to the wise… threesomes are better than foursome."

I try to run but he firmly grabs me. "I will say it's flattering to be propositioned, and look at you with your jealousy. Jokes aside, those days are over, so don't get any ideas. I'll never be able to share you with anyone. Ever."

"Ditto." We kiss overhearing Sandra reprimanding Tomasz.

"Don't pull that shit ever again. Especially with my friends."

"Okay… okay, but you know me… I have a problem."

We enjoyed the rest of the night over heated plum wine while playing trivia by the fire pit. Originally Ethan suggested playing Twister, but in lieu of the evenings atmosphere we figured playing it safe was a better choice. After Sandra and Tomasz left to go home, Ethan and I cleaned up and collapsed on the bed. I awoke to loud heavy rain pelleting off of the windows and noticed we never changed out

188

of our clothes before retiring. Ethan looked angelic sleeping, his light brown hair whisking over his forehead. He had asked me to wake him up before I go to work, but I don't have the heart to disturb him. I left a half hour earlier to get a run in. By the time I get to the station, I receive a text from Ethan. *Why didn't you wake me up? Miss you already.*

"Who are you texting at this godforsaken hour, Canoli?"

"Who do you think? Shane, I'm in the mood to shake things up today... so just follow my lead."

"No doubt just say when. What shall we start with?"

"How about The Toadies 'Possum Kingdom.' Then maybe segue into 'Hanging on the Telephone,' Blondie's version not the The Nerves... that's for you, Jared."

Jared smiles. "Oh yes, and don't forget Cat Power's version, holla!"

One time when I asked him to play a tune, I didn't specify the artist and well, that can make or break the audio logical flow of what I'm spinning. Oh man, I sound like a supercilious movie producer. We break for commercials, I give the song choice reigns to both of them that I'll set up announcing. I felt like taking a back seat today, they couldn't have been happier. The fellas chose impressive tunes from The Who, Stained, Prince, Def Leppard, Tribe Called Quest, and The Allman Brothers. I caught up on e-mails, liaising with LA job prospects. Jared suggests an awesome Cars song to play, "Since You're Gone," one of my favorites. Lana's radio contact in Santa Monica replied back in the interim confirming an interview for seasonal work. The Adult Contemporary station also replied back, stating the position had been filled— thankfully.

Shane clears his throat. "So what shall we talk about

today? How about what job would you love to have other than your current one?"

Jared sees I'm writing an email and takes the floor.

"Well, I want to be a Radio Producer. Currently I'm a piss-ant in training."

Shane motions to me. "I want to be a piss-ant! Not have so much responsibility, 'cause trust me, once you escalate... mo power, mo money, mo problems. Or a race car driver, but the foreign exotics like Ferrari. Screw NASCAR."

"That's a good answer, C Note... I may have to change mine. I was thinking NFL Coach but driving is way more fun. Alright, so since I am obsessed with Meryl Streep and yes I know she's too old for me... but as you both know, I don't give a damn about age. So with that, here's the next question."

"No Shanester, I have no desire to have sex with her." Jared's quick retort made me chuckle.

"Let's not get back on that subject now, J Bone. Anyway... what I was going to ask was have you seen *Sophie's Choice*? If so, do you think she made the right or wrong choice?"

Jared and I quizzically look at each other. By his wide eyed expression, I can read his mind and we're both unanimous. Some of Shane's questions are beyond aberrant, some are just balls out barmy. I immediately think about that dreadful scene where she hesitates choosing, then at last minute says *take my baby* and gives up her daughter who's taken away by a monster to the slaughter house. As usual, my curious mind asks, why? Out of all the movies this unprecedented actress, who evokes pure emotion from anyone watching her morph into character, would he bring up that sorrowful one? Shane is bristling with sighs of impatience while Jared and I dawdle from his level of battiness.

"Shane, I have to ask... why out of all the..."

Shane cuts me off. "It was on last night, and I had never seen it before... I knew you were going to ask that. Seriously though, what a performance, hah? I just figured it's good food for thought... could you make that choice? I felt bad for Sophie, and that scene freaked me out."

"Same here. To answer your question, I feel she made the wrong choice. Even though it was an unbearable Catch-22 situation, I would have rather died with them together than to have them take one... poor girl carried away like that. I wouldn't be able to choose between them. Her guilt winds up killing her in the end... so sad. I will say the author of the book, overtly addressed the necessity to choose between two unbearable options—a paradigm relatable to many facets of life, thankfully not as extreme for most but tragic nonetheless."

"Impressive answer, very percipient of you, Captain. I agree but I would have ripped that bastard's eyes out before being gassed. Jasta, what do you think?"

"Don't know... I never saw the movie. Thanks you, spoiler bitches."

"Woops, sorry dude...and yes, we're assholes. You should see the movie anyway, especially for her performance."

Jared waves off Shane's attempt at redemption and I tell him he can spoil a movie I had on my list to see. He appeases me by blaming it on Shane for bringing it up in the first place. Jared looks up the movie online, after reading the synopsis he agreed with us. I look at the clock and see it's almost time to wrap up. I need inspiration for the last set, but where to find it? I had a few minutes before announcing, I check out my horoscope online that reads: *After many months of drudgery and personal hardships, you have finally reached the end of the*

191

tunnel and the scene is illuminated, the air feels new and you feel recharged. Embrace your so-called new life. It will have unforeseen turns that you'll be better equipped to handle this time around. Instead of worrying just take a deep breath and enjoy the ride.

If that's not apropos I don't know what is. Shane alerts me for my queue, I quickly type songs I would like to end with.

"Well listeners, thanks for sticking with me this fine morning. During our last commercial break, I read something that inspired the last two songs, dedicated to everyone who's dared to try something new by burying something old. Sit back and give yourselves a hand, fellow Jedi Masters… surviving as best we can. Till our next breakfast date, stay tuned in at 97.2 WLDM, the effervescent Kurt Hanson is on next. I leave you with a couple of classics, Bee Gee's 'Stayin' Alive' and Bryan Adams "The Best Was Yet To Come.""

Jared throws a football at me and I catch it getting up from my desk. "To think, this song or any song from that amazing soundtrack was never nominated for an Oscar… dumb Academy fucks."

"Holy shit Jared, how did you know that? Someone's been doing their research, and I couldn't be more impressed. Holla."

"Yes Captain, I have been… there's hope for me yet."

Shane throws the football to Jared. "I'd say… I'm jealous. I didn't know that about *Saturday Night Fever*, nice dude. Claire, I'm still trying to find Bryan's song, I think we have only have vinyl…"

"That's all we have so use it. Bonus-impress-me question: which members of The Beatles played on the song, 'The Ballad Of John And Yoko?' Shane, put your iPhone down now."

Shane rubs his forehead. "Fuck... I know this, I just can't think of it... "

"I know Ringo didn't play drums on it, I think Paul did."

"Very good Parker, you're getting close... one Beatle down. Salinger, come on."

"It was right after they got married... they wrote and recorded in a day... I'm at a loss on who played what."

"Anything else, Parker?"

"I know it was only John and Paul but I don't know who played what."

"Good effort... you're both right. It was written and recorded in nine hours. Paul played drums on the up-tempo beat... it's actually not a ballad. John's idea of the song came quickly and he wanted it released around the time of his wedding to Yoko. Apparently Ringo and George weren't available for the impromptu time frame. This was John and Paul's last collaboration together in the same room, a couple of years prior to that, they had written separately. We better bounce, more next time."

"Jesus, you're a music encyclopedia. I'll never get to your level."

"Is that doubt I hear? That's not the Salinger I know... I like it. That's what will get you to *my* level... and age of course."

Shane climbs up onto his desk, Jared follows and Shane whispers into his ear.

They both bellow. "Oh Captain, our captain."

CHAPTER 18 / *MERCURY RETROGRADE AND THIS SPIN WAS A DOOZIE!*

"Why would the Universe give us Mercury retrograde? Because to move forward it is sometimes necessary to backtrack and reconfigure our paths in life. It is important to reconsider, repair, reflect, and reconnect. Mercury forces us to slow down and fix what's broken, and in so doing, rethink things. It also gives us time to get to projects we have put on the back-burner. Some activities are lucky or actually improve when Mercury retrogrades. You are likely to bump into old friends that you haven't seen in years. Adopted children tend to find their birth parents during Mercury retrograde periods, or people locate their long lost siblings. Prosecutors often find clues to crimes that had previously remained unsolved for years. (Although sometimes the reverse is true—there is a greater danger, for example, that police can bungle evidence during a Mercury retrograde period, for clear thinking doesn't come easy for any of us then.) Mail that went astray weeks or even years ago shows up during Mercury retrograde. Some things that were lost reappear. A Mercury retrograde period is also a good time to dress old wounds, clean up relationships or to simply bury the hatchet. Some people have great breakthroughs in psychotherapy during these phases. For salesmen, it is a positive time to backtrack over previous contacts rather than call on new ones, for former clients are likely to produce the best business. It is a perfect time to schedule work on projects that you haven't had time to do and you've let pile up. Bring your resume or portfolio up to date, and clean out your closets. Take time to paint the house. Clear your decks." —Susan Miller, Astrologer (from her website *AstrologyZone.com*)

I did not catch the bride's bouquet at Bass's wedding. I put forth great effort but this oversized behemoth of a woman, body slammed me so hard, I plunged to the floor falling on my ass. It's all yours lady, congratulations, I hope you can find a sorry ass sucker to marry you. Ethan raced over to help me up. We made light of the situation looking at my beat red hands and the whale in a dress, smiling gripping her flowers with no apologies. It was a touching wedding filled with laughs, tears, and sore hands in my case. The food and music were exceptional; I wouldn't expect anything less from someone in the music industry. Bass and his new wife, Sara, gave me an extra hug for the pseudo death match episode with who turned out to be Sara's aunt, whom she apologized for. During the ceremony I imagined what my wedding would be like. What would the color scheme be? Ostentatious merengue-esque dress or bohemian chic hat with straight line frill? Small or grandiose? One thing's for sure, there is no way in hell my Aunt Aida will be invited. It may pose strife between me and my dad, probably not though because he's in agreement that she's a judgmental heffer. It never failed, any wedding Jake and I went to, it was always the same thing: *When are you getting married? Why aren't you married yet? What are you waiting for? You're not getting any younger.* I finally pacified her at the last family event, when I snarled back in drunken disdain, *It's time to let the cat out of the bag—I'm a lesbian and have no ambition of ever getting married, so stop asking.* It was comical revenge, my brother spit his drink on her dress laughing at my "when keeping it real goes wrong" moment.

The day after the wedding, Ethan took us on a road trip to San Diego. The Pacific Coast Highway supplied pictures that looked like postcards on our two-and-half-hour drive. We finally had our first spat, disagreeing on stuff like why I haven't moved out to join him yet and when was it happening. How many kids we want, I want two, he wants one. It peeved me to hear him say he thought Forest Gump deserved winning for best film over Pulp Fiction. In many ways this trip helped us grow as a realistically functioning couple assuring me our dynamic was more than just physical. Somehow we always managed to laugh at the end of each other's losing battle of frustration. After dinner, I checked my emails for a response from Camden's friend at the station who set up the interview on the first day arrived. I had told Ethan I had to stop by to check out potential job leads, I didn't want to get his hopes up if the interview didn't go in my favor since the stress of our long distance relationship has already become a sore point. I sensed a good vibe from the manager but the job change would be a drastic one. WKROC didn't comprise of free-flow radio segments—this was the big leagues or as Lana put it, "The white shoe station." I've never owned a pair of white shoes or a pair of madras printed shorts for that matter because it will never be me. I would have a strict repetitive format to follow of programmed medleys no matter if I liked them or not. The positives: a drive-time shift of three to seven PM and no more red-eyes with a salary increase. I would be able to keep my place in Long Beach without subletting it out if I chose not to, making better bank. I received compliments across the boards from the three people I interviewed stating they want to see me be the next voice on their sound waves provided I follow their formulaic rules. Decisions, decisions, decisions.

While Ethan was taking a shower, I emailed Camden thanking her and called Lana. "Have you decided? Do we have to set the wheels in motion for your replacement? I have a strong feeling this position's in the bag as long as you want it."

"I'm still deciding if I'll be okay producing formulaic song rotations. I'm an independent rebel at heart... you know that."

"I know what you mean kid. I was in your shoes once... I stayed with the underdog and look at me now. Our station is in the big league. Just follow your gut, no matter what."

"You're right. If I decide to take this job would I... well in case things don't work out for me here, would I be able to get my gig back? I know that's a tall order so I understand if not. I have to set up a security blanket because I'm scared frankly. You're the only one I've admitted that to."

"I'm glad you're comfortable now to confide in me... you'll be fine, it's normal to worry. I would have to pull major strings but I'll do everything I can to help you get back your position here or at least something similar."

"Thanks, that takes a load off. Something similar is fine or contract would work. I wouldn't think of putting someone out of a job over my insane needs. Lana, you're a godsend, especially for bearing with me these days. Honestly, I think I'm losing it."

"Relax honey... it's all part of the process of potential moves. I don't think your idea is crazy at all. I'd rather have you under contract than lose you completely. We'll figure something out. Only thing is... who the hell would want a part-time gig with you? Maybe that dude, one of your interns from four years ago who's in Boston I think? What was his name?"

"Do you mean, McKenzie?"

"Yes, that's him. He was cool and may be interested."

"Possibly, let me think about some options and I'll get back to you. By the way, what's your favorite wine?"

After we finished talking, I ordered two cases and had them shipped out to her.

The next afternoon, Ethan had to unexpectedly go to the studio to re-record a couple of parts of a new song he wrote. I went with him and watched him work. The group's publicist stopped by to go over their upcoming promotions at radio stations and an interview for *Spin Magazine*. Ethan warned me they were going to be a while so I decided to go out and check out The Grove at Farmers Market, for some air. Driving through town, surrounded by vintage store signs and palm trees, I still wasn't a step closer to a final decision on chucking it all to move here. When I arrive at The Grove, I receive a text from Ethan saying he'll be another hour or so and asked if I could pick up wine for the party we are going to later. That's the luxury I admire, you can go to virtually any store here and the aisles are stacked with wine to your heart's content. As soon as I step into Mr. Marcel Gourmet Market, I hear my name.

"Claire, is that you? *C'est vous!* How are you?"

Holy shit. It's Guillaume Cloutier, a guy I knew at Columbia, a hot exchange student I made out with once from Paris. What the hell are the odds of running into him out here of all places? That Mercury Retrograde blurb Sandra emailed me is no joke.

"Oh wow, Guillaume... what a surprise. How's things been?"

He hugs me with a tight hold and surprisingly kisses my lips, unable to avoid his swiftness. I forgot how forward the French could be.

"You look wonderful, Claire. You're so thin... I like you better fuller."

"So I've been told. You look well."

"It must be eight years or more since I saw you last... how have you been?"

198

"Very good thanks. Columbia days are far behind us for sure. *Alors, est LA raison detre votre?*"

"Ooh, your French is still *très bon*. I am in LA for a few months on a writing project... been here for a few weeks. How about you?"

"I'm toying with the idea of moving actually. I'm still in New York for now... I'm here visiting my boyfriend till Monday."

"Oh... Jake's based here now?"

"Actually, we broke up last year. My new boyfriend, Ethan Kilgore."

His eyes widen. "Of Acoustic Division?"

"That's him... you've heard of him."

He grabs my arm. "I know Ethan through some friends in the music scene. He's a cool guy. Can I buy you a drink, for old time's sake? I would love to hear where life's taken you since we last saw each other."

"Well, I have another half hour till I have to go... we can grab a quick drink around here."

"Good, there's a bar down the way."

We walk to the bar and I recollect when Guillaume had kissed me at a party my roommate had. It was right before Jake and I became an item. It could've had potential of getting hot and heavy till Sandra luckily broke up our *tête-à-tête* because she hated him. He wasn't kind to her for some strange reason when I had introduced them and his pompousness didn't shine through till that night. Prior to that, he was tolerable and funny but after that night, I kept his friendship at arm's length. Four months later he went back to school in France and we kept in touch through friends group get together emails.

"Um Guill... you are forewarned, I can only have one drink since I'm pressed for time. *Je répète que je suis d'être coupé à un vodka cranz de vous comprendre?*"

"*Oooh Claire... je ne peux pas être tenu pour responsable de ce que je peut faire pour vous quand vous parlez de français sexy!*"

Oh boy, he can't be held responsible for when I talk to him in French. Translation: he still wants to have sex with me after all this time, great. Does any man exist that actually loses interest in a woman that he didn't conquer and got away? I need to play this cool for the twenty minutes I'm limiting myself to him.

"So tell me, who has won the heart of Guillaume?"

"I am keeping company with a woman from Germany. We're not too serious... besides geography is a sore factor."

"Do you see any progression there? From what I remember, you had no ambition of settling down, have things changed?"

He orders us two drinks. "Somewhat. I have no problem committing as long as she is worth committing to. I was in a long-term relationship with Ariella, a few years after I graduated. We were almost married but she broke off with me when she ran into a college friend... I caught them in bed. It was horrible. *J'étais un mess pour un certain temps... croyez-moi.*"

"Oh Guil, I am sorry to hear that. Let's toast to bumping into old cronies by chance and better days ahead." We clank our glasses.

"So weren't you writing a book or something to that effect?"

"Good memory Claire, yes… I am almost done with it."

"Great to hear, what's it about?"

"The book is about this foreigner who meets this girl at Columbia and they fall madly in love. He impregnates her and they live together happily ever after."

"Really? A fiction novel… nice. Stop playing around and tell me what it's about."

He repeatedly touches my arm as I keep pulling away.

"It's a travel book. The concept was inspired from that semester I got to know all you fools. I wrote about my experiences while in flight which may entail a beautiful stranger talking with me or a fat man who doesn't let me have any space on the armrest. It should be entertaining."

"It sounds it… I look forward to reading it. I've met some pretty interesting characters in my time, especially this lovely lady on my last trip."

"So Claire, how's life been treating you? Why did you and Jake split?"

"Things just fell apart, I don't want it rehash it. Everything's good now. "

"Did he cheat on you?"

"No he didn't." I didn't want to drag out Jake's personal substance problem to anyone other than a close few.

"Did you cheat on him with Ethan or someone else?"

What a douche-bag. "Ahh the European lack of tact… ease up. No I didn't cheat."

He smiles as he downs the last drop of liquid from his glass. "You broke his heart, didn't you?"

"Are you being serious or joking?"

"Look, I'm just calling it like it is."

"Really… why would you say that?"

"You seem the type. I had a thing for you back then and thought I was blatantly obvious about it… you didn't look my way."

"Wow… you're calling me a heartbreaker. This doesn't have to do with our kiss at that party, does it? I chalked it up as us all having a good time. If memory serves correct, you were trying to get with Veronica… that bitch from my biology class. In fact, you kept telling me that night to introduce you two so you could work your magic and I did."

He orders another round. "That is correct and I did hook up with her. She was the biggest bitch on two feet who surprisingly gave *magnifique* blow jobs. But, I liked you and thought by making you jealous… it would spark you, yet it didn't. Don't you remember that time at Lance's party when we were on the balcony smoking something hazy and I basically poured my heart out to you?"

"From a girl's point of view, the jealous ploy of trying to woo us usually backfires. And I don't remember you confessing anything to me at Lance's that night… you kept talking about Veronica. Look, if I hurt your feelings back then I didn't mean to."

"I can't believe you didn't realize… alright then. Here, let's drink and all is good."

"Oh shoot, I'm gonna be late… I have to motor. It was good seeing you, let's keep in touch and thanks again for the drink."

He grabs my arm. "Stay and have your drink, then we'll get out of here."

"I can't, I have to go. Please get your hand off my arm. As I explained earlier, I am pressed for time, finish the drink for me."

"I can't believe you are just going to leave without finishing your drink, what the hell is wrong with you? Do you always making excuses when you don't want to deal with something? That's a bitch move..."

"Fuck you. I've had enough berating for one afternoon... you know, you were always a malcontent asshole but I gave you the benefit of the doubt back then. No more."

He shoots up from his chair and it falls to the floor. I grab my bag and dash out towards the entrance. The bartender meets me at the door and asks if I'm okay. Before I can answer, Guillaume grabs my arm and I scream at him to not touch me. The bartender and another bystander grab Guillaume and tell him to calm down or they'll call the police. I run out in a panic towards the parking lot. I kept running, afraid he was following me. I get to my car and grab my keys to click the alarm. I look behind me and didn't see him. I get in the car and drive home slowly trying to calm my shaking from nervousness. I couldn't understand why he lost it back there like that, it's fucked up. On the ride home, I debate if I should tell Ethan about the ordeal. It's weird how people from yesteryear appear in your head or in person randomly transporting you back to the past. Sandra believes when the planet Mercury is retrograde, spinning in reverse it intensifies your chances of bumping into someone you haven't seen in forever. It's rousing to know people you were acquainted with at some point in your life, whether you met them in grade school or in passing on a security line at the airport, they will be with you for the rest of your life. Whether in a brief thought or inevitably become cyber friends on facebook. Whatever the scenario, they're with you for an infinite reason, as celestial conduits destined to be in your life. I don't believe in reincarnation but I do believe in this present life, we are all connected in some way by fortuitist chance. I'll tell you what else I can't believe, that Veronica gives great head. She was the most ridged bitch to deal with in class. She's probably that typical piranha that treats women like shit and sucks the life out of guys to mooch off them. I bet she purposely got herself pregnant to snag a sap, because there was no way she was marrying a guy with her demeanor and sub-par looks. After Guillaume's Jekyll and Hyde episode, I can safely say they were a match made in heaven. I pull up to Ethan's place and get a text from him saying he's getting a ride home from his manager.

"Oh darlin', I'm sorry work took longer than anticipated, such a draining day... how was the rest of yours?"

"Not bad, glad you're home. I ordered in from Leela Thai, should be here soon. How about we eat and go for a night swim instead of heading to that party you mentioned. "

"Perfect, I'm spent. It'd be nice just to stay home and unwind."

After we ate, we changed into our swimsuits and went next door to his friend, Scout's, place. He's the band's booking agent and helped Ethan get into his current condominium since he knew the owners. Scout has an erratic work schedule, he's hardly home so Ethan keeps an eye on his place while he's away. The pool is heated and has smoke on its surface mixing with the cold air.

"What a day at the studio. We had to remix a bunch of parts and our publicist thinks we're amateurs who don't know interviewing rules 101. Anyway, enough of my ranting… how nice is this? How was The Grove?"

"This pool is heavenly, just what the doctor ordered. The Grove was okay… too crowded for my taste." I decided not to mention my irate ordeal with Guillaume. It would upset him a great deal and I didn't want to add unnecessary stress.

He swims to me. "Are you doing okay? You seem like you got things on your mind."

"I'm good sweetie… I think the time adjustment is makes me groggy."

"Well if there's anything you need or want to talk about… I'm here for you."

"I know… let's enjoy and get some rest."

The next morning Ethan left a note on the table saying he didn't want to wake and he would be back in a couple of hours from the studio. I got dressed and headed to Runyon Canyon Park to go running. Any endurance I gained back home on flat land didn't make a dent in this neck of the woods—these hills are a killer. I veered off the path to rest by a scenic overlook. I scroll through my work blackberry to check messages. Shane and Jared sent funny jokes and notes from the latest staff meeting. I miss them oddly enough. There's a message from Griffin Bettinger.

Hello Claire,

How are you? It's been a long time. I'm headed to NY next week. I need to catch up with the famous deejay I used to know so well. How's Sandra doing? Give her my best. I'll be at my friend's apartment on the UES all week. I can't wait to see you!

Xx – Griffin

It really is Griffin. Add another blast from the past to the list. Unlike wretched Guillaume, I dated Griffin. Besides his zeal and alluring English accent, he was the complete package of charm, wealth, dashing good looks, and sincerity. I used to always joke with him that he's England's version of John F. Kennedy, Jr. I met him when Jake and I were on a break for seven months. During that time of freedom, I worked on a benefit event the station put together with Amnesty International. One of the perks was meeting Bono among other celebrities. We needed volunteers, so I enlisted Sandra among others. We had fun helping out a great cause. Griffin was working at Amnesty as a Marketing Manager for their Public Relations Department. I helped out with promotions and our worlds collided. The first week we worked together, we had an instant rapport and great chemistry. Interestingly, we didn't hook up right away. Considering we were only twenty-seven, we were both overly cautious about ruining our work relationship. After six weeks of combustible sexual tension, a finished project celebrated over drinks, we finally caved into each other. Griffin was my second lover. He was nothing like the so-called uptight British stereotype you hear about despite his proper disposition. He was a sensuous intense lover, elegantly wrapped within a dual persona. During our time, we were both adamant in our non-committal phase that hindered any chance for the long haul. Admittedly, I still wasn't through with Jake when I was with Griffin. I loved him but somehow Jake's impetus lured me back. Griffin's hang-up was his freedom; he loved it more than anything else. Looking back, it was the perfect arrangement for us at the time. We were both exactly what we needed in our five months together. We ended on a sad note when he had to move back to London for his job. We kept in touch for a while but when I reconciled with Jake, I stopped responding. That's one of the reasons I'm on the fence to meet up with him. I never had temptations when I was with Jake in my twenties till we were broken up. Now in my third decade, I have an amazing boyfriend and yet I can feel Griffin's hands all over my body and the shivers I would get from his touch as I sit here. I thought maturing is supposed to suppress these types of urges. I would be back in New York by Monday. Question is, if I meet up with Griffin, can I be strong and keep it platonic? I don't even know what his deal is; he could be married with children and I'm already having us in bed together. I need John to help me with this. Actually, he's another allurement I probably should stay away from. Why do I have these irrational feelings? Is it because I haven't gotten *playing the field* days out of my system? I have now had three lovers in my time and I'm almost thirty-one. In your twenties, lack of confidence, invincibility, and fear of rejection are the norm. You undoubtedly screw up relationships across the board because of it. Now in my thirties, I may have gained confidence but the potential of me messing up a stable connection is dismally greater. I need Sandra's advice. She knew Griffin well when I was with him and what went down between us. What time is it? She should be around, she better be around.

"Hey California girl, what's shakin'?"

"Hey Sands, I need your help."

"Sure, what's up? I know I'm picking you up at JKF on Monday so..."

"Yes, but something else. Out of curiosity, have you run into anyone from the past this week?"

"Now that you mention it, yeah... our old boss from summer camp. He got hair plugs and they look God awful."

"Mr. Ramsey? Get out of here, how is that old geezer? Wait before we get into that, guess who I ran into and got an email from?"

"I don't have time, just spill it."

"First I ran into Guillaume and second... I just got an email from Griffin."

"No shit... really? Wow, is it International flavors week out there? First off, did you kick that fucking French toad sucker in the balls for me? He was such a chauvinist prick. Now as for Griffin, well he'll always have my love, respect and wet dreams. How is he... what did his email say?"

"Oh I have a fucked-up story for you regarding that toad sucker, let's just say he fell head first in the bell jar and should be locked away. Griffin just emailed me saying he'll be in New York next week and wants to hang out, just like that after four years. He asked about you too. I don't know what to do... meet him or decline?"

"Why wouldn't you meet him? Oh, is it because you're afraid of a rematch in bed? I know you... you've been torturing yourself contemplating this, haven't you."

"Of course I have... and yes, I'm afraid of finding myself in a compromisingly tempting position with him if we meet up. Maybe I'm worrying for nothing and I won't feel anything."

"True... but he's the type of guy that has that intoxicating effect on any woman... such a fine work of art and genuine. I say meet him and don't look back."

"Just like that, hah? I guess I don't have to ask if you think I'm horrible for even considering cheating. Would you cheat on your boyfriend? Sandra, Ethan's is wonderful. Seriously, I'm a piece of shit."

"Stop that, stop doing that to yourself... you're not so just chill out. Look, I know Ethan is amazing... I adore him. Here's the thing, you were in something faithful for so long with Jake that fell apart and then eight months later, you're bound to another relationship again. You never had a chance to just mess around like the rest of us did. Truth be told, I think you needed more time to heal from what happened...to have fun. You're obviously stirred up over this, which means you have your answer. If it were me, I would be feeling the same way because he wasn't just some guy and like you, I'm not married. So I approve and in some way... this could be a sign telling you something."

"Telling me what? I'm not in love with Ethan as much as I was with Jake? Because this has never happened to me before. I think you're right... but what am I going to do? Put Ethan on hold while I get my sanity back? I don't want to hurt him."

"Possibly... and I know that. One thing's certain, you need to stop beating yourself up. Just go with your heart, whatever it entails instead of fighting it like you always do. Stop questioning yourself and be happy. It's not just you... we're all conflicted at one time or another. It's life."

"I just wish it were that easy. I think Jake put a hex on me. If he can't have me then no one else will or I'll be a deceiving slut. I don't recognize myself right now. Be honest, you're not having enticing thoughts of other guys since you're with Tomasz, right?"

"Well if we're not counting celebrities then no... but when do I have time to be tempted since he's on me every day? You and Ethan get grace periods with the distance. If you both were with each other all the time, I bet you wouldn't think about wandering. I say it's a phase because of the separations. You are fine... you're a phenomenal girlfriend so stop thinking otherwise. These things happen to all of us. Even happily married couples who bump into their exes... nine times out of ten, they'll get nostalgic and all the old feelings come flooding back. Just catch up with him and see what happens. Remember, you're still technically free... so let the chips fall where they may. Get away with it now while you can, there's a reason for everything, Claire. No one has to know except you and Griffin. I know that's not what you

209

wanted to hear but I'm being honest."

"It wasn't but I appreciate it. It's true, no one has to know but can I deal with the guilt of knowing. It may eat at me… harboring that."

"Yes… or it may not. On the bright side, you know Griffin will definitely eat… and yes I know I'm evil."

"Yes but a lovable one. Sands… we're both sex addicts. To think how innocent we used to be back in the day. Oh I need help."

"Wait, what constitutes a sex addict? Oh who the hell am I kidding, guilty as charged. What can I say? The cowboy brings it out in me. Listen, I'm here no matter what time you need to talk, just call me. Promise me you won't be your worst enemy."

"I promise and thanks for always being there for me… especially for putting up with my craziness. Love ya."

"I love you too. No worries okay… enjoy the rest of your trip and I'll pick you up Monday at the airport. I gotta race… I have to teach six year-olds now."

"You got it. See you Monday."

I'll figure out what I want to do and then write him back. Even if I don't wind up meeting him, I'll respond.

CHAPTER 19 / *ASTRA INCLINANT... NON NECESSITANT*

"Good morning listeners... how are you doing? I'll tell you how one lucky listener is doing. Bob Tennant of Forest Hills... congratulations. You're the winner of our Dysfunctional Family Picnic Weekend Extravaganza. Lucky Bob will be partying with the best of them... some off-the-charts bands like Spoon and Cake and many more. Hmm... just from those two alone I'm a happy camper. If you're craving for a chance to break bread with this bunch, you'll have to answer these four questions in the next hour. On the next song I'm about to play, I'll need to know who played drums, what the singers name is, who produced the record... and the song title. If you're caller or email number ninety-seven with the correct four answers, you will be joining Bob with a set of tickets to the picnic. Good luck and I'll be back after this twenty-minute commercial-free set. Here's the song."

"Wow... did you even breathe during that soliloquy? Got the rap flow like Notorious B.I.G. I know the answers... Phil Collins played drums, Frida is the singer, and the title is 'I Know There's Something Going On' and... "

"And it doesn't count Julio, since you're reading it from the album cover. If you had just listened to the tune, you'd know it was Phil Collin's playing... his sound, especially his snare work is distinct. By the way, he also produced it.

211

Hey thanks for the iced tea… is there any more butter of some kind over there? I have a corn muffin that's feeling neglected."

He reaches around grabbing peanut butter and hands it to me. Shane comes in with foam-topped cappuccinos. Out of the three of us, he's the only one that knows how to make them taste amazing. Usually Jared's are too sweet and mine are too strong so Shane is the designated Goldilocks coffee wench. He likes the chore since it gives him a chance to talk to the new intern, Heather. I hope he gets a chance with her because he's overly ripe for a girlfriend.

"Can I just say that sweet Heather has got this boy hooked."

"Music to my ears… seems the mighty Shane has fallen and what a sight it is. She is fine so play your cards right. It's a shame things fell through with Gwen. My only concern for you is Nina, selling your arrangement down the river so make sure she keeps her mouth shut."

"Agreed, Miss C. Yeah, Gwen still isn't over her ex and she wasn't ready to get serious. And as for Nina, she has no choice. I'll show up on her fiancé's doorstep with explicit details of his future bride if she doesn't. Besides, she knows we're coming to an end and luckily her work gig is almost finished."

"No way… she got engaged to that sap? What a piece of shit she is."

Shane raises his eyebrows. "You said it best, Captain… can't make a ho a housewife."

"Actually Jay Z said it. Fun aside, doesn't it bother you to… well, you know."

"It does actually and that's why it's being quashed. I know it's a fucked-up situation." Jared shakes his head.

"I couldn't fathom marrying someone doing that to me... sad he'll never know what he's getting into."

We nod at each other in agreement. "Shane do me a favor and monitor the ninety-seventh caller's answer... we're at fifty-four right now, thanks."

I'm debating if I should bring up the whole Griffin thing with the guys since I already arranged to meet him tomorrow evening. Would the guys give me judgmental grief or solid insight on the potential stray situation? It would be helpful to have a guy's perspective on this.

"So fellas, I have a friend's dilemma that could use your opinion. My friend Elena, back in LA, is with this great guy for the past seven months. About five years ago she met this dude named Trevor when she wasn't involved with anyone. They started off as friends and then became an item. After six months of dating they both cooled their jets since they weren't ready for the next step of heavy. They parted as friends and distant geography helped the cooling period of their break. About two weeks ago, Elena received an email from Trevor, who's coming to LA soon and wants to meet her for a catch up. Now Elena finds herself on the fence if she should meet him or not... due to possibly sleeping with him in their nostalgic states. Keep in mind, she's not going into it with the intention of doing that per say, but she's scared that old feelings will mess her up. So before I give my take on this, what do you think?"

Shane shakes his head looking unconvinced as Jared smiles eagerly standing up with a response.

"Well I say she should meet up with him, she's not guaranteed to mess up and maybe she needs this test to solidify if Trevor is who she's destined to be with."

"Well said, Jared... that's what I told her to do. Shane, care to reflect?"

"If she's even thinking about this Trevor dude in the first place, she's already cheating on her boyfriend. I don't think it matters if she meets up or not... she's guilty."

Oh Jesus. "Just like that, hah? You sure your damaged heart isn't talking?"

"Claire, you know all too well, when you love someone... you're not swayed to look elsewhere let alone think about another in that way, am I right?"

"Well yes and no. Yes, you won't look elsewhere but as far as think... come on... even a clergyman is entitled to his private impure thoughts. I feel it's possible for a person to be attracted to two people at the same time. Don't look at me like that... wait and hear me out before you judge. What I mean is, you can be in love with someone and find another attractive that you don't necessarily love but you have admiration for. Does that make sense?"

Jared raises his hand. "It makes sense to me, because I've been there. Shane, come on... you can't agree?"

"Look, you're both fooling yourselves if you believe that bullshit. Let me give you a scenario. Say the person in question who's in love with a person, who's 'thinking' about someone else, is you. Here you are all smitten with your dude or girl and all of sudden you see your partner flirting or acting a little too kind to someone else. How would you feel? Grant it, it's just conversation but you'd be a little threatened and jealous no? (We both nod our head yes.) Okay, I have you so far... good. Now let's add while you're in bed and you notice your significant other in their sleep, all sweaty with a big smile because they're having a wet dream about someone else. Now, if you knew that, how would you feel? I know how I would

214

feel. So you're going to tell me that your friend truly loves who she's currently with? I think not. I think if she did, it wouldn't be a question of her letting herself get into a compromising position, blaming it on the ah ah ah… alcohol. If she's secure with her dude, she'd have no reason or thoughts of messing around. I'll give you finding someone else attractive while with someone… hell yes. If Kate Beckinsale was in front of me… well, don't get me started. I know we're only human, I get that. But I'm not going to fuck up a committed relationship by cheating or contemplate doing it, on the one I love. Claire, out of Jared and me… you were in a solid commitment the longest, so tell us. Did you ever think about messing around on Jake?"

It kills me that he's right. "Honestly? No, not till the bitter end. I did find other guys attractive, yes. And after we broke up the first time, I did date someone else. That ended as soon as Jake and I got back together. I think your point's lucid. It's strange though, as I hear more and more people claiming they're in love with two people at once. I don't agree with it, but I do think it's possible."

"I hear that as well and I plan to stay clear of chicks that are capable of that because no one deserves to be shared. Intimate love should be between two people, not three or any other screwed-up triangle scenario. The only reason I've been throwing the stones to Nina is because I am free and not in love with her. I would never think of doing this if I was in love and you know that. It's just physical as I'm passing time till the next one comes along."

It bothers me to even question tomorrow night. I will meet up with Griffin for lunch instead of dinner and not drink.

"I appreciate the feedback boys… I'll let you know what happens for her."

Jared leaves to go grab lunch for us and Shane watches him

close the door.

"How's Ethan, doing?"

I avoid eye contact with Shane because I know he knows Elena is me. I really am a shitty actress.

"He's good… we're both good."

"Claire, if you're having doubts or intrigued by another… don't beat yourself up. You have a good head on your shoulders so give yourself some rope."

I didn't know how to respond. Denying it would dig a deeper hole. I smile and troll the internet waiting for Jared to come back with our food.

"So I'm getting the silent treatment? I didn't mean to pry but it's obvious as shit, Elena is you. You can just tell us, considering all we have been through."

My face burn up as I sink into embarrassment. "Okay, you're right. I just didn't want to be judged… who does? I'm not in love with Griffin, it was a long time ago. I love Ethan, but the damn distance is straining us. I felt reminiscent of that time in my life when Griffin reached out and that's also weighing me down. I would never hurt Ethan and I don't plan to. I've never experienced these emotions before so I'm trying to understand them and get a grip… so let's just drop it now. All will be fine when I see him tomorrow."

His eyes widen as his mouth drops. "You're seeing this dude tomorrow? Why would you sign up for that? Do you want to ruin what you have?"

I never imagined a pragmatic moment of reason from someone eight years younger than me.

"I'm not setting myself up for doom, will you chill out.

He's just a friend I knew years ago. A few of us are hanging out tomorrow while he's in town. Give me some credit."

"But didn't you just present to us that you dated this guy?"

I want to crawl in a hole. "Yes I did. When Jake and I were broken up."

"Take it from me… a guy's point of view. We will constantly pursue a woman till she submits to our advances by having sex with us. When we finally conquer her, the women falls into one of two categories: 1. The sex was okay… we may or may not keep in touch or hook up occasionally. 2. The sex was so good that the guy is struck with her and she'll always have a special place in his heart. That same guy will always try to have sex with her, even if he or she is taken. If he's contacted you, that means he still has those feelings… and you're not married so that equals a probable Greek tragedy."

I felt an anxiety attack coming on. I need to shut this down before I lose the nerve to meet up with Griffin.

"Dude, the only thing Greek is your dramatic bravado. I'm done with this. It will take too much exertion for me to try and reason with you. Like you said, I have a good head on my shoulders. End of discussion."

"It's not your head I'm worried about."

After I raised my eyebrows he desisted. The room was silent till Jared came back with lunch. As soon as the show ended, Shane walks over to me, leaning in to whisper.

"Please don't let him manipulate you, because he will. If you need anything, just call and remember, the stars incline… they do not determine."

"I appreciate you looking out for me. I love the end

note by the way… I may steal it."

I walked home thinking about how I never told Griffin about Jake and I could never peg the reason why. I just didn't. When I got into the apartment, I receive a text from Griffin that reads, *24 hours… countdown begins!* I didn't respond. I don't want to deal with the hassle of changing plans. I'll check in with him before I head out tomorrow night. He had asked to meet for dinner and I suggested ABC Kitchen. My game plan is to have dinner and then head to his friend's party for an hour and do an impressive Irish exit. After Skyping with Ethan, I felt duplicitous. I couldn't fall asleep as midnight approached. I went downstairs to the fridge and found the bag of edibles I snuck on the plane from my last visit to LA. I popped one to numb the degrading nerves that vibrated loudly.

* * * * * * *

I raced over the Williamsburg Bridge in a panic for my lunch date with Bianca and her friends at the Brooklyn Flea. I blamed my twenty minutes of tardiness on the foot traffic instead of oversleeping. We picked up a couple of vintage albums and caught up with each other. I had mentioned I was hanging out with friends along with Griffin later that evening, instead of telling her the truth. I didn't feel comfortable talking to her about what might possibly happen, especially with her two friends present. We all left around 4:30 PM, I hopped on the empty subway to save time to get ready for dinner. I couldn't decide what to wear. Griffin always complimented and preferred me dressed up in heels. I poured myself a generous glass of wine to calm down, so much for not drinking. I catch a cab as soon as I walk onto the street in my finest stilettos and favorite blue dress I haven't worn in a while. I answer Sandra's texts and let her know I'll check in with her tomorrow. I look out the cab window and see we're in front of ABC Kitchen. I step out of the taxi and reach for my phone. I feel a hand on my back.

"Hello lovely, it's really you."

I immediately notice his face has improved with age. He looks like a man now rather than his lanky boyish good looks I remember. I'm familiar with his penchant for Paul Smith suits, embellished with a Jean Paul Gaultier scent complimenting his pH levels.

"It's good to see you… still handsome as ever. How are you?"

He compliments me as we walk in with his hand on my back till I sit down. I can feel him looking me up and down when I am not making eye contact which is making me even more nervous.

"Let me see… if memory serves correct, your drinks were a vodka concoction of sorts… Cabernet or my country's staple, Pimm's Cup. Are we feeling wine tonight?"

"Good memory Griff… wine would be nice."

"I don't see Ravenswood or Merryvale unfortunately but I think this DeLoach will suffice."

Not only did he remember my favorite wines, he substituted with another one I like and regrettably, Ethan is now here at the table with us.

"So… how are things in London?"

"London is changing but good. You may have heard my marketing venture company is soaring. Not bad since our launch two years ago."

"That's wonderful to hear, congratulations. I remember you had mentioned you wanted to start your own endeavor back then… cheers to that."

"Thanks… how is ravishing Claire doing? You look exceptional by the way."

"You're too sweet. I'm well. We're older now and it shows on me."

He nods as he butters his bread. "You don't look older. You actually, well… you're more womanly now and a refined one at that. When I got closer to you outside, your scent came back to me like it was four and half years ago. You're the only woman I know that rocks Dior's *Addict* and it's not fair. I have bought it for girlfriends since and the fragrance isn't the same on them. You're an anomaly."

Now Shane is at our table telling me: *He wants to have sex with you. I told you so!*

"What can I say… when you've got it, rock it. I also wore another scent, first round on me if you can guess."

His brown eyes brighten as he smiles. "*Chance* by Chanel, don't insult me darling. I fancied you awful back in the day."

I already needed another glass of wine.

"Your show is excellent… you did what you set out to do, you're one of the greats."

"That means a lot… thanks, Griff."

"Just being truthful. Are you seeing anyone these days?"

And here we go. "I am indeed… Ethan, he's a musician. How about you?"

He grips his wine glass touching the rim with his fingers. Before he answers, our appetizers and second helping

220

of wine arrive at the table.

"Yes… Haley. We have been together for the past seven months… and you? Long term or short stop?"

"We've been together for the past four months… but we've known each other for ten years. We were friends first… then it morphed when we reconnected and now we're in love."

"Bloody hell… I'm jealous of this bloke already. Do you see yourself married to him?"

And now John just sat down at the table.

"I do… yes. He's a big deal. What about you?"

"Maybe. I know you have every right to look at me like that (we snicker) but I'm not quite sure. I do fancy her and she gets on well with my mates. A bit materialistic for my own good… if she can temper that, we may be right as rain."

"Well that's something you can work on with her. Thank God for prenups, right?"

We laugh. I can safely say all the wine has officially kicked in. I am now not responsible for any responses. When Griffin talks to the waiter, I stick a fork into my palm and can hardly feel it.

"This place is proper, nice job again on choosing this spot. I haven't had rabbit cooked that well in a while. Look at you… you're pissed already, nice."

"I'm happily buzzed… yes."

He holds my arm with one hand and cups the right side of my face with his other. "Yes you are. I need to catch up… I better order another. Did you drink before dinner?"

"How did… of course you know, silly me. Truth be

told, I was nervous meeting up with you. I needed to relax."

"Aww darling, why would you be nervous? It's just me… you were never nervous with me, especially when…"

"Behave Griffin. You have to admit, this is a bit…"

"Nostalgically nerve racking? Yes."

"Glad to hear it's not just me."

"Not at all… but at least I was able to wait for dinner to drink, look at you."

"Very funny."

"I do appreciate the honesty. While we're bearing our souls truthfully, would it be presumptuous to ask if we can have a replay of our magical bliss from yesteryear?"

I hate Shane. "Are you really asking me to have sex with you? Just like that? Wow."

"Yes I am. Why the hell not? We are two adults that are still not legally bound. You do remember how extraordinary it was?"

"Because we're with other people now and it's wrong. You don't have to remind me of how great it was. Why don't we grab the check and head over to your friends."

"Whatever you want to do, I didn't mean to upset you. I'll get the check. Here, let me help you get your coat on. You know you're safe with me."

The white elephant has finally left the room, and yet I keep questioning if I should sleep with him. All this time, I thought the grating voice in your head only transmits under calamitous circumstances—I was wrong. I keep hearing Sandra say, *No one has to know except you and Griffin.* But I would know, every time I looked at Ethan. Griffin tickles me in our cab ride. There was no doubt I was in safe hands with him, despite his lack of subtly, he is a gentleman.

"Lighten up please... I didn't mean to cause an awkward moment there. You know I'm tactless."

"No I'm fine... sorry."

I tickle him back. I'd be dammed if an Englishman was going to call me uptight. We arrive at his friend's apartment on the Upper West Side. From what I can tell, it has a sick view of the park. Before we walk to the doorway, a man approaches us, pointing his finger towards the inside hall saying "The party is ah that ah way." We proceed 'ah that ah way' hearing bass driven beats of Bebel Gilberto's "August Song." You don't hear this gem very often; I need to play this on Monday. From the looks of the crowd they would be best described as characters straight out of a Bret Easton Ellis novel. I have never seen so many Armani suits in one room and the chicks? If they should dare walk on the sidewalks, a protester would crucify them for their chinchilla. The blood red lips on these felines would leave Patrick Bateman drooling with his axe behind him. I looked good in my blue Carolina Herrera dress and coat, embellished with Jimmy Choo heels and clutch, but I was more Carrie Bradshaw on Valium than Holly Golightly on speed. The cigarette smoke was suffocating me. Who the hell smokes anymore these days? Apparently the saturation of Euro trash beatniks does.

"Hey Oliver, this is Claire... a great love of my life. Claire, this is one of my best friends from Oxford."

"Pleasure to meet you Oliver, thanks for having me."

He looks me up and down, kissing my hand. "The pleasure is mine. I've heard a lot about you. It is nice to finally place the beautiful face with the infamous name." Oliver gets interrupted by a coked-up-model-looking waif that resembles a drawn-out Jessica Biel. I need to probe Griffin.

"Care to tell me why I'm supposedly infamous and just what has Oliver been told about me?"

He puts his arm around my neck nuzzling his face on mine. "All good things of course. I blew you out of proportion at some point at the pub over pints."

"Is it true Griffin? Am I really one of the great loves of your life?"

He grabs my hand to sway. "Of course, why wouldn't you be? I know our time together was short but it was truly significant."

"Yes it was. You... we... just didn't say it often enough back then. It takes on a new meaning when you hear it point blank. We did love each other, that's for sure."

"That's where I beg to differ. I did express it many times. You seemed preoccupied at the time as if you were thinking of someone else. Maybe you just didn't want to hear it. Also, I feel once you're in love with somebody like that, you never quite lose the feeling unless the breakup was a tumultuous mess. That wasn't our case. Come on, let's get a drink and go check out the rooftop."

While I waited for him to return with our drinks, I thought about his logic. It is true. Part of me didn't want to hear it because I knew I wasn't finished with Jake yet. I understand once you love someone they're held dear to you, but that feeling lessens when you're in love with someone else. I struggled, engaging in idle chatter with a group of guests, most of them models that haven't been discovered. The repartee was anything but stimulating, I wasn't missing much. One of them had heard of me. Not that I was looking for notoriety, but it would have been more pleasurable if they had been around the block so to speak.

Griffin hands me a glass of wine. "Claire... how nice is this view?"

"It never loses appeal for me. Hey, do you remember when were at that party for our gala event? Such a crazy night. Being up here kind of reminds me of it."

"One of my favorite nights. Didn't Sandra vomit on an innocent bystander... we had a hard time hailing a cab. That was also the first time we kissed. I wanted you so bad that night and you left me standing there... in pain."

"I had a sick friend to tend to, trust me... I wanted you too. Come on now, wasn't it worth the wait?"

He stands up. "Oh yes! Ooh... do you hear that? They're playing Cary Brothers 'Ride.' Let's dance."

I lean in towards him and he holds me. I didn't feel uncomfortable considering the inappropriateness of the situation. How could anyone not treasure a moment like this? The song ends segueing into The Church's "Under the Milky Way." I need to shake hands with the maestro at the turntable. He puts his forehead to mine just like he used to. He kisses me gently on the lips and I don't flinch.

He puts his head to mine stroking my hair. "Tell me again why we didn't last?"

"The good old *we're too young to tie ourselves down at this point* story."

"That's right. Now look at us... what's our excuse? Maybe this is our second chance?"

"Griffin, I have a good man in my life right now and I'm hopeful for my future with him. Listen to me, please. If she's not the one or you're having doubts… move on. You will find a better choice. We have one shot at life… don't wind up a passionless settler. I don't worry about you because you're special on so many levels and one of the best characters I know… I mean that. If I wasn't spoken for… things would be different. But I am and it took this dance with you to fully realize that. Please don't hate me."

"Oh Claire… I wish you wouldn't have said any of that, Christ. Now I want you even more. Hate you? Never. Granted, I'm upset about the timing of everything. Answer me this… have you thought about me? Especially after I wrote to you? I will say that if I was truly in love with Haley I wouldn't be holding you, dancing here right now. I know you and you're the same way… yet you're here as well. I think we both need to know for sure since we left unfinished. I know we're not done yet. I reckon you're as curious as I am."

"I am here catching up with an old friend… love. That's why I'm here."

He pours another glass of wine. "Here's the thing, we are still fresh in our relationships with no rings in sight. Technically we wouldn't be cheating. How ridiculous were we as a couple… especially in bed."

Instead of his manipulation deterring me, I felt turned-on. Our old short film we had starred in was a magnificently compassionate story. Who would know except us and whatever gods are dancing above right now?

"You were always the master of persuasion Griffin, and you're right. Then explain to me why I'm stressing out with guilt… deception and all the repercussions that come with it. That's what it is by the way, even though we're not married to others. We would still be cheating on people we are supposed to be exclusive with. We haven't done anything and already I feel this… that's not good. How would you feel if

226

you were him? Hypothetically we dance in bed again... then what? If you knew the woman you're in love with has cheated on you with an old flame how would you feel? I know how I'd feel... heartbroken."

"Yes, of course I would. But we're not in their position at the moment... we're on the opposite side coincidentally enough. I'm not here to manipulate you so alright then, cheers to you darling. I expect an invite to your wedding of course."

We hug swaying to the Cure's "A Night Like This." I want to carry the deejay's first born. He pops another cork off a wine bottle.

"I have a good feeling you will beat me to the alter so don't forget about inviting me."

"Why? Don't you remember I suffer from gamophobia? Actually I'm recovered now. Are you scared of having kids?"

"No. I'm scared of how I'll be when I can't control their mistakes and being a successful working mom. Do you know how much I hide from my parents so they don't worry? Who isn't scared of that and all the other responsibilities attached to it? What about you?"

He holds my face in his hands. "You have nothing to worry about... you'll be a wonderful mum. I'm not scared... actually I can't wait to have them. I'm financially set and things are beyond comfortable so I look forward to it. In answer to your question about what we'd gain. We wake up tomorrow and have more salacious fun. That's what we'd get out of it."

I snicker to myself thinking about Shane's caveat.

"That goes without saying but that's not necessarily a

gain."

Griffin smile turns into a frown, his tone turns serious, as if he's about to cross examine a witness.

"Why do we need to have anything other than a euphoric time? What are you looking to gain? You stated very clearly that you're not available to date me. I am pouring my intensions out which is a lot for me to do as you know... that I would date you and continue where we left off in a heartbeat. Just say the word. If I can't have you on a permanent level then I will settle for whatever you're willing to spare. This is not a furtive attempt to have sex with you, it's a desperate longing. I don't need to stress the significance of what you mean to me. I feel we would have been together now if I didn't have to move back to London at that time. Whilst I settled after a few months, I wanted us to try and make it work and you wrote me that you were already involved with someone. That pummeled me by the way. Did it pain you to lose me? Apparently not, since you were already with someone else. I don't blame you, looking back I understand since I didn't plan for our future together... we were young. I miss our mornings of conversation. How we stayed in all day watching shit TV shows and taking the piss out of each other on rainy days. I miss how you strummed your fingers up and down the back of my head when you kissed me. The way the sweat dripped down from your neck when I was inside you. Can you honestly tell me, you don't? I maybe an artful bugger but it doesn't change the way I feel about you. Claire, say something... please."

Another vulnerable outcry enmeshing me. Sandra's words scroll in front of my eyes. She said I never had a chance to be frivolous, have fun like her and the rest of my friends. After what Griffin just said, I want to rip his clothes off and ravish him like I had many times before. This defective desire is consuming me. Whether this feeling with Griffin is love or lust on heroin, I just want to go with it and stop thinking about the tedious trivialities.

"Griffin... let's walk to your place."

I hold his hand leading the way down the stairs as he clutched his other hand onto mine with his lips pressed. We walk out the front as LCD Sound System "Someone Great" blares, its sound waves reach the stretch of the block.

"Look at the stars, Claire... *pultra stellas*. Look at how they are perfectly aligned. Is that Orion or Venus to the right?"

I couldn't look up as my eyes swelled. He asks what's wrong and I assure him my tears are from the cold brisk air.

CHAPTER 20 / *FACE THE MUSIC*

"Get out… they want to hire me? Considering my lack of producing skills…not that I'm not grateful, but there weren't any deejay openings? Lana, did you change your hair color? It looks great."

"I can believe it because I don't want to lose you. I darkened it… yes, thanks for noticing. It's hard to get a decent announcer job. So tell me… are you okay being a full-time producer and ready to relocate?"

"I've given it serious thought for some time and I keep coming back to a proposal I have in mind. You'll probably think I'm crazy but what else is new? I remain here under seasonal or part-time contingency, so I can divide time with Ethan in LA. I have no preference… so whatever you think could work. I've decided to keep my condo as an investment and in case the sublet falls through, we have a hub here. Now I'm sure you're asking who will fill in during my absence. Well I have the perfect person to recommend. Shane. What do you think?"

There's a long pause as Lana gathers her presentation documents for her next meeting.

"What do I think? I think your idea is great. The

question is how do I sell it to the big man? If I can emphasize to the committee how it would benefit the station by having you here most of the month... a more realistic span of time as opposed to seasonal, they'll hopefully sway in our favor. As far as Shane... he's a high risk gamble. He's still wet behind the ears for this huge opportunity you're recommending him for. He hasn't had commercial experience other than as an intern. People will think I'm deranged for even considering it."

"You did the exact same thing for me back in the day, and look at how I turned out. I hear you, but here's the deal. Shane is a natural born talent... you even said it yourself. Lana, this past year I cannot begin to describe the assurance I feel in both of them, steering the ship... no joke. Ideally I would like it to be a package deal. Jared wants to be a producer... would it be possible to have him train on Kurt's show? They are a man short and they both get along really well, they'd make a great team. When I'm here, Shane will assist as a co-producer with me, so we can save on expense. When I'm not here, Les or Barnaby can help out. I mentioned it to them and they're on board. Saving money should bowl over Warren, no? They're hard workers and I know they can do this... in fact, I'll wager on it. Please consider this. Not working here and giving up my show is not an option for me. I'll do whatever you see fit.

"Wow... I've never seen you like this, you're on fire. I like it. Here's the thing... when I gave you a chance, the station wasn't where it is now. But I hear where you're coming from... you're sensing in them what I sensed in your ability so that's enough for me. The obstacle is convincing Warren. Truthfully, I have some doubts of course but the kid is good and his voice so turns me on... keep that between you and me. I'll set up a meeting with the heavy weights. With my persuasion, we may just have a shot. As for Jared, we have been very happy with his performance and Kurt has raved about him too. If it doesn't wind up happening for them, you have to promise me you'll be okay with it and still stay on. I agree… replacing you is not an option."

"Talk about fire… I'm floored boss. We have a deal. You don't know what this means to me… having your support. I'm speechless."

"For the last ten years you've worked your ass off and then some. We may not be the savviest station but we're loyal and you've earned a medal kid. You went through hell and back in your personal life and not once did you ever bail out. You kept your show alive and you showed up every day. To others, that may be viewed as crazy but to me… well I think it's admirable. I've been where you were Claire, and in a fucked up way… work was my only salvation that got me through the tough times. It's like I told you when you were down there for a while and Lord knows you were… I'm here for you. You just didn't want to reach out to me and I understand why so… "

"It wasn't that I didn't want to talk to you about it Lana, I was in bad shape. I didn't want to concern you with my turmoil that's all. The show, you and the rest saved me in many ways. Thanks for being my rock here since day one."

We hug each other and she strategically exits without the guys seeing her as they come into the studio. I contemplated if I should say something to them yet. How crushed would they be if it doesn't turn out in their favor?

"Okay, Claire I give… what's up with you? You seem off in a distant planet. You're not preggers… are you?"

"Oh shit, am I showing already? (His eyebrows rise up as his mouth drops.) No, I'm not, you douche. I'm in the process of working out a proposal with management that involves us. Just don't ask me what that is."

"Now who's pulling a douche move? You can't wave a steak in our face and not let us have a bite? Please throw us a bone for Christ's sake."

Jared looks at us like we are playing a ping pong match.

"Do you have provisions? I can't say this straight."

He grins knowing he's won out. "Silly girl... how many times must I remind you? I'm always packin'. Let's go blaze outside. Jared, put us on autopilot for ten."

We walked down the long hallway with such swagger. Our steps are in line with one another.

Kurt steps out into the hall. "Aww... look at the second best radio personalities. Want to stop by number one? I'll show you how it's done."

"Screw you Kurt. Don't cry when I take your title away, we're only five points behind, you supercilious jack off!"

Shane and Jared cackle.

"Language lady... there are kids present. Actually, that was a good one... albeit delusional of course."

He fist pumps my hand, winking as we head outside hiding behind the big dumpster. We take a couple of tokes while I figure out how to phrase what I need to say.

"Okay... please promise me you will not tell anyone what I'm about to tell you. I need a proclamation swear." They both raise their right hands to their chest and look me in the eye.

"I swear on my mother, Claire... you have my word."

That suffices. Jared follows. "I swear on my grandparent's souls I will not repeat this to anyone."

"Okay, here's the deal. I'm looking into staying here

either seasonally or whatever days they can spare me so I can make this long distance thing work with Ethan. I have recommended Jared to be a producer-in-training for Kurt's show. Shane, I'm hoping you can share the show announcing for me in my absence. Lana is setting the wheels in motion with Warren and the rest. Unfortunately, we can't guarantee anything but there's a strong possibility it could happen. If it doesn't, I'll reference you both for something at the station or wherever you may want to go. So tell me... what do you think?"

They both look like sad stoned puppy dogs. Shane doesn't say anything, faintly smiling fighting back tears as Jared wipes his eyes and gives me a hug, Shane joins in clutching us tightly.

"I don't know what to say... to even consider me to fill in for you while you're catching West Coast rays. Fuck, I'm an emotional mess... and stoked you're not going out there permanently. I'm beyond grateful... but I have to ask, why me? This is a big time gig for someone seasoned."

"You're right, it is. This is my chance to mold someone into something great, like my predecessors did for me. You don't have that luxury when someone comes in already experienced. But most importantly, you have a gift and I see so much potential. Also, you graduated to having doubts, stepping up, challenging yourself to be better. You need that edge in order to succeed and I know you'll keep the integrity of my show. Jared, you have expressed to me many times your desire to be a back-office wizard, working on Kurt's show will garner you that. In all my years doing this, I've never seen an engineer geek with such precision and knack. Here's the thing, if you want a career on-air then we'll have to gear you towards that. Producing, you'll master in no time. I need you both to seriously think about this... especially when you're not lit. It won't be the same job you have now, far greater responsibility and longer hours are guaranteed. You have to be certain you're willing to do what it takes for the long haul.

"To go out on a limb for us... that you hold me and Shane in this incredible regard. We won't let you down, we promise."

"Hey Parker, that's my line."

"Not anymore, Salinger."

I tear up as Shane hands me EZ wrap strips to wipe my face. We head back inside to finish the show.

"Fellas, I'm in the mood for something to dance to... what are we feeling?"

Jared shouts out. "How about Iggy Pop's 'Lust for Life'?"

"No thanks, Mr. Trainspotting... Shanester?"

Jared waves Shane off. "Wait... remember that song from *Kids* 'Natural One' by Folk Implosion?"

"Ooh that's a good one, love the snare drum. It's not danceable but you can roll it out.

I look up seeing a familiar set of eyes peer through the door's window. I gasp, falling into my chair.

Shane looks at the door and then back at me. "That's Jake, isn't it? Do you want to see him or should I ask him to leave?"

"I can't avoid this. I have to meet with him... please close out the show for me."

Shane goes to the door and opens it. "Hello, I'm Shane. Claire will be right out to see you."

"Thanks for letting me know. I'll wait in the hall."

Shane holds the door for me. "You need anything, just ring. Be strong."

I nodded, mustering whatever courage I had to walk out the door. This was it, the day I imagined so many times in my dreams/nightmares. I wish John was here, to guide me along and cut out this unseemly parasite squeezing my lungs. I feel Jared's hand on my back while I pass—it is time to face the music. Jake stands a few feet away, looking out the window. He is thinner, looking ten years older than when I last saw him. The sun-kissed pallor he used to have is now overcast. He turns around. His eyes that looked into mine so many times before are still visceral.

"Hi. I didn't mean to come unannounced. I was a few blocks away for a meeting and figured if you were available, we could talk. Is now a good time?"

"It's fine. Let's go outside on the bench."

As he walks ahead, I leave staring faces behind me.

"How are you feeling, Jake?"

"Better, I know I don't look it, but I'm on an upswing, and you? You always look great... a little thin though."

We faintly smile to one another. "I'm doing better, too."

"Claire, as of late I've become more at peace since our break. I know we're overdue for closure. I wanted to call a few times... but I wasn't ready."

"I understand. Where should we start?"

"Did you have an affair with Ethan while we were

together?"

I shake my head in insulted disgust. "That's where you want to start. You already know the answer to that. Don't disrespect me with your unwarranted jealousy. I have nothing to justify to you. I never strayed on you while we were together... you know that."

He tries to put his hand on my shoulder, I pull away.

"Okay, I'm sorry. It's just fitting to know you're together now. He always had a thing for you. I didn't know it was mutual."

He also knew? I fidget as my face warms up. "It became mutual well after we broke up. If this conversation doesn't change subjects soon, I'm going back to work."

His mouth drops in surprise by my tone. "What happened to docile Claire? I didn't come here to upset you."

"I've changed. I got hurt. I suppressed many feelings when you fell ill. Unfortunately, you're attached to a very sore part of my life. This is the anger I didn't have a chance to express when you were recovering. I would like to bring up something... what happened after you left Sandra's that night? I know you were coked out before you arrived. What happened after you stormed out? Help me understand what you were so riled up about."

He faces away from me, looking at people walking past us on Sixth Avenue.

"I was at work and overheard a couple of the guys on my team, Bill and Todd talking about me. They said... *How long has he been engaged? Two and half years? Why isn't he married yet? What's wrong with him... her? Did you see what she looks like? I would love to fuck some sense into her. She looks like she'd be a whore in the sack. I'm more in her league than his drugging ass.* Those fucks didn't know I was listening. It made me sick hearing it. I knew my problem was causing you to stall. I felt like there was no way out. I wanted us to be married and have children. But something always got in the way and you wouldn't budge. I felt like the second fiddle to your career. You kept insisting I needed to stay on the wagon. Understandably. I resented that ultimatum... you and your morphing career, undeserved since you were a victim of my doing. I knew I had health issues... it didn't matter. I had no desire to stop using and that was also part of my vexation. I wanted it all and couldn't understand any part of no. No matter what, in the end I always got my way but with us... I couldn't win. It's as if you always had the upper hand, unbeknownst to you. I gave into a substance to numb the pain of that. Inevitably, it took the love of my life away from me." He takes out two water bottles and hands me one. We take sips and he clears his throat.

"Before I headed to Sandy's, I got drunk with Hank. We did a couple of lines together. I wasn't coked out. I was still riled up by what those bastards said. When I got to the party, what did I see? That dude holding your arm, both of you holding each other without a care in the world. I lost it. It threw me over the edge. All I could think was you were into him since we were strained... our love turned into ultimatums and wherefore clauses that we both didn't want to adhere to. Who was he and why were you so affectionate to him? Claire, are you okay?"

I sobbed unable to look at Jake. "Well it makes better sense now. That guy is a high school friend. We were hugging each other because he had just told me he got engaged. I was congratulating him. Had you showed up five minutes later, you would have met his fiancé who was getting us drinks. I thought you were assured of us. Why would you let two trouble-making fucks leave you doubting me... us after all our years together? Jake, I should have expressed to you clearer at the time that I had no desire to raise a kid whose father's a drug addict. I wanted us to function well without your problem hindering us. But no matter how many attempts you tried staying clean, you always fell back into it. The pressure and stress it caused made me resentful too and I resisted. I became drained dealing with it, especially your relentless drive to always win... having things done your way. You rarely took any of my needs into consideration."

"I know. I know this is mostly my fault. I thought I could change... control us... you. Once I learned I couldn't, that's when it became unmanageable for me to deal with it. Back to that night, why wouldn't go home with me? When you threw me out of the party, I binged on coke. It hurt so much when you asked me to leave because I just wanted to hold you and..."

"And what? You were so fucking outraged... it wouldn't have been loving and you know that. When you were in that state, it wasn't you. It was a distorted... hurtfully aggressive, fast-forward version of you. Do you remember what you were like that time after your work party? You practically raped me that night, remember? No matter how many times I asked you to stop... you didn't. You were out of control. And it wasn't just that one time either and stupidly, I let you get away with it."

"I am so sorry. It was never my intension to hurt or force you to... it's inexcusable. But you still left me alone. I just wish you would've come home with me. I know I wasn't appealing when I was strung out... you never deserved that, especially seeing me slowly kill myself. I think the rejection and judgment enabled my habit as well. I'm not blaming you... just acknowledging it."

"I never meant to make you feel rejected or be an enabler of your substance problem. We evolved into different realms and dissension set in. I wish it hadn't but it did. I tried so many times to talk to you about things that I wanted for us but you didn't hear me."

"You're right. I didn't hear you and I regret that. Despite it all, you were nothing but supportive to me the whole time, even the low points. Look, you need to know I don't hate you or at least not anymore. I... was just hurt you wouldn't give it another go, like you did the times before. You gave up on me... us. That's what hurt the most. There were no more chances. I wish I knew there were no more get out of jail free cards. You finally calling it quits made me realize the monster I had become. I wish things had turned out different and regrettably sorry for all of the hurt it caused you and my family."

I needed to hear him say this. All the therapy in the world pales in comparison to being face to face with the person who has caused the affliction. Therapy is a band aid— pain killer for the wounds, release and clarity is what heals you.

"Jake, I had no idea that would be the last chance for both of us. I can't explain it, but that night, after finding you dead on our floor... seeing you with tubes out of your mouth... needles in your arms. Something in me snapped. I couldn't stand the pain of seeing you die like that, leaving all we had. It was a harsh dose of invincibility for us."

"So leaving me made it easier for you to deal with... I understand that."

"Yes. I always submitted to you... your intensity. Breaking away from it helped me gain balance again. I went into shock when I found you lifeless. Something in me died that night and my struggle then became living with the guilt of not sticking it out... being stronger. I understand you're hurt because I felt pained each time you snorted a line. I'm sorry for bowing out... waving the white flag." We both tear up holding hands as justified gawkers stare at us.

"I didn't realize, Claire. If I could take it all back, all the horribleness, I would."

He embraces me. I didn't think I would be held in his arms again. It wasn't the same as I remembered. It didn't have the safe tender feeling it once had. Now it's unfamiliar.

"Jake, please promise me you'll get back to that guy you once were and be happy. Please take care of yourself."

"I can't promise anything other than I'm doing the best I can each day. My parents and Greer have been amazing, standing by me. They... we... want nothing but the best for you. As much as it pains me to say it, I know Ethan and he's a stand-up guy. You have my approval, not that you need it."

"Thank you, that means a lot. No matter who I talked to, it didn't matter. I needed to hear it from you. We're both out of exile now."

"Yes, the worst of it is behind us. Just promise me, when you remember our time... don't think the worst of me. I hope I've redeemed whatever I could."

"I never thought the worst of you, through it all. And I never will."

It killed me knowing I would never have the chance to gaze at his mesmerizing eyes again. I will miss them. I will miss all of our great times. I will miss him.

"Who would've thought we'd end up with our last conversation on this bench? Did you?"

I nodded my head yes and said "No."

Tears surface to his eyes again, remembering the night he asked me out. He hugs me and turns around, walking towards Sixth Avenue and doesn't look back. That was it—the end of our story. I now knew what bittersweet meant. After sitting by myself for a few moments, I returned to the studio to get my stuff. The guys had been long gone after I went outside. What seemed like fifteen minutes turned out to be well over two hours. The guys left me a note reading:

Captain,

We hope everything went well. We are down at Croxley Ales for Barnaby's birthday bash. Join us!
Your grateful shipmates

Considering the emotional episode I just had, I wanted to join in, celebrating my new life chapter. More like a new book, the old one has now been placed on the shelf to collect dust. I walk downtown to meet everyone at the party. I texted to Bianca, Sandra, Lana, and Fez that I finally achieved closure with Jake and everything went well; also to join the party at Croxley's. I heard back from Bianca and Sandra right away, they were thrilled about the news and would join after they get out of work. Lana's was touchingly sweet: I'm so happy for you, it feels good doesn't it? I'm already here, so shake your ass and take a cab... don't walk! Fez's took the prize for warped comedy: Congratulations! Is it cool if I take a swing at dating Jake? Drugs don't faze me... Love you ;) I'll stop by soon! I left a message on my parent's phone with the news; I know they'll be pleased to hear it. I reached out to Ethan letting him know I would Skype with him later and he quickly wrote back: Better yet, tell me in person tomorrow morning. I'm heading to LAX tonight... love you! What a wonderful surprise, I miss him so much, timing couldn't be better. Having Ethan in my life to share this milestone makes me even more grateful for everything I have. I grip my jade necklace in my pocket as I walk down St. Marks Place. I remember the touching note I read in the jewelry store window. Bleed no more. I will always cherish this gem as a reminder of an unforgettable time in my life.

CHAPTER 21 / *THE WHAT IFS?*

The kitchen smells so good, I'm about to burst. Bianca has outdone herself again on the dinner she made.

"Here, have a piece of bruschetta... I can see you're drooling. Dinner should be done soon. It's gonna bother me, not having you here all the time. It's so far away... I don't want you to leave."

"I know. Part of me doesn't want to go. It's nice to hear you feel that way along with Mom and Dad because when I dropped the potential news to Dante, he didn't even flinch.

We giggle. "You know he'll miss you, he'd have the same reaction if it were me. He's a bona fide shit though at times... gotta love family.

"Oh yes. I know it's far but with Skype and visits, it'll be fine. I might not get the go ahead at work since they're still deciding. I'm sitting tight because if it doesn't work out, I'm not moving without a job."

"I don't blame you... we're too clever to be kept women. Not to throw on the guilt but Mom's been a basket case with all of this. Dad on the other hand is psyched, another place for him to visit."

"I've been talking with Mom, she'll be fine after she gets used to it. It takes time for her to adjust to anything new. Oh my God, I can't stop eating this. I need the recipe for this red snapper dish… it's so good, did you use dill too?"

"Yes and I'll forward it to you, if you stay."

"You're not playing fair, B."

"You know me. Do you think management will decide in your favor?"

"Lana let on that Warren's being difficult because he doesn't want to rock the boat since the show is high on the ratings again. He also has reservations about Shane filling in for me during my absence. I think it will add freshness to the show and the fans like him. That's what we have in our favor… but it's anyone's guess at this point. "

"He'd be a moron if he didn't meet you half way. You created that show from the ground up and personally, I feel they should kiss your ass for any request you have. My gut tells me it'll go in your favor because I don't want you to go."

"And I do want to go… so you never know. Thanks for feeding me before dinnertime. Are you sure you don't need help with anything else? I have time before I have to walk Fez's dogs. After you guys finish, you should stop by and hang. He's left me unlimited rentals on demand so if you want to hang."

"That sounds like a plan. Mark will be game, we'll head over later. Where did Fez go?"

"St. Thomas, he went with his new boyfriend Darryl. They're getting serious; I'm happy for him."

Bianca shakes her head while she sets the dinner table. "It's tough out there. I've been married for the past six years so I don't know how it is now but…"

"It has worsened, trust me. Men now pass out on their entrees for Christ's sake."

She giggles. "Oh that's right… what a shithead. Didn't he try to go out with you again?"

"He sure did and no go."

"So you never had a chance to have some fun before you jumped back into monogamyland again."

"Well… I did, actually. It wasn't with someone new though."

Bianca's eyes widen as she puts the tray down. "And you didn't tell me… who?"

"Remember I mentioned having dinner with Griffin a few weeks back."

"Oh yes, your ex-boyfriend, I remember him. Wait, that was recent… "

"I know. And I know what you're thinking and you're right. I fucked up. If it's any consolation, I've been filled with remorse since it happened. I didn't tell you because I was ashamed… trying to get a grip on this unfamiliar territory I stumbled upon."

"Oh Claire, that's so unlike you. Look, we all have skeletons in the closet so cut yourself some slack. I'm not judging you because I know you probably had a good reason and I was no angel before I got hitched. This may sound screwy but, it's good to hear you finally didn't play it safe like you always do. Now who should be judged?"

"Really? You don't think I'm a cheating whore?"

"No and don't say that. Did you tell anyone else?"

"Sandra's the only one besides you."

"How did it happen?"

"Ever since he reached out over a month ago, I don't know... I became uneasy. All the old feelings I had resurfaced. I contemplated meeting him because I was afraid that we'd hook up again. I tried to be strong, when we met up... but his intoxicated outcry of feelings mixed with loaded libidos got the best of me. He had brought up our past together... how we parted and he wished we would've had more of a chance. He still wants us to be together and doesn't care I'm with Ethan. That alone, has been gnawing at me since it happened... leaving me slightly torn. I love Ethan but a part of me is insecure with the whole rock star women at his feet shit... and that's where my feelings for Griffin kick in."

"Oh sweetie, I didn't realize you were going through this. You seem so secure with... "

"I know... but I have some doubts and now I've cheated on him. At the time, my rational was we were suffering from the long times apart from each other but it was still wrong. I can't lie and say I didn't enjoy myself because I did. It was the first time I didn't do what scrupulous Claire would do. It was all about that moment and I went with it. Since that night, I've had a dual existence. In a sad way, I don't regret it completely. I spent the whole week with Griffin when he was in town and it was lovely. When he went back, we both took it harder than we thought we would, especially him. My regret clouded my reaction when he left, debating if I should tell Ethan... come clean."

"You can't tell him. You'll lose him. Have you figured out what you want? Who you want to be with? Sometimes we have to experience something extreme in order to understand what will make us happy. Do you still feel you're at a crossroad?"

"No, I want to be with Ethan. For it to work with Griffin, he would need to live here. As far as I'm concerned it was a fling that can't happen again. I'm so in tuned with Ethan now and I love him, despite what I did. For the little fun being naughty provided... I wouldn't do it again. I hate lying. That's why I figured if I come out with it, to put it behind us and start fresh."

"If Ethan is a typical guy, he'll never understand it, especially when it comes to sex. Who the hell am I kidding? We women and everyone for that matter don't wish to understand it... especially you, no? Can you honestly say if he posed this to you, you would be fine with it?"

"No, I wouldn't. Just when I thought I was cured from my Jake tragedy, I cause another one, just like that."

"It happens to more people than you think. You don't feel Griffin would... he wouldn't sell you out, right?"

"He doesn't have a spiteful bone in his epicurean body... so no. He understands everything I just told you because he's also torn and in agreement with me that it was what it was, and if anything's meant it will happen on its own."

"I hope so... for your sake. I'm weary something might come up or a ball comes out of nowhere from left field. Have you heard from him since?"

"Yes, he sent me a handwritten letter... it was sweet and basically a reiteration of our pact to keep our situation under wraps. We're friends and it will be fine. Hey, I better skedaddle sis. Kit and Kaboodle will go for my throat if I don't walk them soon. See you later."

"You got it and keep me posted."

I rode my bike to Fez's and along the way I kept looking at the scenery familiar since childhood. Will I miss all of this? The roads and sidewalks in need of fixing, being in biking distance from my family and friends. The owners of my neighborhood coffee shop who've saved me many mornings when I had no time to make my own cup. What will I do without Washington Square Park or Brooklyn Bridge? Maybe that's what I need. Start anew, break away from all I know. The dogs are happy to see me as I play with them putting their leashes on. Earlier at work, the guys were unusually inquisitive with questions like, what if you chose a different course other than the one you're living on. Would your life be significantly different—enhanced for the better or worse? Jared spurred the questions when he confessed to us he was offered an internship at another station in DC, but he chose to work at ours. Shane reflected on matters of the heart, saying he would have been engaged by now if he and his ex-girlfriend stayed together. Like me, he now has trust issues. He also stated he's trying to come to terms with having to eventually settle with someone who will most likely love him more than he loves her. I hated hearing him say such a thing, it's a sad reality how it's more onerous for men than it is for women to live alone. They had both asked about *my what if?* And if it pertained to Jake. It didn't anymore since we were remedied by acknowledging we were no longer an option to each other. My latest what ifs were, how will my life be away from New York? How would things have worked out if I quit everything and moved in with Ethan six months ago? What if I accidentally become pregnant? What if I told Ethan about my indiscretion and came clean? It seems no matter how many what ifs you bury, other ones are born in an instant to dwell on. The saving grace is these current what ifs aren't enabling enervation and depressive malaise like last year's did. After I walked the dogs I checked my emails for any word from KROQ with potential spots up for grabs. Kamden gave me a smashing reference, I know they liked me when I interviewed but they're apprehensive about having a seasonal employee. When I got back to Fez's, I see a Gchat message pop up on my laptop from Ethan: How is my angel doing? I just booked a flight for Thursday night. I'll be in Friday morning before you head to work. Love you!

I'm no angel babe and I'm sorrier than you'll ever know. I relied on his visits to numb the loneliness I'd grown accustomed to when he's away.

I respond back: Can you talk? I'd rather hear your voice.

My phone rings. "Ethan, it's getting tougher each day apart... I miss you. Friday can't come soon enough."

"I know babe... I can't wait to get there."

"How was the Kimmel show taping? I have the DVR set... soon I'll be seeing your fine ass live."

"Oh yes... I was nervous as hell."

"You nervous? I don't believe it. You're usually chill when you take the stage."

"Yeah, but this was different. They had five cameras rolling at you and I could see some old people looking at us blankly, highly doubt they were fans. It was tough but Jimmy was cool. Ooh, guess who was on?"

"Wasn't Gwyneth Paltrow the guest?"

"Originally, yes but they're having her on tomorrow. I'll give you a hint... he didn't get an Oscar nomination for one of the best parts ever in movie history and you think he's smokin'."

"The Dude? I mean, Jeff Bridges?"

"Yes... very good. He's was really cool and a really good musician; we wound up jamming after the taping. Bass

249

took a video of it… we'll watch together."

"I'm jealous, that's great to hear babe."

"See, if you were living here, you would've been there along with Charlize Theron, who also appeared on the show. Sweetie, do you remember our pact of celebrity hookups that we allowed ourselves? If we should just so happen…"

"I know, thanks for rubbing it in. Wait, please don't tell me you hooked up with Charlize."

"No… but I'd like to add her to the list, is that cool?"

"You can add anyone you want. Let me clarify… as long as they're a once in a lifetime celebrity."

He purrs into the phone. "So I have an idea. Why don't we take your co-workers out for dinner this weekend? It'd be nice to finally meet those two."

"That's a great idea, yes. I definitely owe them a dinner too so I'll run it by them… they'll be excited. Do you prefer Saturday or…?"

"Friday night… Saturday, let's just chill out alone. Choose wherever you want to go. I hate to run but I'm way late for an early dinner with the guys. Resume with you later, beautiful."

"Sounds good, my hero… love you."

"Love you more."

I hear a knock at the door, the party has arrived. Bianca and Mark come in with some rum mixers. We couldn't decide what to watch on demand and wound up watching the Yankee game instead. Ethan should have been here, he would have enjoyed the time. I have come to a point in my life that I don't want to be alone anymore. It's alarming to know I will probably move and leave my show to be with him. Seeing the silhouettes of my sister and her husband dancing affectionately is an inspiration. Each day I'm inching up to the edge of the pool, ready to dive into the deep end, feet first without knowing if I'll come out swimming or sinking. I am ready. No more excuses and fears hindering away at me.

The next morning, I spent Sunday sorting through closets for clothes and shoes I don't use anymore to donate to charity. This beach apartment has never looked so disheveled; a long overdue spring cleaning is in order. After I clean out the file bin, discarding old copies of useless bills, I think about my dream earlier. This one entailed the same train scenario I had before. The same two conductors, with white noise faces, wait while I decide which train to board. They both looked at me shouting: *Come on aboard, don't be afraid!* I shouted back: *Where are you going?* They don't respond. I glanced at each train and said: *Maybe I'm not supposed to know.* I boarded the one to the right of me as the bells were ringing. I walked through the aisle of the shaky train with my heart beating on my sleeve. The conductor, who now has a regular face resembling Bill Murray in his Saturday Night Live days, said: *You made a good choice. Now, sit back... relax and enjoy the ride.*

* * * * * * * *

I commuted into the city and brought my bicycle so I could ride to work on nice days from Ethan's place. Jared spots me outside as I'm locking up.

"Hey Clarabelle... nice bike. Thanks for the invite to dinner, I'd love to join. Also, are you planning on going to My Morning Jacket's show on Saturday night? Taran and I are going and we'd love to hang if you can make it."

"Oh I wish... thanks for the offer but Ethan and I have plans."

Shane hugs me from behind. "To be indisposed until he leaves. It's so nice to have a rock star boyfriend, isn't it J Bone? We peasants don't exist when he's around."

"And your point being, player? Haven't I told you before... don't knock the hustler, baby. Are you joining us for dinner on Friday? We'd like to take you guys out like my email mentioned."

Shane frowns quizzically at me. "What email? I didn't get it. Oh wait a minute... there it is unopened... oops."

"It's okay Salinger, we all have blonde moments from time to time."

Shane reads the message. "That's mighty kind of you both, we finally get to meet the man. I'm there... where are thinking of going?"

"Excellent. We're thinking Morimoto if that's cool with you guys? It's on me by the way... just a small token of appreciation for all you both do."

"Claire you don't have to do that, besides Morimoto's is bucco bucks. That's a huge gesture... we're fine with a corner joint somewhere. Why don't we check out that Japanese place in the West Village instead?"

"That's nice to offer but it's the least I can do. You guys have earned it and don't worry about the money... I make bank."

We walk into the studio and Jared hands me the set list. "So we're allowed to bring dates? You rock."

"Yes J Shizzle, feel free to bring anyone you want as your co-pilots."

"I'll see if Taran can join."

"Cool player, okay, we're almost ready to roll. Shane can you hand me the PSA log sheet, thanks."

I IM Shane: You're not thinking of bringing Nina, right? You had mentioned things didn't work out for you and Gwen.

He IM's back: Hell no... are you crazy? I have my first date with Heather on Saturday so I'm probably going stag. I don't mind being the 5th wheel.

I IM Jared: Hey buddy, Shane may wind up going alone, if so, is it cool for you to fly solo if he doesn't? I just feel bad for him as the fifth wheel and all... thoughts?

Jared IM's back: Sure, I totally agree. It'll just be the four of us.

I respond: Thanks for taking one for the team, Parker.

* * * * * * * *

Friday rolled around and Ethan texts me he's close by, on his way over to the apartment. I texted him back to detour to the radio station for a surprise.

"Hey guys do me a favor and steer the ship for a half hour or so. I need to run an errand. Thanks."

Jared gives me thumbs up. "You got it, take your time."

I head outside to the entrance and wait for Ethan to arrive. After a couple of minutes, I pace back and forth and he surprises me from behind, kissing my neck. I tell him to "Follow me." I lead him down a corridor to one of the conference room's that has a wall of one way windows that enables people inside the room to see out in the hall. We used to use this room for office parties, until they decided to have them offsite. Lana had given me a key, in case I ever wanted to take a break since it had couches and bathrooms.

"So what's the surprise, darlin'?"

I unzip his pants and go down on him. "Oh, that's the best surprise ever... wow. I have never received a... oh... in a conf.... oh oh... wait... Claire, someone's looking at us... stop!"

"We can see them, they can't see us. Now relax...or shall I not continue?"

"You naughty girl...love you, don't ever change."

I turn his tense nervousness into putty. After a few moments I wiggle myself up to him while he gasps, stretched out looking up at the ceiling.

"You were saying, Ethan?"

"That just happened. It was the hottest... yet most disturbing head I've ever received. I didn't think you could outdo yourself... I was wrong."

As we have sex, I now felt the thrilling sensation since my back wasn't to the spectators. It really is alarming how you see people walking by, who can potentially unlock the door walking in, seeing us sprawled out on the table. After we collect ourselves, we freshen up and get dressed.

"Just come home with me please... they can finish it out. Please, we were apart for too long."

"I know... that's why I had you make a pit stop. Let me finish up and I'll be home soon. You make me laugh since you just had me... don't you ever wear out? Actually, I'm so glad you don't so scratch what I just asked."

He put his head to mine. "Why don't I come upstairs with you, meet them before we head over to dinner?"

"Well I told them I had to run an errand… if you come with, they may put two and two together. And we so… have nasty slut hair right now…"

"Yeah we do. (We both laugh.) Alright, I see your point. I'll be a good boy and let you finish. I'm going to go home and play with myself till you join me."

"You're not making this easy on me, Kilgore. Now that's all I'll see… unable to concentrate at work, thanks."

"Serves you right… love you."

"Ditto. Well, strike another one off the bucket list. I have wanted to whore it up in that room since they built it four years ago. It was well worth the wait. See you soon."

After Ethan left, I went to the ladies room to fix my bed hair and smeared makeup.

"Hey guys, sorry it took longer than I thought. How's everything going? We're almost in the home stretch. So remember we'll meet later at Morimoto… 7:00 PM."

Shane nods his head yes. "Can't wait. Oh and by the way kids, keep your fingers crossed for me with Heather tomorrow."

Jared smiles at him as I answer. "Of course… you'll be fine. Hey, you never told us what happened between you and Gwen."

Jared crossed his arms and throws a foam football at Shane. "Yeah, tell us."

"It just didn't work out. She's on the ambitious marriage track, moving way too fast for me. After six weeks she was talking about moving in together… chick turned out to be loco."

"Yikes... Maybe you brought that out in her, you know once they have Salinger lovin' they lose their mind."

"Maybe J Bone, but I'z got no time for ultra-clingers. Claire, was that Ethan you were with when you were out earlier?"

"Whoa... you saw us?"

"Yeah, out front, I went to get a bagel and saw you with him. You should have brought him up to introduce us."

"He just flew in from LA and was tired... he stopped by for keys to the apartment. He's looking forward to meeting you guys tonight."

Jared says softly. "We are too... fun awaits."

On my way home, I called John's office and made an appointment. I needed to have a session after a long break, so much has happened since my last time there. The apartment was empty with a note and flowers:

> It was no fun without you, so I decided to work at the studio instead. I'll be home with lunch in hand around 1ish.
> Love ya lots,
> E.

I get out of the shower to find Ethan sitting on the counter waiting to watch me dry my hair.

"Why don't you let your hair go wavy tonight... it looks so good that way."

"I don't agree but there's something about wild cave woman hair that you men love spewing over."

I nod yes to him while I put the brush down and put mousse in my hair, scrunch drying it.

He rummages through his shirts and slacks in the closet. "What do you think I should wear? That place is dressy, right?"

"Yeah somewhat… I think a pair of jeans with a nice shirt and jacket will look good. I'm thinking of wearing my black dress with that funky zebra print coat you love so much."

He turns around. "Anything Gwen Stefani designs or does is cool with me. This also looks nice, hey how come you've never worn this blue dress? Maybe tonight, we can be cheesy and match… I'll wear my navy jacket."

Ethan pulls out the same dress I wore from my week of shame with Griffin. My stomach sunk with hard-hitting guilt.

"That's a fun suggestion but it needs to be dry cleaned… so definitely another time. I do have another blue one that'll work."

I went into the other room to collect myself from the clamminess. No matter how pleasurable my week with Griffin was, it didn't matter because I'm overpowered with regret. We finish getting ready and arrive at Morimoto, the guys are at the bar looking quite dapper.

Ethan whispers to me. "They are exactly how I pictured them… except you didn't mention how handsome Shane is."

"You have no reason to be jealous, he'll be lucky if he's up to half your caliber in ten years." Ethan kisses me and we tap their shoulders for attention.

"Hello Ethan, pleasure to meet you finally. I'm Shane."

I could tell Shane was nervous by the tone in his voice.

"The pleasure is mine... and you must be Jared, hello... Claire raves about you both. What are you guys drinking?"

Jared holds his glass up. "We have Jack and cokes... can we get you drinks?"

"Night is on me so order another round. Claire, what are you feeling tonight?"

Anything to suppress the malfeasance I'm hazed with.

"No offense to Jack, but I'll have a vanilla stoli and diet coke, thanks."

We have a group cheer as our hostess tells us our table is ready. We're unanimous in sharing different maki rolls and a few appetizers. Ethan holds the guys attention with how the band started and I listen in fond remembrance. After we finish eating, Jared and Shane rub their stomachs.

Shane raises his glass. "Great meal... great time, thanks again for taking us out."

Ethan says. "Our pleasure, thanks for joining us."

"I'd like to make a toast... for your support, hard work, and especially for making work fun again. You all inspire me in your way and I'm very fortunate. Cheers to more amazing times ahead."

Jared motions to me. "Claire, we're the ones that lucked out... you're the best boss ever. On that note, I need to use the restroom. I'm drunk... yay."

We chuckle as Shane fixes Jared's jacket lapels and says "You're not alone, buddy."

I excuse myself from the table and join Jared, walking towards the bathrooms. Shane and Ethan stayed at the table. On my way back, I notice an eye-catching sculpture with a vivid floral arrangement. As I lean in, I hear Shane's voice, behind the art decoration.

"So tell me, what does it feel like to be a rock star?"

"It's pretty surreal most of the time, I won't lie. Aside from the sacrifices and pressure, it's amazing... indescribable really. Each artist has a different take on it. For me, just seeing the audience faces light up from our songs makes it all worthwhile. The creative process on a whole is mind-blowing yet grueling as well. So tell me, how it feels to be a disc jockey?"

"Not quite yet, but hope to get at some point. It's a lot of hard work, but I wouldn't change it for anything. We truly did luck out with her, she's a gem to work with and Jared's like a brother. Speaking of lucking out, look at you."

"You mean being with Claire, oh I know."

"She's a dime... always treasure her."

"She is and trust me... I do."

"Cheers to dimes, man... best women in the world. Who'll move cross country, leaving everything if they have to, for the one they love. Promise you'll be good to her... she deserves it. I'm sorry... I'm a mess right now so just mind me blabbering."

"I understand. It's nice that you look out for her. I don't want her to give up anything, we're working it out. As soon as I can, I'm moving here. Unlike her, I can live anywhere."

"I apologize. I'm just so... who do you know would give a chance like that to an amateur like me? I didn't mean to pry… I just know how musicians can be… with all the women around."

"I know all too well, it's not my deal. I'm out of that phase and would never hurt Claire."

"I'm sorry. She's amazing and human too… and we humans make mistakes. I need coffee."

"What do you mean by that, Shane?"

Why did he just say that? If only I could throw something out him. He's not even answering Ethan back. I run back to the table and put my arm around Ethan's shoulder.

Jared puts his hand on Shane's shoulder. "Are you okay? You look properly drunk my friend, here have some water."

He takes off his glasses and rubs his eyes. "Yeah, I had way too many. I'm going to use the restroom."

Shane leaves and I rub Ethan's arm. "He's officially cut off. How are you, babe?"

He kisses my hand. "I'm fine. He's definitely three sheets… I'll order some coffee."

I leaned over to kiss him. "Are you sure? Did he say something… he's known for being overly direct so mind him if that's the case."

"He really cares about you. He was just making sure my intentions are good. I love you more than anything… I know the distance has been tough on us."

"I love you and don't worry about that. Let's resume later and talk to Jared."

I face Jared and Ethan catches on. "Hey, sorry Jared.

We were just reminiscing about something. How does coffee and dessert sound?"

Jared assures Ethan no offense was taken. Shane returns and he looks as if he put his head under the faucet.

"We ordered some coffee and dessert. How are you doing over there, Salinger? Did you go for a swim?" I ask as he coyly smiles.

"You could say that. I was sweating so I ran some water through my hair and face and it helped. Thanks again for tonight."

The mood was a little heavier when dessert arrived. We said our goodbyes and put the guys in the car I arranged for them. It was nice out and we decided to walk back to apartment.

"So tell me, what were you guys talking about?"

Ethan looks at the brown stones as we walk up Waverly Place. "Nothing much. Just about how great it is to work with you and Jared. I'm spent. You would tell me if there was anything to tell right? I want you to be happy, so no matter what, you can tell me, okay?"

I felt tension knot up in my neck. Shane sort of opened Pandora's Box and no matter how I could try explaining my infidelity, it wouldn't matter. It would crush him. I assured him everything is fine and slowly changed the subject to lighter fare, emphasizing what a great night it turned out to be. I was tired too and figured a good night's sleep would help us both. We got home and stumbled into bed. I must have of dozed off because Ethan awoke me with kisses around my ear whispering "You're not that tired are you?"

As he amuses me in my sleep haze, I tell him "You're gonna have to do all the work, playa."

He softly kisses me. "No problem beautiful (yawn)... I'll take care of (yawn)..."

He passes out instead. The warmth of his body prevents me from getting back to the date I was on with the dream police. I tear up staring at the ceiling thinking about my week with Griffin.

CHAPTER 22 / *THE ROAD NOT TAKEN*

I am sitting in a conference room with Warren, his assistant Julie, and Lana. My nerves are shot and I can't stop fidgeting. This is the second and final round of negotiations. Lana had pioneered for the seasonal contract proposal and the Committee didn't approve it; she's prepared me for the worst with their counteroffer. Now I await the verdict of their proposal. Once again, it's showtime.

"Claire, I have met with the managing members regarding their disapproval for the initial proposal you and Lana presented. I had given much thought to it and like the rest of the members, I too have concerns. First being, you are one of our most valued deejays here. Your show has brought in so much revenue over the years… we can't afford to lose that now. I understand your personal situation of having to consider relocation out West. We have gone back and forth for possible options that could benefit all of us. Here is what we are prepared to do. We are willing to extend your weekends, shortening your work week. Meaning you will have Friday or Monday off and work four days, to give you time to travel and arrange what you need to personally. Of course, if a situation arises during the day you are out, you'll be expected to either work remotely or be here. I think starting off with a three-day weekend is generous, and after a couple of months we'll determine by how the ratings are. If they do not decrease after the first quarter, we can further discuss any suggestions you may have for this arrangement. Please understand this is in no way a reflection on you. In fact it should solidify how much you're valued. We are also aware that you are overdue for a raise. You will have a salary increase of eight percent effective on Monday. Before I open up the forum I'd like to add we're optimistic to open a West Coast hub in roughly eighteen months. If this endeavor happens, you will be first in consideration to relocate with our new entity. Please think about this proposal carefully and let me know as soon as you can, no later than Friday. The floor is open... any thoughts?"

Holy shit. They are giving me an extended weekend and a salary increase. But how can I possibly have quality time for travel with only three days to work with? Warren's clearing his throat, that's my queue to speak.

"Warren, I would like to thank you and Lana again, for considering my initial proposal. As for your alternative, I am grateful. However, it doesn't seem feasible for me to have enough travel time squeezed in three days with a roughly twelve hour commute roundtrip when all's said and done. I think a more realistic option would be having Friday and Monday off two times a month... four days is barely doable. I can't stress enough how much I love working here, but after nine years of loyalty and no questions asked, I feel I should be granted this request. We can go back to the drawing board, in conjunction with what I suggested originally. Have Shane cover for me in my absence, two days a week, bimonthly with either Les or Barnaby producing. The three days I'm here, I'll gladly run the show along with producing tasks while Shane assists. It will save on cost and make all parties happy. I'm very confident the ratings will only be affected in a positive way. If for some reason they slip, then you can do as you see fit. Also, have we determined an answer in regards to Jared? They're both solid choices and I feel will do very well if given the chance."

Lana winks and smiles at me pleasingly while Warren's expression lines on his face look like they're throbbing. I had nothing to lose and was prepared for the worst case scenario.

"We are in the process of finalizing our decision in regards to Jared. As for two days a week, that's a big gamble. Claire, you know it's unheard of for an intern to take over a show for a seasoned deejay. Why are you pressing for this?"

"Warren, I completely understand your concerns but I know for a fact my ratings have risen with their collaborative efforts. Their hard work and performance should be acknowledged... the fan mail accolades I sent you confirm that. They're both willing to start at entry level pay to prove themselves. Considering they have a year's worth of hands-on experience under my wing, they'll knock it out of the park and keep my show intact. What could it hurt to try? Like you said, we can see how we do in the first quarter. If we don't exceed your expectations, you can hire replacements and consider my standing. It will save the nuisance of interviewing others and Shane would only cover for four days a month, and I'm available by Skype if my assistance is needed during those days. And lastly, I'm willing to forfeit my raise to have those four days off a month. Warren, with all due respect, you and the station have nothing to lose. With that, I have nothing else to negotiate."

His façade had softened as he absorbed my plea. "Just like that? You don't want time to think about this?"

"I have thought about it for some time and I stand firm on my decision."

"I give you credit Claire... it's extremely gutsy to take a bold gamble like this on an opportunity of a lifetime. One thing's certain, you've made cogent points. It would save us an exorbitant amount of money to hire them both instead of seasoned outsiders. The ratings as you mentioned, have been doing great… the three of you do have a dynamic chemistry. Well, I know Lana supports you and I think the Committee will be willing to try this out. You have been heard. I will back this proposal as well… with contingencies of course. We try this out… two month probation for Shane covering you on Monday and Friday bimonthly. Tuesday through Thursday, it will only be you on on-air. He can assist without having airtime while you carry the show and there's no negotiation on that. I can see by your look, you're wondering about Jared."

I smile nodding yes.

"He will have six months probation as a contingent hire. If he does well in the two quarters, he'll be hired full-time. Jared can work with Kurt and still help your show intermittently if coverage is needed. Lana expressed Kurt has happily approved this request so I'm willing to give it a try. After Shane's initial two month probation, he will have the same deal as Jared, four more months of temporary employment. And lastly, you will still receive an increase in salary as I mentioned before. If they can prove to me what they've proven to you, I will personally take you all out for a celebratory dinner after they're hired. Since my final vote is the deciding factor, can we just call it a day and all systems go?"

"Yes, we have deal. Thank you so much for accepting my proposal. I… we won't let you down. When will this be effective?"

"First day of next month. We'll need time to coordinate and finalize your contract along with the contingent contracts for Shane and Jared. Let's meet on Friday to go over scheduling and format details. Julie, check my calendar and see when's good, forward an invite to Lana and Claire. Good day everyone."

As he escorted us out of the conference room, Lana motions

to me to join her in her office.

"I'm so proud of you. You kicked major ass is there, how do you feel? I'm so relieved to know we're not losing you. I won't lie... I was a little scared there when you didn't budge."

"I know it's so unlike me... It felt great laying it on the line like that. I was scared too but I had to go for it and you have a lot to do with that. Thanks again for backing me on this, you've been amazing. I think Ethan will be happy with this, I know I am. I didn't want to give up my show so frequent flyer it is."

"Yes, and I still get to bust your chops indefinitely... oh happy day. Oh crap! I'm late for my lunch meeting, see you later."

I put my hand to my heart. "You're the best boss ever." She turns around and salutes me.

I needed to burn off the day's anxious energy. I ran the long way home to find Ethan napping on the couch with a book on his chest looking so peaceful. I cooked dinner and relaxed with a joint and mindless reality TV while he slept. I must have zoned out because I awoke smelling smoke from the oven.

"Let me help you there. "

"Oh, I'm sorry... I didn't mean to wake you. I'm a little baked at the moment. Is the roast a goner?"

"No I think it's salvageable. I didn't hear you come in, must have passed out reading. Hey, how did everything go today?"

"It went pretty well, the only thing is they completely shot down the seasonal idea, they counteroffered with a four day work week where we would have Friday through Sunday together. You would've been proud because I told him it wouldn't work and stood firm with a final offer... three day in office work week bimonthly and he accepted. I'll be able to fly out two times a month, and hopefully you can fit in a visit so it's manageable. I know it's not ideal, but at least we're both happy and it's workable. He did mention they may have an LA sector open in a year-and-a-half and depending on where we'll be at that time, they'll transfer me. What do you think?"

"I think that's great, I'm proud of you. We can definitely make that work... we've been apart longer than that at times. Now we're guaranteed not to get sick of each other, so yay."

A little part of me senses he's placating me and I feel helpless. "Are you ready for a spectacular dinner? Charred London broil with sautéed egg noodles and roasted veggies."

He chuckles as he grabs dishes from the cabinet and utensils to set the table. "It smells amazingly burnt... let's eat."

After dinner, we cleared the table. "So... tell me, how do you really feel? I don't have to stay and I can tell them to shove it. Be honest, are you okay with this? I want to do whatever it takes."

"I know that. The thing is... you won't be happy in the long run. You'd be happy with me on some level but unfulfilled without your show and I couldn't bear being the reason for that. So it's simple... we do the best we can with what we have to work with. I can set up shop here for in between band commitments and on the times I can't, you'll be out there with me, okay? The sublet may get extended depending on my buddy's plans and if not, we'll get another one or just stay out in Long Beach. We have plenty of options. I say we can go another year or so with this arrangement, then we'll focus on a permanent home."

"Absolutely… let's see how it goes because honestly if traveling becomes a strain, then I'll just move out permanently."

He dances with me in the kitchen. I meant what I said. I am willing to do whatever it takes to make our relationship work, inspired by him meeting me halfway, making a sacrifice for my happiness as well. I never had that with Jake—a love that compromises.

* * * * * * * *

The next week went by smoothly, relaying news to all my friends and family about the latest developments. Shane and Jared were ecstatic and beyond grateful. Ethan was especially considerate and with each day, expressing excitement for our new details. When I went into work the next day, the guys had already set up earlier than usual.

"Good morning fellas, in nice and early I see… such kiss asses."

"That be us… Captain. Good morning, we got you a house omelet you love with a chocolate chip muffin, further brown nosing." Shane quips.

"You both spoil me… thanks."

As we ate, I update the show program task list for Shane to follow on my absent days.

"So he wouldn't budge with Jared co-producing our show, ha? It sucks that Jared can't stay with us. With all due respect, Les seems uptight." Jared nods attentively while he finishes a listener request call.

"Yeah Shanester, he's way uptight, hence the reason he needs to be here when I'm out. You need the strict conditioning dude… at least you'll have it easy for three days.

269

Besides, this is an incredible opportunity for Jared. Our show doesn't need two interns anymore, Kurt's does. Jared, I'd say in two years' time, you'll be an accomplished producer and on a happy note, help us out when you're able. Who knows… if things go well for all of us, we may be on one show again, that is if radio still uses live heads instead of programmed robots."

"I couldn't be happier, Captain… no offense Shane, but I need a break from your gold bricking ass confidence, I don't like your jerk-off face and I don't like you, jerk-off…"

Shane throws the foam football at him and I get out my water gun pretending to shoot at them for laughs.

"I can't believe we're being hired under contract, just like that. We owe you big time, boss. I know it's not what you originally wanted… but I'm happy you're sticking around. How are you with this?"

"I'm elated, it'll give me the chance to stick around and build this show back to number one status. And yes Jasta, it will happen, so look out."

"I know you'll kick our asses and I'll do everything I can, surreptitiously to help you claim that. I'm going to miss working with you guy's every day."

"I know same here. Don't worry… we'll still annoy the shit out of you any chance we get."

"So are you going to stop and see the Grand Canyon on your trip?"

Before I answer Jared, I look at a postcard I received yesterday from Ethan that reads: See you in St. Louis next week. The promotional tour needs your flair! Make sure to stop for me on the road. Xoxo

"Yes, basically, it's the only spot we have time for. We

270

have nine days travel time… with a rest stop in LA to drop off some of my stuff."

Shane throws the football to me. "It's cool your dad's taking the trip with you, you'll have a nice time... like National Lampoon's Vacation."

"Nice… yeah, out of the three of us, I'll probably wind up being Clark Griswold."

Shane sends us Lindsey Buckingham's "Holiday Road" YouTube video via IM and proceeds to play it over the loud speakers.

"Good one!"

"I had a feeling you'd like it. I road tripped after I graduated College with my friends and it was one of the best times of my life. Of course, your time will definitely be tamer."

"What kind of shenanigans did you get into?"

He takes off his glasses and looks at us with a coy smile. "The question is what trouble didn't we get into? Let's just say it involved your typical balls out blast in Vegas where we got thrown out of the Bellagio for our belligerence. We got speeding tickets in four states… hallucinated on the finest 'shrooms in New Mexico. And of course, the highlight of having my ass worn out in a threesome with two smokin' chicks on X in LA. Sweet Jesus, I was a porn star that night. It feels like forever ago. Life speeds by too fast after you hit twenty-one."

"If you think it's going fast now, wait till you hit thirty. It speeds by in light years and you'll have harsh reminders telling you you're one step closer to death."

Jared hands me the request list. "You'll never get old,

wise one, just more refined like wine."

"Kiss ass."

While the show ran, I cleaned out my office drawers thinking about the past year. The new crop of assistants will be starting in a few weeks; this time my show gets one instead of two. It's unbelievable how my life radically changed for the better, aside from my indiscretion. Last year I was so low with despair and heartache. Now I have love and support around me with no hurdles except my guilt. I am counting the minutes till I see John later.

Shane clears his throat. "Claire, do you want to join us after work, there's a happy hour going on at the Gansevoort Park Rooftop."

"I would love to but I have plans with Sandra and Fez for dinner, rain check when I get back."

"Of course and don't worry about a thing here for two weeks, we have everything covered."

"Cool… much appreciated. Hey, how are things going with Heather?"

"We're doing good. She's a dime… we're almost there."

"Ooh… almost where?"

"Well it's almost a month since our first date… you know what that means."

"Gotcha… nice to hear you waited. How's Nina?"

He takes a sip of his coffee. "I broke off with her right after my first date with Heather… I know she's special so I cut my losses with the jump-off. She was a little bitter at first but understood."

Jared throws the football at him. "So it's been about a month since you've had that love and feeling?"

"Yes J Dog, thanks for reminding me. My right hand is shot by the way. Jokes aside, I've gone without sex for longer than that. I'm not the depraved junkie you make me out to be. The only reason I hooked up with Nina is because she put the move on me when I was a free agent. I will admit though, after she got engaged it felt wrong and I learned a lesson. So yes, I have a little regret there. How about you guys? Any regrets?"

"Wasting valuable time depressing over my breakup... how about you, Claire?"

I was accustomed to Shane's modus operandi of seeking out information. It would be unfair of me to not share with them since they're both always unabashedly honest. Could I daringly bring myself to confess my latest screw up? No matter how I could convincingly rationalize my nefarious actions, I couldn't muster up the nerve.

"Do I have regrets? Sure I do... everyone does in different calibers. I truly believe anyone who says they don't have regrets in their lifetime is kidding themselves. If it's any consolation Shane, don't judge yourself too harshly with Nina. You weren't the one messing around on your fiancé, she was and that's for her to contend with. Be proud of the fact you realized it didn't feel right anymore and you ended the tryst before it caused further damage. You're maturing and learning from your mistake... that's one of the many perks of being older and wiser."

Jared's phone rings and he steps outside to take the call.

"So as I get older, I can look forward to no longer making jackass mistakes?"

"I wouldn't say that... I know sixty-year-olds that still make jackasses out of themselves. My point is, learning from your errors is what counts."

"Can I ask you a personal question?"

"Let me guess, how did things go when I met up with Griffin that night, right?"

"Yes."

"It went fine... nothing happened. We bragged about Ethan and his girlfriend Haley with the others over drinks."

He focuses on my eyes for a moment as if he's looking for the truth. "Good to hear."

"Yes. Oh shoot, I have to peace out for my Dr. Appointment. If anything pressing comes up or you guys need me, just call or email... it's no bother."

Shane gets up to help me with my bags. "All will be fine, just have a ball and remember whatever you do... do not under any circumstance take drugs in Vegas. Drinking yes. Drugs no. Give my best to Ethan and your dad. What time are you guys heading out?"

He holds the door open for me. I motion to Jared while he's on the phone and he hugs me, mouthing he will call me later.

"Five thirty. Even on vacation I have to fly with the friggin' roosters."

"Be sure to tune in to the show. You'll only have roughly two hours of broadcast then static city."

We walk to the curb and I hail a cab. "Look at you with knowing that fact... of course, what else would I listen to? Hey, don't let smelly Berkeley Stephen stink up my desk."

He opens the cab door for me. "Sure thing. I plan on fumigating that shit right after his coverage is over. I don't know why they couldn't have me fill in for you the whole time. Claire, one more thing... thanks again for everything."

"You're very welcome. Now, I'll leave you off with what all my friends tell say when we skip town. Don't get pregnant!"

He snickers. "I like that one... stealing it for sure. Bon voyage, Captain."

I arrive at John's office and there's a new receptionist that greets me. After the nurse escorts me in, I notice his office has been redecorated with new furniture and a pale yellow color on the walls. It looks brighter than the grey blue shade it was. I'm glad to see he kept the cow pictures. I missed coming to therapy. John knocks and then opens the door.

"Hello Claire... it's good to see you again."

I stand up and we shake hands. "Hello, likewise... thanks for accommodating my last minute appointment request. How have you been? I like the new pieces of furniture."

"Thanks, I'm doing good. My girlfriend helped me spruce up the place. How have things been with you? Shall we start with where we left off the last time or anything new that's pressing you would like to address?"

"I have a new dilemma. Five weeks ago... I cheated on Ethan. I need a refresher course on that guilt problem we worked on previously."

John's eyebrows widen as his mouth drops open for a moment. If I were sitting in his seat, I would nosh on popcorn for my viewing pleasure.

"How did the infidelity start? Did you have a falling out with your boyfriend?"

I told him about my history with Griffin and the details of the incident as he listened pensively. I also explained how Jake and I finally made at peace and how much better I feel.

"Claire, from what you have described, it sounded like you were having doubts with the whole distance issue and your attraction to your former boyfriend was reawakened. On a scale of one to ten, how would you rate the guilt?"

"I'd say a seven or eight. It was wrong and I feel awful... having a futile indiscretion. How can I overcome this?"

He writes in his notebook. "Well, there are a couple of ways. You could confess to him what happened or try dissecting why you gave into your desires with someone else. You mentioned earlier, how therapeutic it was to finally have closure with Jake. Maybe coming clean to Ethan will help reap the same benefit."

"Ethan would never forgive me if I told him the truth. From a man's point of view, you tell me hypothetically. Would you forgive your girlfriend if she slept with someone else behind your back? Or would you break up with her?"

He stands up and looks out the window while gathering his response. "Hypothetically of course... I would forgive her over time, but most likely part ways. I see your point. Coming to terms with your actions it is. So let's start with a couple of things. Have you ever had an affair like this before? When did this recent desire win over the reluctance?"

"No, I've never cheated before. When I was with Griffin, it brought me back to the days when we were together. At first I was adamant about not sleeping with him but as the night went on... nostalgia clouded my judgment and..."

"And what?"

"His vulnerable plea. Expressing his feelings for me. He went out on a limb considering the odds, and it moved me. That bravery doesn't happen very often. He kept saying we were still fresh in our relationships so it was no big deal... then I wanted him all over again. I was lonely while Ethan was away recording and doing shows for a few weeks. I know it's a weak excuse but the attention and admiration from Griffin distorted my rationale. Also, I had never just had fun before and wanted to finally do what I wanted without having my responsible side sabotage me. Now as I sit here, I feel those reasons aren't valid enough. And the old adage of once a cheater always a cheater doesn't help. I don't agree with that by the way..."

He sits down and pours me a glass of water. "It's brave when one expresses deep feelings or admissions... like you are now and feeling sorry for it. That's a huge step towards healing from it. It's not easy to be standing in front of someone you're attracted to who audaciously declares their feelings to you, even when you're not available. Do you still see Griffin... did you express the same feelings to him?"

"No, he's written me and has said that if things don't work out he wants us to be together. I told him I have love for him but I'm torn because I'm in love with someone else. Our fling lasted a week when he was here visiting from London. I will never cheat on Ethan again. We've progressed as a couple and we've since built a strong foundation, I don't want to ruin that. I played with fire... the one lapse of reasoning I submitted to. I just wish I could take it back, the moments of pleasure it provided wasn't worth the price of admission."

"But you did enjoy yourself at the time, right? Why would you want to take that back? Why are you going back to the state of exigency you worked so hard to overcome? You're torn between them both and what you need to attain is a balance within yourself. Think about that for a moment. Instead of being your own worst enemy with blame and guilt, try forgiving the situation. If you can do that, I bet that infamous narrator of yours would be silenced. Some patients react to stress with anxiety or high blood pressure or binge eating, etcetera—every person reacts differently. For you, it's that uncontrollable voice. You may think it's your conscience, but I think it's your confusion. A conflict battling with your desires you're unable to communicate with the person in question. Instead, you fight it out with yourself. Maybe because you're afraid of the outcome or what the person's reaction will be if you truthfully communicate with them? Remember you said in our fourth session, you were *thankful that screeching distorted sound was quiet.* At that time you were dating Ethan and things overall had improved. Also, you weren't going on deaf ear by having me and people surrounding you who listen, most importantly, understand you. It's reasonable to equate the so-called positives in your life with silencing the voice of damnation. When you're being heard authentically, that's what really makes you happy. Tell me... do you hear the voice when you're here?"

"Not so much. The only time it squawks is when I'm debating if I should bring up something... like a reasoning mechanism."

"Really? Why would you struggle with talking about things here?"

I didn't answer right away, he'd probably respond in a professional manner by denying any attraction we may have had. I need to play it safe now.

"I don't censor myself... more like how to approach a subject, that's what I meant."

"Oh... okay well that's usually how everyone hears

their inner voices. What we need to work on is balancing out energy with your ability to communicate and feeling complacent while doing so. One of our goals is to listen to our bodies signal when it's overloaded and/or needs help."

I could hear his passion, proving his point in his tonality as his voice deepened.

"That sounds good, John. I agree... if I could achieve more balance that would be clutch. I'll come in more often to work on this. I wanted to get back to what you said about being torn between two men... isn't that supposed to be impossible? Or what is it called... um..."

John clears his throat. "Logical contradiction."

"That's it. I remember reading about that when I looked it up. I don't think... I mean, I love them both differently. John, why aren't you chastising me for my mess up."

"I'm not here to criticize you. It would be a different session if you were married, where we would then have to determine if the marriage could be saved. You were five months into your budding relationship. Focus on what we worked on in the first few sessions. Stop being so hard on yourself. You've mentioned many times about your loyalty and high regard when you were in an intimate relationship with Jake. Unfortunately, Claire... we're not perfect and desires outweigh so-called logic at times at any age. There are different levels of mistakes, temptations. I think what's important is recognizing the mishap and learning from it, which you are currently doing. Sometimes people move us in such a way, we succumb to our feelings... good or bad and it clouds our better judgment. Maybe you were attracted to the different characteristics they both provide, and that's what you're drawn to... the ultimate guy. Or maybe the reason you never experienced this before is because you have different needs now than you did previously in your first relationship.

"Or maybe I'm not as struck with Ethan as I was with Jake. I'm beating myself up because I'm damaged from the heartbreak I sustained. Ethan isn't damaged. He's never been hurt badly like me or Griffin and maybe subconsciously I'm wrecking my relationship with him. From that alone, I sound like some sort of monster. It's grating to act is if nothing happened when I'm with him. I hate dealing with whatever you call this."

"Emotional dissonance. A good example is when someone is hurt by another's rude comment and instead of reacting hastily they exude kindness instead—hiding their true feelings. This applies to many things. You made a good point... how secure do you feel with Ethan? If you're doubting things... we'll look into this. It's not just you, this happens to many people and you're not any type of monster."

"Have you ever experienced anything like this?"

He looks up from writing. The sun's glare illuminates his brown eyes with gold amber hues. His hands clenched the arms of his chair. The corners of his mouth turned slightly upward.

"Claire, our goal here is to focus on helping you. It's not ethical for me to talk about my personal experience. It may cause..."

"Emotional transference."

"Yes."

"I'm just curious since it helps hearing from other people if they can relate. I didn't mean to imply any inappropriateness."

"I know, I didn't mean to insinuate that."

He gets up from his chair and walks to his desk grabbing the pitcher of water, pouring himself a glass. His shoulders look tense, as if perilousness weighs heavy on them.

"Claire, are you comfortable during our sessions or have I made you feel uneasy at all?"

"No. Everything's good… I just figured we were on a different level considering our conversations outside the office. I understand the necessary boundaries, so no problem."

"You're right. I was a fan of yours long before treating you, so it's different. If at any time, you don't feel comfortable, please let me know. It's important that you do. Yes… yes I have experienced what you're going through. It gets easier… once you get a grip on it."

"I appreciate you sharing that. John, are you okay with treating me?"

He unblinkingly looks at me, delaying his response.

"Yes."

I don't believe him. I've sat where he is right now, in front of him and Shane, when I lied about my night with Griffin. I could probe into this tension further but as I look at the clock, our time is almost up. I didn't know how to safely respond so I smile instead.

"Was there anything else you wanted to talk about? We have a few more minutes."

"Nothing in particular, just how ecstatic I am keeping my show. Despite my ongoing laundry list of issues we have to work on… I feel much healthier since first sitting here. I'm optimistic my new schedule and living arrangement will work out. Lately, I've been thinking about the long term ahead like marriage and kids."

"I'm happy to hear you're feeling better these days. The long term road ahead... we'll focus on helping you with that balance I mentioned when you get back. Let's skip back to where we were before. Aside from the dissonance, do you feel you're communication has improved?"

"Yes, it has. I never knew I could be this assertive, clearing the air with Jake and proposing my non-negotiable plea at work would have never happened a year ago. As I'm moving forward, I'll play it safe by saying in regards to my communication... it's a work in progress."

"Hey, that's one of my lines..."

We chuckle as we stand up.

"...very good, in the meantime, I'd like for you to write down any thoughts you may have, especially if that ranting narrator shows up. Here's a notebook and pen. Write the dialogue out in free flow without editing. Bring in your notebook and we'll review what you've written together. I'll go over therapeutic exercises that you can use and benefit greatly from, sound good? I look forward to seeing when you get back from vacation."

"It sounds great, I feel like I'm school again. I wish I had come to therapy years ago... do you know how long this puppy's been barking in here? Better late than never I suppose. This was by far my favorite session... thanks John. I'll see you when I get back with pages in hand."

He holds his hand on my back escorting me out.

CHAPTER 23 / *"THIS IS DEDICATED TO..."*

I still have packing to do and the trip starts in less than six hours. Why did I wait till the last minute to get organized? Instead of going out to dinner with my friends having a fabulous time, I should've been home with a check list. Who am I kidding? Like packing ever had a chance over festivities. There's a bunch of messages on my blackberry I need to read. One's from Ethan wishing us a safe trip along with a reminder of food spots to check out on the way. Another one from Bianca saying yet again how jealous she is I'm taking a road trip along with one from my niece that reads: We heart you! Wally World, Woot woot! Jared sent me a follow up email with good wishes and to have a blast. Shane sent a simple text: Tune in at 6AM, Captain. The days are far and few between spending times out in my beach digs, I can only imagine how much mail I have to sort through. My neighbor Mr. Frayson, is a gem. He's an older man who's widowed and takes care of my plants and collects mail for me while I'm staying in the City apartment. Anytime I'm out here, I put together a care package for him with his favorite treats, scotch, scotch, and more scotch. I open the garage and in the corner is a box Mr. Frayson has placed on the work table. There's a note on top of the cover.

Have a wonderful road trip, Claire.
Call if you need anything else looked after.
Hugs, W.

I ruffle through the full box of magazines and junk mail sorting out what to toss. There's an invite from Kamden, to her engagement party and a letter from Griffin. It's the second correspondence he's sent since I saw him last. He loves sending old-school mail. I open it to read it with shaking hands.

Hello Claire,

I was happy to read your last letter and all the good news that's been happening for you. You may be skeptical believing my sincerity, but if you know me as well as I think you do, you know it's genuine. I believe things happen for a reason, and I'm happy we're not typical exes that can't sustain a friendship. Since my last write, I'm doing much better whilst being away from you and our week together. I've been out with Haley and after our week, I've realized what I'm missing. Love. I'm breaking off with her tonight, because you're right, no point in going on with someone I'm not struck by. On the work front, things are good. My company's doing very well and we're in negotiations to open a NY sector next year. Brace yourself kid, you may be seeing me more than you bargained for. These wheels were set before I saw you, so don't think it's all about you (even though it might be, but I need to keep some level of pride.) My only complaint is the work hours, a huge strain but I keep telling myself it will pay off. Okay, so a moment of uncensored words. I can't stop thinking about you. I feel comfortable expressing it so don't be upset. I know you feel it too despite your understandable denial. I have reminders of Claire everywhere, especially those fedora hats you mentioned admiring, that's all I see now on the street. I can't control my heart and I'm okay with the fact that you can. But hear this: don't be your worst enemy. I gathered you have been struggling with what happened between us from your letter. It will be fine. Just enjoy the now and don't worry about the what ifs. Bloody hell, I sound like a cheesy pop record, don't I? Haha. I hope you receive this before you go away, have a great time driving out to CA. Send a write or ring me when you get back. Think about what I said. I meant every word. Just say yes and I'm there. I'm glad you'll still be based in NY – match point!

XX
Griffin

I think about the exercise John gave me—jotting down things that come to mind. The first thought I have as I write is, *I am late. My period is a week late and it's always been on time. I'm hoping it's stress because if I'm pregnant, I don't know what I will do. If time calculations are correct, it's Griffin's. As liberal as I'd like to think I am, I couldn't fathom having an abortion. I held Sandra's hand when she had one, consoling her as she cried saying it was the most horrifying experience of her life. I vowed to never go through that. I don't remember skipping a birth control pill so if I am pregnant, it will be a miracle. Maybe Griffin is right, what's meant to happen will happen on its own. I can't blame this punishment on Jake this time since he always wanted me to have a child with him. Besides, he never played the schadenfreude role. No, this is the ultimate warped payment for my indiscretion. I don't know exactly what it is I possess that has Griffin so enamored with me in my unavailable state—maybe it's that reason alone. I'll wait another week or so before I buy a pregnancy test. If it turns out positive, then it's crucial decision time. Live with the secret and pass the child off as Ethan's or come clean and end up with Griffin. If I selfishly choose Ethan, can I be so callous to keep this from Griffin? If I do the right thing and tell him, he'll make sure I don't wind up with Ethan, emphasizing how he's destined to be in my life. I could be very happy with Griffin but I don't know how I'll be, knowing I'm the cause of damaging... crushing Ethan. Therapy is definitely working since I'm not stressing in my usual fashion over this big 'what if' right now like I normally would. I'll cross that bridge if and when I get to it. I'm focusing on the present and what's ahead. I'm embracing the fact that you shouldn't feel guilty when someone leaves a lasting impression on you, like Griffin has for me. Provided I adhere to the boundaries of my situation, it's okay to keep in touch with him. I'm sure Ethan has a woman he knows of a similar caliber in his life and I'm cool with it because it's inevitable. I'm not talking about the ones that got away but more like the ones you've loved and shared time with, always staying in your heart. In the past, I always focused my energy on someone else's happiness. My new found religion is being passionate about me, for better or worse. I used to fall victim neglecting this temple that makes up me. Each day I'm improving, ensuring a more peaceful abode for the visitors in my life. I like this new challenge ahead of me and part of the excitement is not having a clue of what's up ahead with no crystal ball in sight. What am I going to do?*

As I pause I see the time, it's 2:03 AM. I have to get to sleep for the long haul tomorrow. I place all my mail in the drawer except for Griffin's letter, I'll figure out a secure hiding place. I go over my road trip checklist and one by one the items are accounted for. I hear my stomach growl from hunger as I lay down, I could eat two meals. If I eat now, I'll spoil any chances of shut eye. If I pass out now I'm lucky to get two solid hours of rest.

(Beep beep beep beep) Oh I'm hurting and my eyes are burning. I don't remember dreaming, my hunger has left me hazy. I scoff down cereal before I jump in the shower and get ready while the coffee brews. Everything's locked up and ready to roll. I grab extra snacks for later to help me stay awake with seven hundred miles ahead of us. I get in the truck and realize my dad will most likely have a grocery store packed with him as well and he's calling me.

"Hey Daddy, I'm leaving now. Are you ready to rock and roll? Good... I'll be by in ten minutes."

It's chilly out, far cry from a few hours ago. There's not one soul on the road at 5:10 AM. Shouldn't there be bread delivery trucks riding around, isn't this their prime time? I turn on the radio and tune into my station. Stephen sounds good behind the mic; it's been forever since I've heard him live. I roll up to my parent's house and see the door's open.

Dad walks out with luggage. "Right on time, Canoli... you look tired. How much sleep did you get?"

"Oh a couple of hours... you know me, last minute to organize everything. Here, let me help you pack the truck.

"Claire, I have ham and egg Panini's, fruit, and apple crumb muffins your mama made."

"It sounds delightful. Is she up?"

"Yes, she's in the kitchen."

"Where's my beautiful mother? Oh there she is."

She's pouring coffee, unable to hug. "Hello lovey. Please promise me you'll take it slow and be careful. You're both speed demons and I'm already worried. I'll check in with you every few hours."

"Of course we'll take it easy but it's so much fun to drive fast and …"

She punches my arm deservedly. "… I promise, so don't worry. We'll be back before you know it. Thanks again for letting me use the truck… you're a gem swapping cars with me. That Mercedes-Benz GL has so much more room than my decrepit Jetta. It's not a fair trade at all… I promise to take care of her."

She walks me out. "I love you, baby… have fun. Your dad is so happy he's able to take this trip with you, it means a lot to him… and me. I'm so relieved you don't have to move out there permanently. I know, call it selfish but I love you and want you near. You'll see when you're a mom."

I give her a kiss on the cheek and whisper in her ear. "Not selfish at all. Love you."

She walks back into the house with Dad to make sure he hasn't forgotten anything. They come out and we say our goodbyes. She waves as we drive away. I'm forgetting something but can't peg what it is.

"Let's see… it's 5:40 AM, we should be close to I-70 in Pennsylvania by 10:00 AM or so."

"That sounds about right, just don't tell your mother

287

we're going over way over the speed limit."

"My lips are sealed... hey Dad, can you turn up the radio, thanks."

We listen to Stephen broadcast the last portion of his show.

"Is that the smelly pot smoker you introduced me to last year?"

"That's him. If you thought he smelled bad, you should go into his studio... it's wretched. Dad, I have a question for you. Are you okay with me being the way I am? You know... not following the status quo of being married with kids at this point in my life, like Bianca and Dante."

"Of course I am. I'm proud of each of you... glad you're all different. Otherwise, it would be boring for us parents. Claire, you've always had a good head on your shoulders. I never had to worry about you like Dante or Bianca. Life experiences, whether it entails marriage... kids or whatever are yours for the taking. Do what makes you happy, that's what your mother and I always instilled in raising you kids. Take it from me, it's pointless to compare yourself with others... everybody has their something that they have to deal with. Be secure in your decisions and follow your heart. I'll let you in on a little secret... marriage and kids are not the be-all and end-all of existence. I lucked out with your mom and the three of you... but as you know it's tough too and not all days are full of bliss... sadly. Marriage is not for everyone... please don't tell your mother I said that, she feels it is. Focus on what you've accomplished so far and be proud of how things have worked out for you. At the end of the day you have to trust your instincts, that's what I did and things worked out really well."

"I like this side of you, Dad... we don't get to have heart to heart talks like we used to. I was just thinking about

288

life in general and I want to come clean about something. I've been in therapy for ten months. I'm sorry I didn't tell you from the start, I just didn't want to add any more concern for you or Mom. Please don't be mad."

"I'm not mad but you should've told me. I'm not surprised... you went through so much with Jake. Don't ever worry about adding concerns or worry... that's what I'm here for, to help you. Who else knows? How's the treatment going?"

"It's going well, I feel much better. After the breakup, I needed help so I decided to give it a try. Dr. Groundz is good, we meet every other week and he's been helping me resolve issues. I only told Bianca from the family."

"You're definitely doing better than before... you seem like you're happier. I'm glad it's helping. How long will you need to stay in treatment?"

"That's a good question... depends on how quickly I resolve everything. I'm getting there and optimistic it will end early next year. I actually missed a few weeks here and there with traveling and all. It's good to have as a backup, in case I need it."

"What issues are you addressing?"

"Stress and dealing with the aftermath of the breakup... trust issues."

"Trust... that's understandable. If there's anything I can do for you... just say it. You know can talk to me about anything."

"I know that Dad... thanks. Help me figure out how to break it to Mom. Ooh, the show will be starting soon."

He pulls out breakfast sandwiches for us to eat. Oh

no! The letter. What did I do with Griffin's letter? I don't remember where I put it. I hid the first letter he sent in my locked drawer at work so Ethan wouldn't have a chance of seeing it—I have to locate it when I get back. My Dad raises the volume on the radio.

"Top of the morning to you folks. Thanks for joining me, Shane Salinger, on 97.2 WLDM FM. I have the honor of covering for my mentor, Claire Convenzionale, while she's out on a well-deserved vacation. I, along with my counterpart Jared Parker, have a special show for you, dedicated to her. As I speak, she's on the road driving to California. In the next four hours, we'll have a special free flow hour of songs about the West Coast later on the program. The request lines are open so let us know what you want to hear by calling or logging onto our website and we'll make sure to play them. On a side note, I want to commemorate an upcoming year anniversary, when Jared and I started here at 97.2. We'd like to give a special thanks to our program manager, Lana Silson for making the life-altering decision in choosing us to work with Claire, who's an inspiring spirit to everyone she meets. We look forward to celebrating with both of them when she returns. This next hour is dedicated to how far she and the rest of us have come this past year. For some, the significance is being able to play and listen to a song again after a long hiatus in exile. In my case, it's moving forward in merriment instead of past bitterness. With that, this next one goes out to Bill, Helen, Tanya, Kyle, and Claire."

My dad hands me a tissue and put's his hand on my shoulder as Bruce Springsteen's "Tunnel of Love" plays.

"That's touching, they really adore you."

"It is… and it's mutual."

Shane segued into Live's "Horse." One of my favorite songs that just so happened to be another one Jake would sing to me. How did the guys know? It was never requested. Maybe Sandra's the culprit? Or maybe my drunken-ass happened to sing it that infamous night I couldn't remember. This one gets a sing-along. I serenaded the last few bars as my dad listened. I am so happy at this moment; any vexations will have to wait.

For the next hour, we enjoyed what the guys put together. As we reached the middle of New Jersey, inevitable static permeated and Shane's voice faded out. I turned the radio off and decided I'd rather cherish these rare moments with my dad by listening to his soothing voice with what he had to say on our trip. I can't remember a day in my life when I haven't had music seeping in my ears at some point. You have to break away from the tried and true every so often and miss being around it to fully appreciate its significance. We continued our conversation from before as I gained miles with the golden sunlit sky following behind us.

ABOUT THE AUTHOR

Lisa Montanino is the author of "Observations of a Native New Yorker" A short story published and featured in *Divine Caroline* magazine. She's also a freelance contributing writer/blogger, and philanthropist. Lisa's an active member of the Amateur Writers Group of Long Island. *Feedback* is her first fiction novel. She's currently at work on the sequel. In the interim, you may spot her wandering or biking at local boardwalks, book stores, and coffee shops around the greater New York, South Carolina, and California regions. Make sure to say hi and tell her your thoughts of this book.

See more on Lisa at her website:
Lisa.Montanino@wordpress.com
@LDMontanino on Twitter
And facebook at www.facebook.com/lilmountain

www.ingramcontent.com/pod-product-compliance
Lightning Source LLC
Chambersburg PA
CBHW070636260626
47161CB00007B/2717